The Only Shadow in the House

All Good Wishes
Joan Donaldson-Yarmey

The Only Shadow in the House

A SUMACH TRAVEL MYSTERY

Joan Donaldson-Yarmey

Toronto

The Only Shadow in the House
By Joan Donaldson-Yarmey

First published in 2010 by
Sumach Press, an imprint of Three O'Clock Press Inc.
180 Bloor Street West, Suite 801
Toronto, Ontario
M5S 2V6
www.sumachpress.com

Sumach Press gratefully acknowledges financial support for our publishing activities from the Ontario Arts Council, the Canada Council for the Arts, the Government of Canada through the Book Publishing Industry Development Program (BPIDP)and the Government of Ontario.

Library and Archives Canada Cataloguing in Publication

Donaldson-Yarmey, Joan, 1949–
The only shadow in the house : a Sumach mystery / Joan Donaldson-Yarmey.

ISBN 978-1-894549-85-1

I. Title.

PS8607.O63O65 2010 C813'.6 C2010-904784-2

Cover design and interior design by Aldo Fierro
Map by Benjamin Craft
Cover Photo Copyright © lamiel/iStockphoto

09 10 11 12 13 5 4 3 2 1

Printed and bound in Canada by Marquis Book Printing, Inc.

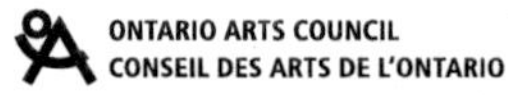

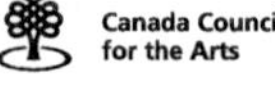

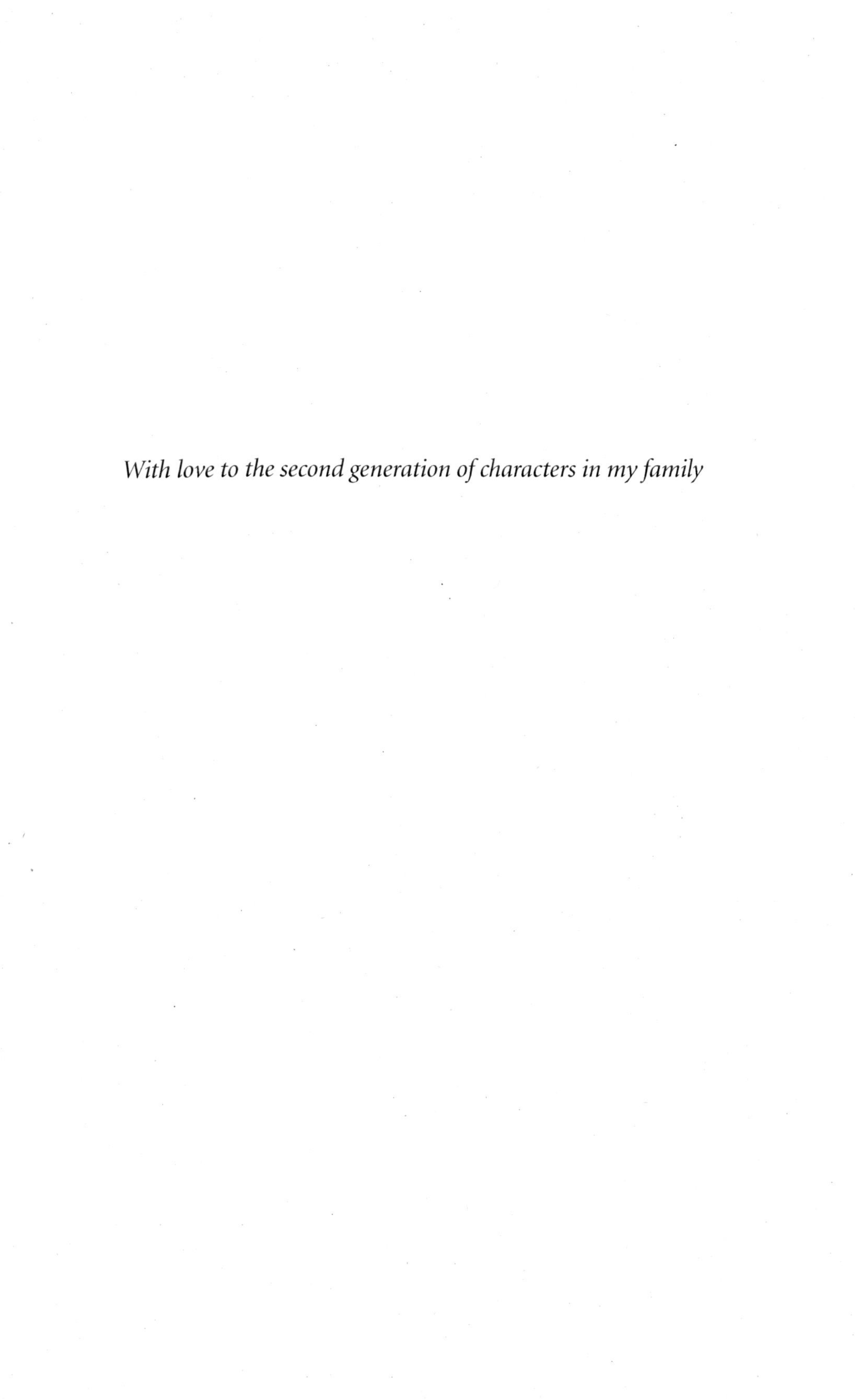

With love to the second generation of characters in my family

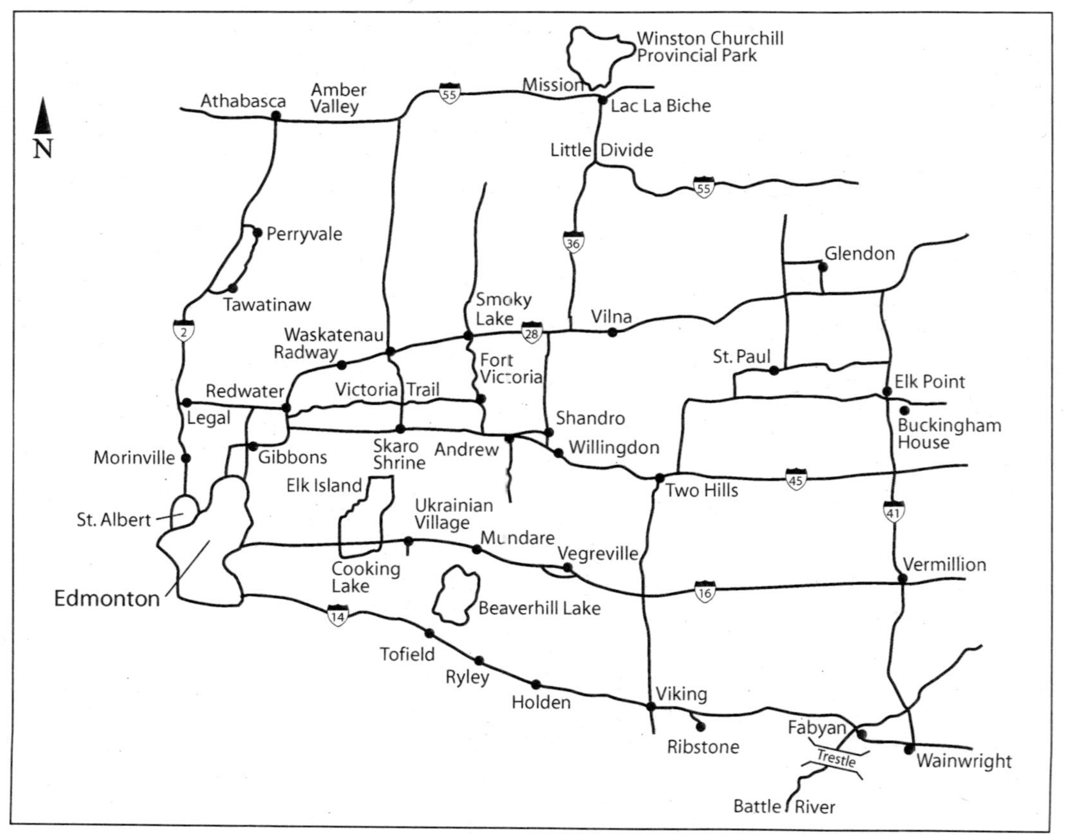
N
Winston Churchill Provincial Park
Athabasca
Amber Valley
55
Mission
Lac La Biche
Little Divide
55
36
Perryvale
Glendon
Tawatinaw
2
Smoky Lake
28
Vilna
Waskatenau
Radway
Fort Victoria
St. Paul
Redwater
Victoria Trail
Elk Point
Legal
Shandro
Buckingham House
Morinville
Gibbons
Skaro Shrine
Andrew
Willingdon
Elk Island
Two Hills
45
Ukrainian Village
41
St. Albert
Mundare
Vegreville
Cooking Lake
Vermillion
Edmonton
16
Beaverhill Lake
14
Tofield
Ryley
Holden
Viking
Fabyan
Ribstone
Trestle
Wainwright
Battle River

Chapter 1

"Hey, Sally, wait up." Elizabeth Oliver hurried to catch up with her best friend. "Are you going for lunch?"

"Yes," Sally Matthews answered. "I'm starving."

"Good. I'm hungry too."

The two women walked down the hallway of the long-term care facility where they worked. Their shifts alternated between days and evenings and between the long-term care and dementia floors. There were times when they saw little of each other but right now their schedules overlapped and they were both on day shifts.

"Do you want to go for drinks tonight with some of us from the second floor?" Sally asked.

"Sorry, I can't," Elizabeth said. "I'm meeting Jared at The Keg."

"You two really hit it off." Sally smiled. "I'm glad."

"And I'm glad you introduced us." Elizabeth pulled her shoulder-length, light brown hair out of its ponytail. She hated ponytails but had to keep her hair out of her face while she worked. She envied her friend's blonde hair, which she kept short and styled. Her own hair was straight and, for the most part, refused to hold any style.

"He's a special man, isn't he?"

They reached the locker room and spun the combinations of their locks.

"He's been helping me with my next travel article, telling me about the places to see in Redwater and surrounding area in case I include it. He grew up on a farm near there," Elizabeth said, reaching for her lunch bag.

"Yeah, and it doesn't sound like he had much of a childhood." Sally took her lunch bag out of her locker.

Elizabeth shook her head. "He's only told me a few things, like his mother committing suicide. You'd think with that and him now being in a wheelchair that he would hate the world."

They pushed open the door to the staff courtyard. It was a sunny July day in Edmonton. The courtyard was square with a high, red-brick wall. The floor was cement with areas left for flowerbeds. Round tables sat under shade trees or in the open for those who wanted to enjoy the sun's rays.

They opened their bags. Sally had two ham and cheese with lettuce sandwiches, three vanilla cookies and a container of milk. Elizabeth had brought a salad with cheddar cheese chunks and pieces of apple in it, a can of Pepsi and a banana.

After the death of Elizabeth's mother last year, she and Sally had moved out of their apartment and into the basement suite at her father's home, more to keep an eye on him than for any other reason. He liked the company and each of them, along with Elizabeth's younger twin siblings, Sherry and Terry, took turns getting him out of the house, a task that was slowly getting easier.

"I hear Jared's coming to the barbecue tomorrow night. So you're finally going to introduce him to your family." Sally bit into her sandwich.

"It was kind of a spur-of-the-moment thing." Elizabeth opened her Pepsi. "With his wheelchair basketball coaching and practices and my shift work, we don't have much time to see each other. When I found out that we had two evenings together in a row, it just seemed that the barbecue would be the perfect time for everyone to meet him." She looked at Sally, as she took a drink of her pop. "What else did he tell you?"

"Just that you'd also invited him to the dragon boat festival tomorrow, but he couldn't make it because of his wheelchair basketball practice."

"There sure are no secrets when my best friend is my boyfriend's caregiver."

Sally grinned.

Elizabeth remembered when Sally had first told her about her decision to take on a private client. She'd interviewed with a few people before finding Jared Jones three months ago. Sally was hired and ably managed her shifts with him around her job at the facility. So far, it seemed to be working well and gave her extra money without taking up much time. Many staff members at the facility had one or two private clients on the side.

Elizabeth had thought about getting into private care but decided to stay with her plan of becoming a writer. To date she had sold eight travel articles and one historical article. She was getting ready to head out on her research trip for another travel one in just under two weeks.

"Hey, Oliver, Matthews, there you are." A heavier woman in a pink pantsuit came over to them.

"Hi, Connie," Elizabeth replied, smiling.

"Sorry I'm late. I had to fill a shift for tomorrow." She pulled out a chair at their table and sat down.

Connie Barkley was in charge of the scheduling and was the one who phoned them if there was a shift that needed filling. She was such a happy, easygoing person that staff often stopped in at the office just to have their spirits lifted and to grab one of the candies from the dish she kept on her desk. Due to her personality, it was sometimes hard to resist her when she called about taking an extra shift.

She always addressed everyone by their last names because, as she put it, "that's how your names are lined up in my files, last name first."

"We still on for the dragon boat races tomorrow?" Connie asked, taking three small plastic containers out of the lunch bag she had set on the table.

"We are unless you call us to work," Sally joked.

"So far, no one has asked for the weekend off, but someone might call in sick."

Elizabeth and Sally watched Connie with interest. Their friend was always trying a new diet, and they never knew what she would be bringing for lunch. This time she opened the containers to reveal vegetables, fruit and three boiled eggs.

"Low carb," Connie explained, noticing their scrutiny.

"Is it working?" Elizabeth asked.

"Just started it this morning." She grinned at them. "Friday, you know."

"I thought diets were started on Mondays," Sally said.

"I used to try that but it never worked so I've decided to change days."

Elizabeth and Sally laughed.

"So where are you travelling to this summer?" Connie asked Elizabeth.

"I'm not sure. I'm supposed to write about three loop tours that can each be done in a day's drive from Edmonton."

"That covers a lot of territory." Connie sprinkled salt on an egg and ate it.

"I know," Elizabeth said ruefully. "That's why I am having such a hard time deciding. I've gathered tourist brochures of central Alberta and checked out the Internet, and I've come up with a lot of fascinating and entertaining ideas but still have to decide on the routes. I even asked the editor of the magazine what she had in mind—towns, attractions or scenery. She told me to go with what interested me."

"Well, that was nice of her," Connie said.

"Yes, it's great that she has faith in me, but it would have been nicer to have had some sort of guidance." Elizabeth wrinkled her nose. "Although, if I concentrate on one area, like to the east or the north, then when I send it in I could mention that I would be willing to do three in the other directions. It would be kind of like creating a special segment for myself in the magazine."

Connie laughed. "Smart."

"Have you narrowed your selection down at all?" Sally asked.

"Yes. There is Highway 16 East with Elk Island Park, Ukrainian Cultural Heritage Village and the Pysanka at Vegreville. Highway 14 has the Viking Ribstones and Fabyan Bridge. Or there is Highway 16 West with the Alberta Fairytale Grounds ..."

Sally held up her hand. "Okay, I get the picture."

"And that's just a few." Elizabeth smiled.

"Sometimes I wish I were a writer," Connie said. "But I wouldn't want to be you right now."

"It's certainly not as easy as it sounds. But I wouldn't trade it for anything else. I love my travel writing."

"Do you think you'll find another mystery while you're gone?" Connie asked. Everyone at work knew about Elizabeth and how she solved murder mysteries while researching her articles.

"I doubt it," Elizabeth said. "The odds of that happening three years in a row would be high."

"Did you know that she wrote about the mystery of the skeleton found in the septic tank near Fort Macleod last summer?" Sally asked.

Connie looked at Elizabeth. "No, I didn't hear that."

Elizabeth smiled. "Yeah, and I have a magazine editor who wrote that he liked it and would let me know when they had space for it."

"Hey, that's great!" exclaimed Connie.

"Yeah, I'm thinking of writing about the first murder I came upon in Red Deer two years ago."

"Sounds as if you like that as much as travel writing," Connie said.

"Oh, travel writing will always come first. At least I have magazine editors who want my articles before I even write them." She held up her hands. "But enough about me. Did you know that Sally's writing a science fiction novel?"

"Really?" Connie turned to her with interest.

Sally blushed and nodded.

"I didn't know you liked sci-fi too. I'm reading a great sci-fi book right now. What made you decide to write one?"

"I've been reading fantasy and science fiction since I was a kid and some of them were pretty bad," Sally explained. "I finally decided that I could at least write as bad as them. I'm taking a summer evening course at a local college."

"Wow, I know two writers. I can hardly wait until you both are famous and I can tell people I worked with you."

Sally looked at her watch. "Well, I have to talk to the nurse before going back to work." She looked at Elizabeth. "I'll meet you at the car after work. We'll go straight home so you can get ready for your date with Jared."

Elizabeth nodded. She and Connie said goodbye to Sally then sat and enjoyed the warmth of the day for a few minutes more before heading in for the afternoon.

Chapter 2

Elizabeth sat at the restaurant table waiting for Jared. She couldn't believe the thrill she was feeling just at the thought of seeing him. She felt it every time they got together. She had to admit that she really liked the man. Her mind went back to the first time she met him. She reddened slightly at the memory of the fool she'd made of herself.

Sally had insisted that she meet her new client. "His name is Jared Jones and he's thirty-four years old. He lives on his own in a condo. He was in a boating accident when he was twenty-two and has been paralyzed from the waist down since then, so he's in a wheelchair. He has a special van that's been adapted for him. It has a side door and a lift for him to get in and out with."

Sally took a breath and continued. "He always has a smile. He isn't angry about his situation, and he tries really hard to make life better for other people in wheelchairs. He's met Rick Hansen and has helped him raise money by taking part in his Man in Motion fundraising. And he belongs to a wheelchair basketball team and has gone to the Paralympics twice."

"Sounds like an active guy," Elizabeth said.

"He is. I've been telling him about you, and he's interested. So, will you come with me and meet him?"

After two weeks of putting her off, Elizabeth had finally agreed. "Okay. I guess it won't hurt."

"Good. He coaches wheelchair basketball in the afternoons so we could go see him after work. I'll call him and let him know that we can meet him at the gym."

"Tonight?"

"Why not?"

Elizabeth couldn't think of a reason. She shrugged. "Might as well get it over with."

When they entered the gymnasium, Elizabeth surveyed the room, watching as the young players deftly manoeuvred their chairs with the basketball on their lap, threw the ball to a teammate and took shots at the basket. She was impressed when one girl made a basket because, even though they were in chairs, the hoop was the same height as for able-bodied players.

The whistle blew and Elizabeth's eyes were drawn to the man who wheeled out on to the court. Her breath caught.

"Yes, he is, isn't he," Sally said beside her.

Elizabeth didn't answer as she stared at the most handsome man she had ever seen. His blond hair was cut short and gently spiked, his face was tanned and he wore wire-rimmed glasses. His body was long and lean, but his shoulders were broad, probably from wheeling his chair. It was hard to judge, but she thought he'd be about six feet tall if he could stand.

"He's our age, and he doesn't have a girlfriend," Sally reported. "And close your mouth."

Elizabeth stopped staring and shook her head. Boy, she had never done that before.

"He's very formal. He'll call you Ms. Oliver until you tell him differently. He addressed me as Ms. Matthews the first couple of times until I realized he needed to be told to call me by my first name."

Jared had noticed them and was wheeling over, a smile on his face. Elizabeth hoped she could speak.

"Hi, Jared," Sally said. "This is Elizabeth Oliver, the writer I was telling you about."

"Hello, Ms. Oliver." Jared held out his hand.

Elizabeth took it, feeling a tingle run down her spine. She suppressed a shiver.

"Mr. Jones," she said, quickly adding, "Call me Elizabeth."

"Okay. And I'm Jared."

She felt a tug at her hand and blushed as she let go of his, realizing she had held it too long. She had to get her mind together and quit acting like an idiot.

"The practice is just about over," Jared said. "Can you wait ten minutes, then we'll go for coffee?"

"Okay," Sally agreed, before Elizabeth could say anything. "We'll wait in the bleachers."

"Talk about making a fool of myself," Elizabeth muttered, when they were seated.

"Well, at least you weren't drooling." Sally laughed.

They watched the rest of the practice and then followed Jared in his van to a nearby café. While they each ate a piece of pie, he seemed to take a genuine interest in her and her writing, asking her how she had gotten into it, what she liked most about it and what was her favourite place in Alberta so far. By the end, she was smitten.

"Well, what do you think of him?" Sally asked on their way home. "Quite a hunk, isn't he?"

"That he is, all right." Elizabeth grinned. "Why didn't you warn me?"

"I did. I told you he was cute. Besides, no one warned me, and I did just what you did when I first met him."

"It was embarrassing." Elizabeth laughed. "He's very nice, isn't he?"

"He's the easiest client I've ever had. He's not bossy or complaining or demanding. He helps when he can. He's just the best."

"So how come you're not dating him?"

"For one thing it's against the rules and for another, as nice and cute as he is, he's just not my type." She glanced over at Elizabeth. "I think he's yours, though."

"I definitely wouldn't mind getting to know him better."

Now, two months later Elizabeth was waiting for him to show up for one of their infrequent dates. Not that they didn't see each other often or talk on the phone every day. It's just that this was a real date, where they got dressed up and she put on makeup and tried to style her hair.

Her delight, though, was quickly turning to worry. He'd never been late before. She checked her watch again. He should have been there fifteen minutes ago. Hopefully, he hadn't been in an accident or had a flat tire. She thought about phoning him, but she was sure he'd call her if there was a problem. She felt a sudden disappointment that maybe he'd forgotten.

Then she saw him come in the door. He hadn't forgotten. He hadn't had an accident. Her relief was quickly replaced with excitement at the prospect of the evening ahead. She didn't care why he was late, only that he had come.

As he wheeled closer she jumped up to give him a kiss. He returned it but just barely. Nor did he greet her with his usual smile and "Hi, sweetheart." He certainly wasn't his normal, happy self.

Her stomach cringed. Something was wrong. Something had happened. Would he tell her? Was their relationship strong enough that she dared to ask?

"I'm sorry I'm late," Jared said quietly.

"That's okay. I haven't been waiting long."

Jared picked up the menu and glanced through it quickly, flipping the pages without really reading. Elizabeth sat and pretended to look through hers. She'd already read everything on it twice while waiting.

Jared closed the menu and looked at her. "I've heard that you've worked on a couple of murders," he said softly.

"And who did you hear that from?" Elizabeth asked.

"Well, it may have come up in one of my conversations with Sally."

"I've only figured out two and not because I knew what I was doing; it just happened," Elizabeth said.

Jared pulled out an envelope from his shirt pocket and removed a photograph. He glanced at it before handing it to her. She looked at him and then down at the photo of a gravestone with an inscription:

> Anna Jones
> She Took Her Own Life
> And That Of Her Unborn Child.

"My mother's grave," Jared explained.

Elizabeth looked at it again. What kind of a person would put this on a gravestone?

"Turn it over."

She complied. The three words "She was murdered" had been cut from a magazine and taped to the back. There was no signature. She raised her eyebrows at Jared.

"I received it yesterday," he said.

"From whom?"

"I don't know." He handed her the envelope. "There was no return address. But the cancelled stamp shows that it was mailed from Redwater. I took it to the Edmonton police as soon as I opened it, but the person at the station said I would have to talk to the RCMP in Redwater where mom died. I phoned that detachment and spoke with an officer. When I explained the story, she told me that they would need more evidence than that to open the old case."

He took the photo and envelope back and looked down at it again. "That engraving is carved into my memory, but it still makes me heartsick to see that Dad had that written on her headstone."

Elizabeth's heart went out to him. She laid her hand on his arm. She wanted to ask why his father had put it on the stone, but she refrained and was glad she did. He began talking.

"This morning I phoned my older half-brother, Willy, who is farming with our father. He laughed at the idea. 'Why would anyone kill her?' he asked. 'She had no money and she didn't have any enemies. She was just a woman who was tired of her life.'"

Jared fell silent, brooding.

"I'm so sorry, Jared," Elizabeth said quietly.

"But why was she tired of her life?" Jared asked, looking at her sadly. "That's what I've never understood. Why did she commit suicide?"

"Did no one ever tell you?"

"I was only told that she had gone to heaven. I wasn't told how or why. Later, when I started school, the other children taunted me, telling me she had committed suicide. When I asked my father what that meant, he refused to talk about it, but I kept asking until he finally said, 'Yes, she committed suicide. She threw herself down the old well. Now leave me alone.'

"After that, Dad barely talked about her or her death. He wouldn't tell me why she'd done it, or even if she'd loved me. He never answered any of my questions. As I grew older I learned that I had grandparents who had moved to Edmonton before Mom's death, but Dad refused to talk about them or give me an address. He never told me anything about her life before they'd met."

"What about your brother, Willy? Did he tell you anything?"

Jared shook his head. "Just like Dad. He told me to forget about it."

"How old were you when it happened?"

"I was only four."

"Do you remember much about her?"

"The only thing I remember is what she told me about how she met my dad at a dance. They married and she moved to his farm. Over the years I guess I've let everything else about her slip into my distant memory."

He paused. "But now, since receiving the picture, some images have come back. I even dreamed about her last night, with her long, dark hair, which she kept pinned back from her face. She used to brush it in the evening. And she always gave me a hug and kiss when she tucked me in bed."

"Did you tell your father about this photograph?"

"No, Willy doesn't want me to. He wants me to throw it away and forget the whole thing. He says Dad doesn't need to be reminded of the past." He paused and looked at the photo. "And that's why I'm late. I've been on the phone with Willy most of the day trying to get him to help me. I wanted to ask Dad about this, but Willy kept intercepting the calls and hanging up on me, like I was a telemarketer or something."

Jared went quiet again, and Elizabeth didn't say anything. She knew expressing words of sympathy would be futile.

He looked up at her imploringly. "I've been thinking about this ever since I received it. What if she didn't commit suicide? What if she was murdered, as the words on the back of this photograph suggest? If I ignore this, then I'd always wonder if a killer got away with my mother's murder. I have to make sure she wasn't murdered, and I need your help."

Chapter 3

"I'm not a detective," Elizabeth protested, feeling a load of weight suddenly settle on her shoulders. She couldn't get caught up in this. The other murders had involved people she didn't know, and she'd had no stake in the outcome. She knew Jared, and the pressure to succeed for him would be immense.

"The police want more evidence. I don't know how to get it, and I can't afford to hire a private investigator. You're the only person I know who could do this for me."

Elizabeth chewed on her lip. "You know I've already taken time off work to research and write my travel article."

"Yes." Jared nodded. "You'll be in the Redwater area, won't you? I could come with you ..."

"I'm still not certain which highways I am taking from Edmonton yet. I might not have time to go out to Redwater and ask questions."

Elizabeth's heart ached at the look of disappointment on his face, and she felt her resolve weakening. She wasn't positive that she could say no to this man she found so alluring.

"Could you do it on weekends or days off?" He quickly held up his hands. "I'm sorry. I didn't mean to plead like that. It's just that I really want to find out what the truth is."

The waiter came to take their orders, and Elizabeth continued after he left.

"I really know nothing about solving crimes," she reiterated. "I just happened to be drawn into them, and it was only luck that I was able to resolve them."

"I'll settle for anything, experience, luck, whatever it takes to find out what this is all about."

"It could just be a prank," Elizabeth said. She was trying everything she could think of.

"I've thought about that too, but I still need to know."

Elizabeth hesitated. Don't get involved, a little voice told her. Don't even ask for more information. You have enough on your plate as it is.

As usual, her natural-born inquisitiveness caused her to ignore that little voice.

"There are just so many questions," she said, her mind working. "Like who sent it? Why now? Why did they send it to you and not your father? What do they think you can do about it after all this time?"

Jared just shook his head. "I wish I knew all that."

"Maybe if you waited long enough they might go to the police."

"But if they don't, then I will never know."

Elizabeth tried not to be swayed by his good looks as her head advised her to say no while her heart yelled yes! Yes!

"Tell me more," Elizabeth finally said. She couldn't help herself; she was intrigued.

"I don't know much. My mother threw herself—supposedly threw herself—down an old well on our farm."

"How much older than you is Willy?"

"Twelve years."

"So he knew your mother."

Jared nodded.

"Other than your brother have you talked to anyone else about the photograph?"

"No."

"Where is the farm from Redwater?" They had been talking about her going out to meet his family sometime. Maybe it would be sooner than expected.

"It's southeast of Redwater."

Elizabeth picked up the photo and turned it over again. "Why do you suppose it was sent now?"

"The only thing I can think of is that this year is the thirtieth anniversary of her death."

Their food was delivered, and Elizabeth breathed a silent sigh of relief. Maybe eating would give her time to come up with a way out of this. They ate in silence for a while.

Her mind failed her, so in the end she said, "Why don't I think it over? After all, I still have a week before I start my research."

Jared's face brightened a bit. "Would you?" he asked.

"Yes," she agreed.

"Thank you," Jared said with a smile.

Elizabeth's heart beat faster. She couldn't be positive yet, but she thought she was in love.

That evening, Elizabeth sat in her bedroom, which also doubled as her office, going over the notes she'd been making on her computer for her trip. But thoughts of Jared kept creeping into her mind. He was so striking in his looks, his demeanour, his attitude. Once she'd agreed to think the idea over, they had had their usual great time, talking and laughing and eating dessert. She was surprised at how quickly the evening had gone. It just seemed that time sped up when they were together.

She hadn't told Jared that she had actually thought to work from Edmonton, leaving early each morning and coming home at night just like her readers would. If she took on his "case," she would have to stay somewhere around Redwater.

Chevy began to whimper at her feet. Jared had met her cockapoo dog, who always went with her on her trips. Another possible complication to consider. She liked staying at bed and breakfasts. Would she be able to find one in the Redwater area that allowed dogs?

"So you think it's time for your walk, do you?" she asked, with a smile.

Chevy wagged his tail.

"Okay, let's get your leash."

They climbed the stairs, and Elizabeth walked through the open door into her father's place. He and Sally were playing a game of Scrabble.

"That makes twenty-four points, Phil," Sally said, as she tallied up her numbers. "I'm ahead by forty points."

"I'm taking Chevy out," Elizabeth called from the doorway.

"See you later," her dad and Sally said together. All three laughed.

It was just growing dusk as Elizabeth and Chevy started out on their route down the alley. Chevy went from fence to fence checking scents while Elizabeth greeted any of her neighbours who were out in their yards. At the end of the alley, Chevy turned left, and they headed towards a park. Here she undid his leash, and he took off on a run. She kept an eye on him so she could clean up after him.

Sally was sitting on their couch when she arrived home. "Thank you for spending the evening with Dad," Elizabeth said. It seemed as if Sally was the one who spent most of the time with him, and Elizabeth felt a little guilty.

Sally waved her hand. "He's fun, and he doesn't mind losing. But I want to know how your date went." She leaned forward eagerly.

Elizabeth sat down and told Sally all about the photograph Jared had received.

Sally leaned back and raised her eyebrows. "Wasn't it just this morning you were saying that the odds of finding a murder to unravel three years in a row would be high?"

Elizabeth grimaced. "I know."

"Are you going to help him with it?"

Elizabeth thought about it. Now that she was away from Jared and the spell he seemed to have cast over her, her common sense took over.

"I really don't know if I can," Elizabeth said. "There would be just too many problems, like having to use his vehicle for the wheelchair and trying to find a place that accepts dogs. And how would I find time do my work if I have to run around asking questions?"

Sally nodded in sympathy. "You have a tough decision to make."

"Not only that. It's almost as if he believes I can do it, that I know how to conduct a proper investigation. All I've done in the past is somehow ask the right questions and read the clues. He wants to know so badly what happened to his mom that I'm scared what will happen to us if I'm not able to find out."

"I'm sure he'd understand."

"I don't know. It was like being with a different Jared when he talked about it. He's holding in a lot of hurt, and it's as if knowing this will make it all better."

"I don't envy you your decision." Sally tried unsuccessfully to stifle a yawn.

"Yeah. I'm kind of caught between two choices. I could turn him down and take a chance that it won't affect our relationship. Or I could try and take the chance that if it doesn't turn out the way he wants, it won't cause problems between us. I really like him, and I want to continue seeing him."

"I'm sorry that I can't help you with your dilemma."

"Thank you for listening, and now I'll let you go to bed."

Elizabeth went into her bedroom and again brought up her notes on her computer. There were at least ten highways leading out of Edmonton to choose from. She studied her Alberta map. Leaving daily from Edmonton, it would take her three days to travel the highways, and then she had planned four days to write the article. Once she'd sent the article away, she wanted to head to the mountains and do some camping. Last summer, her anticipated camping trip had been shelved because of the enticement of the skeleton in the septic tank. This year she wanted to make that trip.

She looked at Redwater on the map. She could have the reader leave Edmonton on Highway 28, which ran past Redwater, and return on Highway 45. Then the next route could begin on Highway 16 East and return on Highway 14. The third would also begin on Highway 28 but head north and then back to Edmonton. They would all keep her in the vicinity of Redwater. It might just work out.

What to do. To get away from it for a while, she let her mind consider Jared's anonymous message.

The person who had sent the photograph to Jared either knew his mother had been murdered or was trying to cause some trouble for that family. And why send it to Jared? He'd been a child when his mother had died, and anyone who knew him could see he didn't have much money and couldn't afford a professional investigator. How was he going to do anything about it?

What about the person who sent it? Who could it be, and why now after all these years did they feel the need for something to be done? Maybe they had been protecting someone all these years who didn't need protecting anymore. Someone who had recently died, she thought. Or maybe the sender was dying and wanted to clear their conscience.

Elizabeth felt a familiar stirring in her stomach and goosebumps on her arms and realized in dismay that she was being hooked. She felt her detective instincts begin to surface, her solving juices flow.

"Oh stop it," she said out loud. "You don't have any detective instincts or solving juices. You just love a mystery."

Chapter 4

Anna's Story

Anna had just finished giving four-year-old Jared his breakfast when she heard Paul stumble around in the bedroom, and then go into the bathroom. He'd been at the bar until it closed last night.

Paul's eyes were red and he gave Anna a venomous look when he came into the kitchen.

"Would you like some ham and eggs?" she asked, sweetly.

He glared at her, as his face turned a sickly green. He spun around and went back to the bathroom. Hearing him retch gave her a small feeling of satisfaction. Paul headed for the bedroom again, and she heard the bed creak when he lay down.

She leaned her arms on the table and rested her head on them. Was it really only six years ago that she'd been planning to go to university in Edmonton? It seemed a lifetime had passed. Her parents had agreed to pay for her tuition and books and the rent for an apartment. She would have to find a job to buy her groceries and other essentials.

"We want you to learn what it's like to start paying your own way," her father had said.

Hers had been a stern upbringing. She was an only child and for as long as she could remember her parents had told her she was going to go to university and become a lawyer. And she'd believed it, thinking that was what she wanted to do. Then she'd met Paul at a wedding.

He was older, a farmer like her father, and he had a twelve-year-old son. He was a great dancer and was very courteous and caring towards her. Her boyfriend had just broken up with her, and even though she really wanted to get back together with him, she went on a date with Paul.

"Stay away from him," her father had warned. "He's too old for you."

But suddenly, at eighteen, she'd realized that she was tired of her parents telling her what do to. She wanted to make her own decisions and one of them was to say yes every time Paul asked her out. Deep down, she'd known that she didn't want to be a lawyer. If anything, she wanted to be a nurse.

When she discovered she was pregnant, she'd been afraid to tell her parents. She thought about using that as a way to get her ex-boyfriend to marry her, but he'd already left the area to take a job. Then it finally got to the point where she had to tell them. Her mother was quietly sympathetic, but she hadn't been prepared for her father's reaction. The words were barely out of her mouth when he began to rant and rave about what a no-good daughter she was, and then, to her shock, he actually threw some of her clothes into a suitcase and, grabbing her elbow, shoved her out the door. He then slammed the door and locked it. She stood on the step totally bewildered. She tried banging on the door, thinking her mother would let her back in, but there was only silence inside.

Finally, she began walking down the road and was picked up by a neighbour, who took her to Paul's place. He was her only choice. Would he believe her, though?

When she told him about her pregnancy, he immediately said, "I guess you'll have to marry me."

A week later, they were married at the house of the local marriage commissioner. Her parents refused to come, so it was just Paul's mother, his son, Willy, and the two of them.

Everything was fine until Jared was born almost six months later. Then Paul suddenly changed. He began to drink and not come home until early morning. And he had begun to yell at her and Willy. Then one night, when she yelled back, he hit her. That surprised both of them, but he didn't apologize. Anna immediately phoned her parents and asked them to let her come home. But they refused, even after she told them how Paul drank all the time and had hit her.

"You are married now, and you have to stay with your husband," her father replied.

She knew they had been humiliated by her pregnancy and her quick wedding. And now, in the almost five years since her marriage, her parents had come only once to see her and that was to drop off a little blue suit for Jared when he was born. She'd invited them in, but they said they had other places to go. She'd sent them a picture of Jared on each of his birthdays.

Without her parents' help, she'd been forced to stay with Paul. His drinking and erratic behaviour had continued, and he'd occasionally hit her over the years, not always hard but just enough to let her know that he was mad about something.

Anna lifted her head. There might be a way out. She'd been thinking about it for the past few days. Her old boyfriend from high school, Nick, was back. She'd go see him.

It was early April and still cool, but the little snow they'd had was gone and the ground had begun to thaw. Later, when Paul had headed out to move some hay bales off one of their fields, she went to her closet and found her best jeans, the ones that showed off her butt, the butt that Nick had liked so much. She pulled on her tightest sweater and then a short jacket, which she left open. She took special care to style her long dark hair so it framed her face. Then she picked up Jared and carried him and his toy tractor to the truck. Paul wouldn't be back for hours. It wasn't far. She had time.

Anna drove into Nick's driveway, hoping he would be in the house or yard. She was glad to see his truck parked by the house. She looked around and saw him standing outside the garage.

"Wait here, honey," she told Jared. "I just have to go see this man."

Anna swayed her hips as she headed to the garage. She could see Nick staring at her. Good. She smiled as she neared him.

"Hi," she said brightly. "Welcome back."

Nick nodded.

"Is that all I get?" She pouted. "There was a time when you would grab me and swing me around when you saw me."

"That was a long time ago," Nick said. "What do you want?"

She kept the smile on her face. "I heard that you're getting married."

Nick nodded again.

Anna went up to him and put her arms around his neck. "I just wanted to give you a chance to change your mind." She kissed him.

"Don't," he mumbled against her lips. He reached up to remove her hands.

She tightened her grasp, pushing her body into his. She could feel him relaxing. Yes.

Suddenly, he stiffened. He pulled her arms away and stepped back. “No,” he said, wiping his lips.

She hid her disappointment. “You still feel something for me,” she wheedled. “We could still have a life together.”

“You’re married and I’m engaged. We have no future together.”

“I’ll get a divorce; you can break off your engagement. It would be easy.”

“No,” Nick said.

“But you loved me when we were in high school.”

“That was years ago. We didn’t know what love was then.”

“I did.”

“Well, I didn’t.”

She wasn’t ready to give up. She stepped closer to him again. “Okay, but just a kiss for old time’s sake.”

“No.”

“Oh, come on. We’re going to be neighbours and friends.” She put her arms around his neck again. This time she opened her mouth and probed with her tongue. She heard him whimper. She knew it. He still cared for her. This had been easier than she thought.

Chapter 5

The next morning, Elizabeth quickly ate a bowl of cereal while Sally had a cup of coffee.

"We'd better get going," Elizabeth said, putting her bowl in the dishwasher. "Sherry's first race is at nine o'clock."

"I'm going with Phil in his truck so we can carry the lawn chairs. Do you and Chevy want to come with us?"

Elizabeth had thought about taking her own vehicle so she could leave between races, but she decided she'd better stay to support Sherry.

"Okay, we'll go with you two." Elizabeth scooped up Chevy and headed up the stairs.

They drove downtown and parked in the underground parking lot close to Louise McKinney Riverfront Park. They left the windows partially down for Chevy, and Elizabeth opened the containers of food and water she'd brought for him. She grabbed her lawn chair from the back of the truck and followed her dad and Sally to the park.

It felt eerie to walk along the grassy plateau above the North Saskatchewan River. The last time they'd been here was when her mother had paddled her last race with Breast Friends. Today, it was Sherry paddling with the breast cancer survivor team.

It had been a long year for the entire family. When Sherry had been diagnosed with breast cancer, everyone had gone into shock. It had been only seven months since their mother's death, and it felt like they were reliving her fight with cancer all over again. Sherry had spent the first month after her lumpectomy living with their dad, and then they had all taken turns going with her for her twenty-five radiation treatments.

She'd joined the dragon boat team in January and had been training with them ever since. Everyone in the family hoped that the cancer had been found in time and there wouldn't be a reoccurrence like there'd been with her mother, whose cancer had spread to her brain.

Elizabeth smiled when she saw Terry coming towards them.

"Sherry's team is up soon," Terry said. "She's in the marshalling area."

"I'll go let her know we're here," Elizabeth piped up, giving Terry her chair. She headed past the vendors' tents to the area where the teams for the upcoming three races were waiting. The ones who would be getting into the boats next were lined up in order at the bottom of the stairs, watching the boats from the last race empty out. The teams for the race after were at the top of the stairs. The teams for the third race were in loose lines on the grass joking and laughing.

Elizabeth spotted Sherry in her life jacket and holding her paddle, and she hurried towards her. Sherry hadn't gone with the team to any of the other festivals during the summer, so this was her first race. She looked nervous.

"Hi," Elizabeth said.

"Oh, you made it," Sherry said, relief in her voice. "Did Dad come too?"

"Yes, and Sally. How are you doing?"

"I am so scared."

"Scared? Why?"

"Because this is an important race. We're the hometown team, and we have to make a good showing."

Another team member, overhearing the conversation, spoke up. "You'll be fine."

"Thank you." Sherry smiled weakly. "But I just don't want to let the team down by not pulling my weight."

"You're a strong paddler," Elizabeth said. "You won't let anyone down."

The race marshal began to call the teams. When he yelled "Breast Friends Juggernauts," Sherry gave Elizabeth a quick hug and hurried to the top of the stairs with her team.

On her way back to the tent area, Elizabeth's cellphone rang. Her stomach did a flip-flop when she saw the name Jared Jones on the display.

"Hi," she said.

"Hi, sweetheart."

Butterflies flitted around in her stomach at the sound of his voice.

"I hope I'm not bothering you, but I forgot to ask what I can bring this evening."

"Nothing, thanks. Just yourself," Elizabeth replied. "We've already got everything we need."

"Are you sure? I really hate to freeload, especially since I don't even know your family."

"You won't be freeloading. Everyone is looking forward to meeting you. Dad even bought some real expensive steak." Elizabeth walked towards the others sitting in their chairs along the edge of the riverbank.

"Have the races started?" Jared asked.

"Yes, Sherry's team is in line for the next one."

"I'm really sorry I can't be there, but I'll see you tonight, sweetheart."

"Bye, Jared." She slipped her phone into her pocket. As much as she was looking forward to seeing him again, she was worried about what to say to him about his request. She shook her head. This was not the time to think about it.

Elizabeth sat in her chair and looked out over the river. One thing about this venue was that everyone who attended had a great view of the races.

"Hey, Oliver, Matthews. I finally found you." Connie came up to the group with her lawn chair. "I've been looking all over for you."

"Hi, Connie," Sally said. She introduced her to Phil and Terry.

"Connie's in charge of scheduling, so she is the one responsible for me taking extra shifts when I really don't want them." Elizabeth laughed.

Connie set her chair up beside Elizabeth. "I've never been to a dragon boat festival before," she said.

Elizabeth pointed to the boats lined up near the foot bridge. "They race from there to that marker, which is four hundred metres. When they are finished, they paddle over to the dock and get out so that the next teams can load. And that's about it. While they are loading, another set of teams are getting ready to race."

"When does your sister race?"

"That's Sherry's team there," Terry said, waving at a boat that was going by on the other side of the river. He cupped his hands around his mouth and yelled, "Hi, Sherry!" No one looked up at him.

"They're supposed to concentrate on their paddling, so they never look when their name is called," Elizabeth clarified for Connie. "It's not that she was ignoring him."

They watched while the boats were lined up and then heard the horn. Everyone was on their feet yelling. When the boats passed by their vantage point, Sherry's team was in second place and that is how they finished the race.

"Wow, second place," Connie said, sounding impressed.

"They aren't actually racing against the other teams in their race," Elizabeth explained. "They're going for best times against all the teams in their section."

When Sherry came up to them after her team debriefing, she was radiant.

"I've done my first race," she said proudly, returning everyone's hugs. "The team captain said that I've gone from a festival virgin to a dock whore."

Elizabeth laughed. The vulgar term was used as a rite of passage in dragon boat circles. But she suddenly felt a tug at her heart at the memory of her mother saying the exact same thing after her first race. It was a like a dragon boat baptism.

"When's your next race?" Elizabeth asked, after introducing Connie.

"At two-thirty," Sherry answered. "I have to be back at the tent by one-thirty."

"Then we've got time to wander around," Terry said. "There's supposed to be a kung fu demonstration that I want to watch."

"I'll come too," Sherry said.

"I need something to eat," Phil added. "What about you, Sally?"

"That sounds great. I only had coffee this morning. You two coming?" She looked at Elizabeth and Connie.

"I'm not hungry," Elizabeth said.

"Sorry, Matthews, but I have to go find my cousin," Connie said. "She's on one of the hospital teams. This is her first festival too, and I said I would cheer for her. Do you want to come with me, Oliver, and then we can look around?"

Elizabeth agreed. "We'll just leave our chairs here. It's pretty safe."

They found Connie's cousin. Her team was warming up, but it would be awhile before their race.

"Let's go to the merchandise tent and see what they have," Elizabeth suggested.

They wandered over to the tent, where they checked out various items of clothing with the Edmonton dragon boat logo on them.

"This would be a nice souvenir," Elizabeth said, holding up a red vest. "I bought a black one at Mom's first race here."

When she'd paid for it they went to a jewellery tent, and Connie bought a necklace with a dragon pendant and matching earrings. At the next tent, Connie held up a black T-shirt with a red dragon on the front. "I like this. I think I'll buy it."

They returned to their chairs, where they found Elizabeth's dad and Sally. After they cheered on Connie's cousin's team, Elizabeth left and took Chevy out for a tour of the grass along the street. When she returned, it was almost time for Sherry's race.

Her team beat their first race time by three seconds, and Sherry was ecstatic when she joined up with her family.

"See, you had nothing to worry about," Elizabeth said, as they gathered up their chairs to head home.

"Well, I'll see you at work, ladies," Connie said, waving goodbye.

That evening, Elizabeth tried not to keep watching the alley for Jared's van. She had told him to park on the cement pad behind the fence. She had also said they would eat around six o'clock and that was still half an hour away. Terry and Sherry had arrived already, with Terry explaining that they would be leaving early to get Sherry home and in bed after her long day.

They were sitting on the patio in the backyard when Elizabeth saw the top of Jared's van over the fence. At last. She jumped up and went to open the gate to let him know he had the right place.

She watched as he pressed the buttons to open the side door and lower his lift from the upright position. He unlocked the brakes that held his wheelchair, swung it around and wheeled on to the lift. Jared smiled at her as he pressed a button and the lift lowered quietly to the pavement.

Once off Jared pushed the button on his key ring to raise the lift and fold it in the doorway. The sliding door closed and locked.

Elizabeth bent towards him. He put his hand behind her neck and held her for such a long and lingering kiss that she had to catch her breath when she pulled back. He grinned impishly as he turned towards the gate. She walked beside him, keeping her hand on his shoulder as he wheeled up the sidewalk to the patio. It would have been better for holding hands if he had an electric chair, but he preferred the manual chair, as wheeling it kept him fit.

"Dad, Terry, Sherry, I want you to meet Jared," she said.

Phil held out his hand. "Great to finally meet you. Elizabeth and Sally have told me a lot about you."

Jared chuckled. "I've heard about you too. It seems you barbecue the best steak in the city."

Terry offered his hand, while Sherry came over and said with a cheeky smile, "Elizabeth did say you were the most gorgeous man she'd ever met, and I have to agree with her."

"Sherry!" Elizabeth felt herself turn bright red, and she noticed that Jared did too.

"What? It's true."

"That's the last time I tell you anything," Elizabeth said, laughing.

Chevy went to the chair, and Jared reached down to pet him. Encouraged, Chevy jumped onto his lap. Elizabeth went to take him off, but Jared held up his hand.

"No, he's fine, aren't you, fellow?" he said, scratching Chevy's ears.

"Would you like a drink?" Terry asked.

Jared shook his head. "Thanks, but I brought some pop with me."

Elizabeth reached into the backpack hanging on the handles of his chair and withdrew a can.

"How do you like your steak, Jared?" Phil asked from the barbecue.

"I'll take it rare, please."

"Good choice."

They chatted while eating their salad, then went over to Phil, who dished up their steak, baked potatoes and corn on the cob. After dessert they settled into their chairs while Sally passed around the coffee.

"Well, I'm stuffed," Jared said. "That was so good! The rumours about you and steak are definitely true, Phil."

"Thank you. I've had years of practice."

"I've got to go home and get some sleep," Sherry said, yawning. "I was scared of missing the alarm this morning, so I didn't sleep very well last night."

Terry jumped up. "Let's go, then. Good night, all."

"Call me after your race and let me know how you did," Elizabeth said.

She had to work tomorrow and hated the idea of missing the final races and maybe not seeing Sherry receive her first medal.

"Come on, Phil," Sally said. "I'll beat you at another game of Scrabble."

"What do you mean, you'll beat me?" He followed her into the house.

"It looks as if my family has, not so discreetly, left us alone together." Elizabeth grinned.

"I don't mind," Jared said. Chevy, who had been gnawing on a bone, jumped into his lap again.

"Would you like some more coffee?" Elizabeth asked.

"No, thank you."

There was a rare lull in their conversation. Usually they talked a mile a minute and had a hard time saying all they wanted to in their time together. Elizabeth had decided to tell him the problems that would arise for her if she took on the job, so he would understand why she had to turn him down. For, after much thought, her head had won out, and she knew she just didn't have enough time to do her research, write her article and also run around town trying to solve a long-ago murder that might not even be a murder.

"I've really thought this over, and I can't see how I can help you. My vehicle isn't set up for your wheelchair, and I'll either be gone all day researching or in my room working on my article. I won't have the time to go with you and dig around for information."

"We can use my van for travelling." Jared leaned forward eagerly. "I'll pay for the gas. And there's plenty of room for Chevy too, if you're bringing him. I could even look after him sometimes if you want. He could keep me company."

"I was planning to work out of Edmonton," Elizabeth said. "I'd drive each road in a day and after the three days begin to write the article. I can't do that and work on your mystery in Redwater."

"Redwater isn't that far from Edmonton. We can stay at my dad's. He's got lots of room and some of the house has been renovated to accommodate my chair. You can leave from there."

Elizabeth sighed. This was not going well. Staying at his father's house was definitely not an option. "I think it would be very awkward, investigating the suspicious death of his previous wife while eating at his table."

"Yes, I guess you are right." Jared's voice was subdued. Then he perked up. "I called my grandmother who lives here in Edmonton, and she said you can come over and meet her. You could ask her some questions about my mom."

"Your grandmother?"

"Yes, my mom's mother."

"Did Sally tell you to do that?" she asked, suspiciously. "Are you trying to get me hooked on this?"

Jared smiled. "Sally may have given me a few hints. Plus, I just plain like your company."

Elizabeth felt herself grow warm at the statement. She knew it wasn't a good idea, but she was having a hard time turning this man down. And she did want to spend more time with him.

"We can go now, if you want," Jared said, as if sensing her wavering.

"Isn't it a bit late?"

"No, I just have to phone her and let her know."

"Okay," she relented. "But this doesn't mean I'm on the case!"

"She doesn't live far from here so we'll take my van, then I'll bring you back," Jared said, a wide smile spreading across his face.

Chevy rode on Jared's lap out to the vehicle. He jumped off when Jared wheeled on to the lift. Elizabeth picked up the cockapoo and climbed into the passenger seat.

"Did you tell your grandmother about the photograph?" Elizabeth asked, holding Chevy on her lap.

"I said that something had come up about Mom's death, and I had someone who wanted to ask her some questions about it."

Elizabeth shook her head with a laugh. "You sure are taking some liberties."

"That's my nature," said Jared, grinning.

Chapter 6

They drove down a tree-lined street in an older section of the city and stopped in front of a small, stucco house. Elizabeth climbed out and waited for Jared to ride down on the lift. There was a ramp for him to wheel up to the landing at the front door. She noticed that the outside door had been removed so it wouldn't be in his way. He pressed the bell.

A woman in her mid-seventies opened the inner door. Her face broke into a smile when she saw Jared.

"Come in." She stood back and gestured for them to enter.

"Grandma, this is Elizabeth Oliver. Elizabeth, my grandmother Olga Dombroski."

"Nice to meet you," Olga said, with a slight Ukrainian accent. "Come into the kitchen. I have a pie in the oven."

Elizabeth let Jared go first, then followed.

"Please, sit down," Olga said to Elizabeth, indicating a chair. Jared wheeled to an empty spot at the table. She sat and put her hands in her lap. "Now tell me what this is about."

Jared reached into his pocket, pulled out the photograph and handed it to her. Just the sight of the stone brought tears to her eyes. "Such a terrible thing to put on her grave. Such a terrible thing."

"Turn it over, Grandma."

She read the words on the back, and her eyes widened. She looked at Jared. "What does this mean? Someone thinks she was murdered?" She held the picture to her chest and began to rock back and forth. "Who would murder my daughter?"

Jared held up his hand. "We don't know that she was murdered, Grandma," he said gently. "I received that in the mail two days ago. I don't know who sent it or why."

Elizabeth was beginning to feel uncomfortable. This wasn't a good idea. Olga was getting upset, and she couldn't blame her.

"Did you go to the police?"

Jared nodded. "I talked to them, but they said they needed more information, so I asked Elizabeth here if she could help me."

"You are a private investigator?" the woman asked sharply, peering at her.

"No, actually, I'm a travel writer."

"A writer?" Her voice rose. "What does a writer know about murder?" Olga turned to Jared.

Jared put his hand on her arm. "Grandma," he said quietly, as if trying to calm her. "Elizabeth has found the killers in two other murders."

"Why don't you hire a real detective?"

"Because I can't afford it."

"I have some money," Olga said.

"No, Grandma. You keep your money."

Elizabeth didn't like the sound of this. She was going from being uncomfortable to becoming resentful that Jared had put her in this position.

Before she could say anything, Jared said, "Grandma, Elizabeth isn't here to try and figure out what happened to Mom."

"Oh? Why not?"

"Because she has a job, and she has to write an article for a magazine."

"So why did you come if you're not going to help?" Olga glared at her.

Elizabeth felt her temper rising. This woman had gone from not wanting her to look into the mystery because she wasn't a real detective to demanding to know why she wouldn't try to help Jared. She bit her tongue. It probably wouldn't do much for their budding relationship if she told off Jared's grandmother.

"She came because she's a friend, and I asked her to," Jared interjected.

"Oh," Olga said, contritely, "I'm sorry. I didn't mean to be rude." She smiled, and then hurried over to the counter and put on her oven mitts. She opened the oven door. The smell of baking pie filled the air, but Elizabeth couldn't tell what type it was.

Olga put the pie on a wooden board and closed the oven door. "Would you like a piece? It's blueberry." Olga cut the pie and set the steaming pieces in front of each of them.

Elizabeth accepted the peace offering with a smile and cut hers up so it would cool quicker.

"Grandma, can you tell me about Mom's death?" Jared asked around his first mouthful.

"I've already told you many times."

"I know, but can you add more, like the little details?"

"I don't know what I can add. I only know what happened." She settled back in her chair and began.

"Someone phoned, I don't remember who. I answered it. She said that Anna was dead. I said no, but she said yes. 'How?' I asked. 'She threw herself down the well,' she answered. I didn't wait to hear more. I hung up."

Elizabeth nodded sympathetically and took a bite of the pie. It was delicious.

"Your Grandpa Victor didn't believe me when I told him." Olga gestured with her hands as she continued. "He grabbed me and shook me. He yelled at me, asking me why she had killed herself. I said, 'Because you didn't let her come home. You forced her to go back to Paul.'"

Elizabeth couldn't help herself. "Why did you say that?"

"Because it was true." Olga jabbed her finger on the table. "Anna stood here at this table and begged him to let her and Jared move in with us for a while. She told us that Paul drank a lot and sometimes hit her." A tear ran down her cheek. "She was pregnant with our second grandchild, and Victor wouldn't let her stay with us."

"Why not?' Elizabeth asked gently.

"Because he was set in his stupid old ways," she said, vehemently. "He thought a woman was supposed to stay with her husband no matter what he was like. Then when he heard the news he kept saying, 'If I'd known it was that bad, I would have let her stay.' I yelled at him, 'You saw her tooth; you heard her story!'"

It was beginning to sound like there may be some merit to what was on the back of the photograph. Elizabeth knew the conversation was drawing her into the vortex and she listened, helpless as it happened.

"Did Paul really beat her?" she asked.

Olga nodded. "She had a chipped tooth when she arrived and a bruise on her cheek."

"And your husband sent her back?" Elizabeth couldn't believe a father would do that to his daughter.

"Yes," Olga said, her breathing agitated. She was reliving the moment. "'You son of a bitch!' I yelled at him. 'You and your almighty ways, worried more about what people think of you than your own daughter; so self-righteous that you wouldn't help her when she really needed you!'"

Elizabeth and Jared could only stare at her. Elizabeth could tell that he was shocked by her outburst.

"'Anna is dead and you murdered her,' I told him." She began to cry. "And, God help me, I let him. I let him."

Olga wrapped her arms around herself and rocked back and forth. "Oh, Anna. Oh, my poor little Anna." The tears ran down her cheeks.

Elizabeth and Jared sat silently, letting her recover from her thirty-year-old grief, and then Jared offered her a tissue. It was obvious that she'd gone over that conversation many times during the past years.

When she was finished wiping her eyes, Elizabeth asked, "Did you go to the funeral?"

"Yes. We still had friends in the area, so I phoned one of them to ask when it was. We went down just for the day. When we got to the funeral home, a woman came up to me, said her name was Meredith and handed me an envelope. 'Anna asked me to give this to you,' she said.

"I asked her when she'd done that, and she said on the day she died," Olga stood. "Wait a minute, and I'll get it for you." Olga left the room and returned a few minutes later with a worn envelope. She handed it to Jared.

Jared slowly opened the envelope and pulled out the yellowing piece of paper.

Olga blinked back the tears as he read it out loud.

Dear Mom and Dad,

If you are reading this letter, then you know that I'm dead. I'm sorry I wasn't the type of daughter you could be proud of. I don't blame you for anything that has happened to me. It was my choice to go out with Paul, and I admit I did it to spite you. So what happened afterwards was a result of my stupidity. I hope you can forgive me for everything I've done to hurt you.

Please find it in your hearts to be caring grandparents to Jared. Let him come to visit you, write him letters, send him birthday and Christmas gifts, phone him, do everything a grandparent does. And tell him about me. Tell him I loved him with all my heart. Please don't let him forget me.

Thank you.

I love you both.

Anna.

There was silence when he finished.

"How come you never showed this to me before?" Jared asked, as he stared at his mother's writing.

"When you first asked about your mother, I thought you were too young to read this, and then you quit asking. I figured I should leave well enough alone."

"Did you show this to the police at the time?" Elizabeth asked.

"Yes, they decided it was a suicide note since everyone they talked to said she was unhappy. Plus, she wrote it as if she knew she was going to die. That suggested suicide."

That could also suggest she might have been afraid of someone, Elizabeth thought. She glanced at Jared before asking Olga, "Did you tell them about Paul beating her?"

"Yes. According to their records, she had never filed a complaint against him, so they said that it could have been a one-time occurrence."

"Do you think this letter was a suicide note?"

"Everybody did," she said defensively, before adding softly, "but I always had my doubts. I never really believed that my Anna would do that."

"You were four when your mother brought you here," Elizabeth said to Jared, as they drove away from his grandmother's house. "Do you remember anything?"

"All I remember is a long bus ride and then Dad coming to pick us up."

"Do you recall your dad ever hitting your mom?" Chevy jumped up onto her lap and lay down.

Jared shook his head.

"Did your dad ever hit you?"

Again, Jared shook his head. He glanced at her. "So did that conversation with Grandma stimulate your interest a little?"

"More than just a little," she admitted.

"And?"

"Okay," she laughed. "I'll do what I can. Just as long as you understand that my research takes priority. And I'll find a B and B for us to stay at." She could put off her camping trip for a few days, if necessary, for this man.

"Thank you, Elizabeth," Jared said with a big grin. "You don't know how much this means to me."

"But," she cautioned, "you have to be prepared for whatever we discover. If that wasn't a suicide note, then maybe she was in fear for her life and was saying goodbye to her parents. And with what we learned about your father, right now it's not looking very good for him."

"I know and that does bother me. But he's my father, and he raised me, so I think I know what he's capable of. He may not have been the best husband, but I don't think he would have killed her."

"I hope you're right." Elizabeth thought a moment. "I have some more questions."

"Ask away. I'll answer every one."

"Did your grandparents fulfil your mother's wishes?" Elizabeth wondered what type of grandparents they had been before.

"They tried, sending gifts on birthdays and at Christmas, but Dad wouldn't let me talk to them when they called, and he wouldn't let me go visit them."

"Do you know why?" Elizabeth scratched Chevy's head.

"He said they never wanted anything to do with me before Mom died, why should he let them now."

"What about the rest of your mother's family. Did you see any of them?"

"Mom was an only child and none of her extended family lived nearby."

"What about on your dad's side?"

"Dad and Willy's mother moved to the farm from the Grande Prairie area when Willy was small. Grandma Jones moved with them, and she was the only family I knew on his side."

"Did you find it lonely without much family around?" She wouldn't have wanted to grow up without her siblings.

Jared shrugged. "It was the only life I knew."

"Okay, that's about all I can think of right now." Elizabeth grew silent, thinking about what else she might need to know. "I'd like a picture of your mother, if you have one."

Jared reached for his wallet in the cup holder and pulled out a photograph. "It's her graduation. Mom is the girl in the centre."

Elizabeth took it and looked down at a group of four young people posing for the camera. The girls wore long gowns; the boys were in suits. Anna's dark hair was piled on top of her head with wisps hanging down the side of her face. She was squeezed between a boy and a girl, with another young man draping his arms over her shoulders. They were all smiling happily.

"She was pretty," Elizabeth said. "And it looks like she was popular. Is this the only one you have?" She'd been hoping for a more updated one, maybe with Jared as a child.

"This is one that Grandma gave me. Dad threw all their pictures away after the funeral."

They'd reached Elizabeth's house and sat for a few minutes in Jared's vehicle.

"I made a list of Mom's friends and neighbours," Jared said.

"You did? You were that sure I would agree to this?"

"I wasn't, but I wanted to be ready if you did." He gave her a sideways smile before reaching into the little pouch on the side of his chair for a folded sheet of paper. He handed it to her.

Elizabeth looked at the long list. "That's a lot of people for us to talk to," she said, a little dismayed. Maybe this was going to be a bad idea.

"I've divided them into groups. Some of them are names of people who were our neighbours when I was growing up, some are friends of ours and the others are a few names that Grandma could recall. I don't know how many of them knew or will even remember Mom."

Elizabeth started reading the list out loud. "Sarah and Nick Thompson, Wayne and Christine Dearden, Ben and Meredith Warren."

"They were neighbours of Mom and Dad. Mr. and Mrs. Thompson still live on their farm. I think she goes by her maiden name of Munter, though. Mr. and Mrs. Dearden are divorced. Mr. Dearden is on the farm; I'm not sure where Mrs. Dearden is. Mr. Warren is dead. Mrs. Warren is a poet and lives in Redwater. She was Mom's closest friend."

"Meredith, the one who gave your Grandma the letter?"

Jared nodded. "Brittany and Tylar Heigh," he continued. "Mrs. Heigh was Ben's sister. They bought the farm after Ben was killed."

Elizabeth noticed how Jared referred to them. Paul had certainly taught him to be polite.

"That's a lot of people," Elizabeth said. "Hopefully we won't have to talk to them all. Let's break it up. Since they knew your mother, we'll start with the first three, and if we can't learn anything from them, then we'll move on to three more."

Jared nodded.

"Do you know where they live?"

"Except for Mrs. Dearden, yes. And maybe we can find out from Mr. Dearden when we talk to him."

"Good," Elizabeth said. "I'll call a few bed and breakfasts in the area and find one that allows dogs and has a wheelchair-accessible room on the ground floor. Unless you want to stay at your dad's."

"No, a B and B is fine with me, and I'll pay for the rooms since this isn't an expense you had considered in your travel plans. Besides, if we stay at the B and B together, then we only have to take one vehicle. Mine will hold all you need as well as Chevy."

Elizabeth shook her head. She needed a vehicle totally at her disposal. Going with Jared in his wasn't an option, even if they were both staying at the same place. In spite of all the talking they had done over the past two months, she really didn't know his morning routine, how long it took him to get up and ready, whether he liked to have a leisurely morning or would be willing to get going early.

"When I am working I get up early and leave, sometimes without breakfast," Elizabeth explained. "And I don't quit until it's dark or I'm finished for the day. If you come with me that might be a long day for you, or if I take your van you are stuck at the B and B for the day."

"Yes, I see your point. How many routes are you planning on doing?"

"I've set up three so I'll be gone at least three days, maybe more."

"That's going to be a lot of work," Jared said.

"Yes, it is."

"And with us taking separate vehicles I can be doing some other things while you are gone, and when we are working on Mom's murder, we can travel together."

"That works for me."

As much as she hated to call it a night, she had to work in the morning. "So I'll book us each a room at a B and B and maybe I should come by your place one evening this week with Sally and learn your morning and bedtime routines."

Elizabeth kissed Jared good night and clambered out of the van with Chevy in hand. She held him in one arm and waved until the van was out of sight.

Elizabeth quickly went on the Internet and looked up B and Bs in the Redwater area. Miraculously, she found one almost immediately that was just perfect for their needs. The phone was answered on the first ring.

"Pine Tree Bed and Breakfast," a young, male voice answered. "Brandon Ulfsten speaking."

"Hi. My name is Elizabeth Oliver, and I would like to book two rooms, one being your wheelchair-accessible room, for next week." That was all the time she wanted to give to Jared's conundrum.

"What day will you be arriving?"

"Saturday."

"Okay. Will you be needing someone to look after the person in the wheelchair?"

"Probably, on the occasional day. I plan on leaving the B and B early on some mornings and might get back late, so my companion, Jared Jones, will need help on those days with his morning and evening routines."

"There is a slight charge for that," Brandon said.

"No problem. Also, I will be bringing a small dog."

"And a pet fee for him."

"That's fine."

Once it was arranged, Elizabeth called Jared to let him know, and then she climbed into bed. She hoped she wouldn't stay awake all night rehashing the conversation with his grandma.

Chapter 7

Anna's Story

Anna lay in bed and listened to the familiar banging noise at the back door. She glanced at the clock. It was five in the morning, and Paul was just coming home from town. She had long since stopped getting up to assist him. Helping didn't improve his mood and not helping didn't worsen it.

At last he was able to open the door, and she could hear him colliding with the table as he struggled to get through the kitchen. She turned her back to the door and feigned sleep as he neared, hoping he would fall on to the bed and pass out. But when the room lit up through her lids, she knew she wouldn't get her wish.

"Anna, geddup!" His words were slurred. He grasped her shoulder and shook it. "I want shomeshing to eat, dammit!"

She pretended not to hear. He pulled her over on to her back. She opened her eyes, fearful that he might strike her.

"I'm hungry." He bent close to her face, his breath reeking of beer. "And I wan' bacon, a whole plate full of bacon." He slumped over, half on the bed, half on the floor.

Anna knew better than to argue. She climbed off the bed and stepped around him. She grabbed her housecoat, covering her swelling belly.

She watched as Paul groped his way to his feet then bounced against the wall in the hallway. He went into his sons' bedroom and turned on the light.

"Time to geddup and milk the cowsh, Willy," he slurred. He leaned against the door frame for support.

Anna hovered behind him. He'd never raised a hand to the two boys, but she didn't trust him. There was a time when he had never hit her either.

Sixteen-year-old Willy groaned from the upper bunk and slowly opened his eyes.

"Get up, you lashy bugger," Paul yelled. He stumbled over and kicked the corner of the bunk bed. "Why do I alwaysh have to wake you? When I wash a kid, I was alwaysh up in time for milking."

Willy threw off his covers and jumped from the top bunk. He looked at four-year-old Jared, who was cowering in the lower bunk.

"I'll be right with you," Willy assured his father. He leaned over and patted Jared soothingly on the shoulder.

"You better be," Paul growled, as he staggered towards the doorway again.

Anna turned quickly and headed to the kitchen. She was standing at the stove putting bacon in the frying pan when Paul finally entered the kitchen.

"Where'sh my coffee?" he demanded, collapsing into a chair at the table.

She grabbed the pot with its leftover coffee from the night before. She poured him a cup and set it in the microwave. The smell of the bacon permeated the room and it was making her nauseous.

"Could you please take over for me?" Anna asked Willy, when he came in.

"He'sh got cowsh to milk," Paul bellowed from his seat at the table.

Willy walked up to her. "What did you do to make him get up so early?" he demanded through clenched teeth.

"He's just come home," Anna said with resignation. She looked up at the kitchen clock as she took the cup from the microwave. Willy followed her glance. It was just after five o'clock.

"See what you've done to him." He glowered at her.

"Whadd're you waidding for," Paul yelled. "Gedd out to the barn."

Willy grabbed his jacket and headed for the door.

Anna fought back the bile in her throat as she turned the bacon then quickly put the lid on the pan to keep as much of the smell in as she could. She made toast, put it on his plate, then forked the bacon beside it. Between the stove and the table, her stomach started to rebel. She threw the plate in front of him and ran to the bathroom. His drunken laughter followed her.

When she had finished, she leaned back against the wall. She didn't know what she was going to do with another child or even what Paul was going to do. For he never once picked Jared up when he was a baby nor did he talk to him in his crib. As Jared grew older, Paul had disciplined him when he needed it, but he never showed any emotion towards him and never hugged him. She'd always wondered if that was just his nature, if he had treated Willy the same way when he was younger. Now she worried about how he was going to treat the new baby, especially after he'd said, "Oh, so you're having another little bastard, are you?" when she'd told him she was pregnant again.

When Anna heard Paul stumble to the bedroom, she came out of the bathroom. She went to the back door and opened it, a signal to Willy, waiting at the bottom of the step, that it was safe to come in.

She didn't go back to sleep. It would mean climbing into bed with Paul. Instead, she sat at the kitchen table for a few moments, then got up to make a start on the bread. It was going to be a scorcher today, so she might as well get at it early.

That afternoon, with the bread in the oven baking, the house felt like it was a sauna. Anna's hair was damp and beads of sweat formed on her forehead. On days like this she just wanted to take her clothes off and sit in front of a fan. But she couldn't do that with the boys around.

Anna picked up a plastic pan and went outside. She set it on the step, then grabbed the pail and rope that sat in the corner of the porch. In the backyard was an old well that had been used by the previous owners before running water had been put into the house. The round metal casing stuck out of the ground up to the height of her calf, and a large rock sat on the metal lid to keep Jared from lifting it off.

Anna pushed the rock over the edge and removed the lid. She stared down the wide mouth of the well into the water below. So many times during the record-breaking temperatures of the summer she had looked at the clear water and wished she could slip into its peaceful, inviting depths, feel its soothing coolness envelop her.

She lowered the pail until it hit the water. The weight on the end of the rope tipped it over so it filled.

Anna grunted as she pulled up the heavy pail. No matter how long she ran the water in the house, it never seemed to come out as cold as this did. She replaced the lid and rock, and then carried the pail to the porch, where she poured the water into the pan. Sinking down on to the step above the pan, she slipped off her sandals and slid her feet into the water with a sigh. This was the best way to cool off on a hot day.

Willy stopped and looked down at her on his way back from the chicken coop with a bowl of eggs. At sixteen, he was almost as big as his father.

"Why don't you just leave?" he asked angrily. "Just get out of our lives?"

Anna continued cooling her feet. When she'd first moved in, he'd done the temper tantrums, the ignoring, the trying for his dad's attention. Little had changed as he'd grown older.

"Did you hear me?" he asked louder. "Dad's had a mad-on ever since you moved in here and Jared was born, and I'm tired of being the brunt of it."

Anna looked up at him. "Willy, I would love to leave your father and this place, but I have no money. With one child, another on the way, and no training, I have little hope of supporting us if I did."

"There's welfare."

"I don't want my children to grow up on welfare."

"I wish you'd never come," he snarled, stomping away.

"Me too," she said softly.

Anna scooped the water up with her hand and let it run down her legs to cool them. Her life was getting worse and worse. If only her parents would give her a chance ... If only Nick had agreed to her wishes.

She heard the door bang open behind her.

"Make me some fresh coffee," Paul demanded gruffly.

Anna jumped up, quickly pushed her wet feet into her sandals and threw the water away.

Chapter 8

Elizabeth took stock of her equipment. She had her laptop with its voice-activated software for recording as she drove, her digital camera with its chain for carrying it around her neck and her cellphone and tape recorder in pouches to hang from her belt. And there was her battery charger and extra batteries and tapes. She used the recorder for anything outside her vehicle, like when she went into buildings, interviewed people or went on a hike.

She carried a credit and a debit card and some cash for donations to some of the attractions she would visit. These she kept in her jeans pockets along with her vehicle keys when she wasn't driving.

Her suitcase, a box containing some granola bars, a few cans of beans, a case of water and a dozen cans of Pepsi were in the back of her Tracker. Chevy's bag of dog food and water dish were also there. Since she wasn't going camping until after she had finished her research, she'd left the back seat intact. When she went to the mountains next week, she would remove it to haul all her camping gear.

As usual, she'd called Sherry and Terry the night before to say goodbye. Sally had had a graveyard shift, so she was sleeping. Elizabeth hugged her dad.

"I obviously can't tell you to stay away from this murder," he said. "So I'll just say to be careful and call often."

"I will, Dad. Anyway, we don't even know if it was a murder. That's what we're trying to find out."

Chevy followed her out to the Tracker and jumped in on his side of the car.

"We're off again," she said, patting him on the head.

Elizabeth drove to Jared's place. He was ready and waiting in his vehicle. She pulled up beside him, waved and carried on. He followed her.

As Elizabeth headed out of Edmonton on Highway 28, she instantly felt a sense of freedom. She was on the road doing what she loved best, researching for her writing. She never seemed to get over the awe she felt knowing that this was her career. And she did consider it her career. Working at the long-term care facility was just a means of supporting herself and her writing.

She looked over at Chevy sleeping on the seat beside her. Her father had offered to take care of him.

"I look after him while you are at work, why not now?" he'd asked.

With the extra time she'd be spending with Jared, she'd actually thought for a few moments that it might be a good idea too. But she'd quickly changed her mind. Chevy had gone with her on her other research trips and this was where he belonged.

She checked in the rear-view mirror to make sure Jared was keeping up with her. She'd given him the directions in case they got separated, but there was little traffic on the highway so it wouldn't be a problem.

Elizabeth turned on her laptop and began recording the route from Edmonton to Redwater. She'd include a map of the routes with the article and advise the reader to take along a road map, which would show the distances between the towns. By not having to give that information in the text of her article, she could focus more on the attractions and sights.

She had told Jared she would be stopping in Gibbons. When she reached the town, she drove to the Emmanuel Anglican Church. Jared parked behind her but waited in his van while she grabbed her tape recorder and camera and entered the church.

"The interior, with its U-joint style and large beams, is modelled after the inside of a ship," she recorded. "It's over one hundred years old and is unique in Alberta. It's still in use today."

Elizabeth continued to the Sturgeon River Historical Museum in Oliver Park. When she'd first read about this on the Internet, she'd wondered if the park was named after anyone related to her. Jared joined her, and they headed down the wide path to the McLean Brothers Store with its antique cash register, desks and an old sewing machine sitting on the hardwood floor. They moved on to a log building with artifacts from the area and a small home with 1920s furnishings. Jared pointed to some of the old farm machinery and explained to Elizabeth what each piece was used for.

"Hey, you're more than just a pretty face." She laughed. "You might actually be helpful for my research on this trip!"

She drove out of Gibbons and at Redwater pulled over to let Jared take the lead. After all, this was his hometown, and he knew it better than she did. He took her to the tourist information centre for the pamphlets and brochures that she enjoyed reading in the evening after a long day. She'd find little tidbits about the background of the area that sometimes fit well in her article.

Then he drove past the site of the tallest oil derrick in North America so that she would know where it was. This was where she planned to start her day off tomorrow.

She followed him until they pulled into the driveway of the Pine Tree B and B, a large, two-storey, red building. When she'd seen it on the Internet, she'd wondered if was an old, converted barn.

The yard was full of animal-shaped evergreen trees. There was a cat and a dog by the driveway, and dotted about were a unicorn, a bear and even an elephant. How on Earth had they been made, and how many years had it taken?

Elizabeth stepped out and put Chevy on his leash. He immediately headed for a walk.

"Not yet, bud," she said. "We've got to check in first." They waited for Jared to be lowered on his lift.

"What an unusual place," she said.

Jared nodded. "It's funny how I was raised in the area, and I never knew this was here."

Elizabeth led the way up the sidewalk to the front door, which was at one end of the building. She rang the bell, wondering if they were supposed to enter or wait for someone to come. A young man opened the door and smiled at them.

"You must be Elizabeth Oliver and Jared Jones," he said, holding the door for them. "I'm Brandon Ulfsten. We spoke on the phone."

"Nice to meet you," Elizabeth said, stepping in. When she'd talked to him, he'd sounded young, but she was surprised to see just how young: he looked to be in his teens.

The entranceway was large with a counter to one side and a couch and two chairs to the other. There was a fireplace on one wall and a stuffed moose head with giant horns hung over it. Brandon went around the counter, and they began the check-in process. Finally, he pulled out two pieces of paper and handed one each to Elizabeth and Jared.

"If you could fill these out before you leave, I'd appreciate it," he said.

Elizabeth glanced at hers and saw that it was a customer questionnaire.

"I'll show you to your rooms now," Brandon said.

He is very efficient and certainly knows what he is doing, Elizabeth thought, as they followed him to Jared's room. Maybe he was older than he looked. That made her wonder if she was starting to judge people's abilities by their age or their looks. She certainly hoped not.

Jared's room was large and sparsely furnished with a double bed, an overstuffed chair and a desk with a flat-screen television on it. There was plenty of space for him to manoeuvre his wheelchair with ease.

Brandon showed them how the bed could be raised and lowered, and he pointed out the ceiling track to which Jared's lift could be attached. In lieu of a dresser, the closet had shelving for clothes. The ensuite had a shower area with a hand-held nozzle and a commode chair with a belt for sitting on. It also had tracking on the ceiling.

"If the overstuffed chair is in your way, I can remove it," Brandon said.

"The room looks perfect," Jared said. Elizabeth agreed.

"I'll be the one assisting you on the mornings when Ms. Oliver isn't here," Brandon said.

Elizabeth and Chevy followed Brandon upstairs to her room. It too was large but held more furniture, a king-sized bed, a desk, a dresser, two night tables, a table with a coffee pot and an entertainment centre with a television. Her ensuite had a whirlpool tub plus a shower.

Brandon returned to the parking lot with Elizabeth. He carried Jared's suitcase and laptop to his room while she lugged her own suitcase and paraphernalia to hers and unpacked. After Chevy's walk, they went back to see how Jared was doing.

He, too, had unpacked and was reading a book, which he closed and handed to her.

She read out loud, "*Slashed Love: Book Three of the Revelations of a Lost Wife Series* by Meredith Warren."

Ah, yes, Jared had said she was a poet. Elizabeth looked at it with interest.

"It's just been published. I brought it so that I could get her to sign it for me."

Elizabeth reread the series title. "*Revelations of a Lost Wife* makes it sound like the poems are sad ones."

"I've just started to read these ones, but if they're like the poems in her other two books, then they are. They're about her life with her husband, Ben, until he was killed."

"Killed? How?"

"Well, it happened when I was young, but from what I've heard, he was stabbed by his lover." He paused for dramatic effect. "Her name was Christine."

Elizabeth raised her eyebrows. "As in Christine and Wayne? One of the couples on your list?"

"Yes."

Elizabeth looked at the cover. On it was an illustration of a heart with a knife in it, and three drops of blood.

He handed her two more books, one titled *We Were One* and the other *The Unravelling*. "These are the first two in her series."

They both had the same cover picture as the latest one. That was unusual. "Are these signed as well?"

"Oh, yes. I bought the first book at a reading and signing that Mrs. Warren did in Edmonton. I went because I sort of knew her. I liked it, so when the second one came out I bought it too. That one I took to her place when I was out here visiting and got her to sign. We've been friends ever since."

"You never mentioned that before."

"With everything else happening, the timing never seemed right. It does now."

"You like reading poetry?" Elizabeth asked. This was something new. She sat down in the overstuffed chair and thumbed through the book.

Jared blushed a bit. "I do, and I also write it."

Elizabeth looked up at him, impressed. There was much more to him than she had realized.

"Meredith is my mentor. Whenever I come to visit Dad, I go see her and we talk poetry. In between, we email each other. I get her to read over my efforts, and she gives me her feedback. She's the one who encouraged me to start sending my poetry to literary magazines."

"Have you had any published?"

"A few." Jared took off his glasses and cleaned the lenses. He looked different without his glasses, younger, more vulnerable.

"How many is a few?"

"Fourteen."

"Hey, that's a lot." Elizabeth put the books on the side table and leaned towards Jared. "Did you bring any for her to look over while we're here?"

"I'm working on a chapbook right now, and I've been emailing some to her for her advice. I'd like to discuss them with her while we are here."

"What's a chapbook? I've heard that word, but I'm not sure what it means."

"A chapbook is a small book that could contain poems, short stories, family recipes, whatever the author wants. It's usually self-published, but some book publishers are now willing to publish them."

"What type of poems do you write?" She was enjoying this.

"I really like the Japanese haiku."

Elizabeth felt a little foolish having to ask. "What's that?"

"There are many types, but the one I like to write has seventeen syllables spaced over three lines. The first line has five syllables, the second has seven and the third has five again. I can show you an example." He turned on his laptop and brought up a long series of poems. "I'm working on this to send to a literary magazine contest. They want a chain of haiku using the different definitions of the word 'operation.' He moved away so she could see them.

She read out loud:

"Secret agents act.
Busy businessmen transact.
Governments enact."

She stopped and counted the syllables in each line. "Five, seven, five," she said, then read one to herself. "Oh, I like this one!" she said and read it out loud:

"Airplane pilots fly.
The smooth talker utters lies.
Store purchasers buy."

She looked up at him. "Those are good."

Jared shrugged. "I don't know. Haiku are not supposed to rhyme, but there are so many types and so many rules that people don't follow, so I decided to do them this way. I'm still working on them, so they might change." He shut down the computer.

"I guess we should get out to Dad's," Jared said, taking the photograph of the gravesite from his suitcase and tucking it in his shirt pocket. He wheeled out the door.

Chapter 9

"Have you decided if you are going to show your dad the photograph?" Elizabeth asked, as she and Chevy settled on to the passenger seat of his van.

"Not yet. I phoned Willy again and had another long talk with him. He's still adamant that I shouldn't, that Mom committed suicide, but there was something missing in his voice. It lacked conviction, almost like he knows something."

"Maybe we should try to speak with him alone," Elizabeth said. She wanted to mention that Willy might know something about their father beating Jared's mother, but she wasn't sure if now was the right time to bring it up.

"What did you tell them about me?" she asked.

"Just what we decided. You're my caregiver. When we get there, I'll ask the questions."

Elizabeth nodded. They'd discussed how to best approach their investigation. They thought people would talk more openly with Jared than they would with her. Jared had been worried that he wouldn't be very good at it. She'd given him some pointers on how to get started with people but added that follow-up questions usually depended on what was said and how it was said.

"Just play it by ear," she suggested. "You'll get the hang of it."

Jared turned down a road, and Elizabeth read the name. Victoria Trail. This was on her agenda for tomorrow's trip.

They pulled up in front of a ranch-style house. Two dogs came over to welcome them. Seeing them, Elizabeth decided to leave Chevy in the van.

"I don't see Dad's truck," Jared said, as he wheeled up the ramp.

"Does he know we were coming?" She hoped this wasn't a surprise visit.

"Yes. I phoned him last night. I finally managed to call when Willy wasn't around so I could talk to him. But I didn't say the exact time we were going to get here."

Jared knocked on the door, then opened it and went in. Elizabeth followed.

"Hello?" Jared yelled.

"In here," a male voice called back.

They went into the kitchen where a man sat at the table. He had thick, dark hair and bushy eyebrows. He was big and burly and wore a black T-shirt that enhanced his protruding stomach.

Elizabeth surmised that he must be Willy, since he was too young to have been Jared's father. Good, they could ask him some questions alone.

Jared introduced Elizabeth to his half-brother. Willy nodded and turned to Jared. "I see you're going to carry through with this."

"Yes, I am, and you can't stop me."

"Oh, I won't try to stop you. Just don't expect much cooperation from me or from Dad."

"Where is he? He knows I'm coming."

"He and Susie went into town to buy some groceries and parts for the swather. Susie insisted that she had to get some of your favourite foods for supper tonight."

Elizabeth didn't know if she liked the idea of staying for a meal. Then again, once Jared had asked his questions, they might not even be invited.

"I was just on my way out to the deck," Willy said. He held up a bottle. "You want a beer?"

Both Elizabeth and Jared shook their heads.

"What about a juice or pop then?"

"I'll have a Pepsi, if you have any," Elizabeth said.

"Me too," Jared added. "But I'll get them." He wheeled over to the refrigerator and opened the door. He rummaged around until he found two cans of Pepsi.

When they were settled on the deck, Jared handed Willy the photograph. He immediately looked on the back.

"It's just a hoax," Willy said, as he passed it back to Jared. "I still don't think you should be showing it to Dad."

"Why not?" Jared asked.

"Because it happened so long ago."

"A murder is still a murder." Elizabeth couldn't help herself.

Willy stared at her. Oops, she thought. A caregiver should keep her mouth shut. But if he thought she was out of line, he didn't say so.

"You think this photo with some words pasted on the back carries more weight than a police investigation?" Willy asked with sarcasm.

Elizabeth bit off her retort. She didn't need to antagonize him the very first day. But she'd already spoken up, so she carried on, trying another tactic. "Don't you think your father should be informed in case whoever sent this to Jared sends it to someone else or even the newspapers?"

Willy stared at her as he raised the bottle of beer to his lips. She saw no resemblance between him and Jared. She wondered what their father looked like.

"He'll certainly find out if you start asking questions," Willy pointed out.

"She's right, though," Jared said. "Dad needs to know."

"You do what you want," Willy said, standing. "But remember that I warned you." He started off the deck. Elizabeth willed Jared to say something to keep him there.

"Uh, Grandma said that Dad beat Mom," Jared fumbled. "Do you know anything about that?"

Willy stopped and looked down at his half-brother. "Leave it alone," he said, his voice devoid of any emotion. He strode off the deck and over to the barn.

"Well, that didn't go very well," Elizabeth said.

"He's always had a short temper," Jared explained. "Don't take it personally."

They had almost finished their drinks when a blue truck drove into the yard and parked near the deck. A man and woman climbed out and began to unload bags of groceries. The woman smiled when she saw Jared. Elizabeth noticed that the man didn't.

"Hello, Jared," the woman said, giving him a hug with one arm.

"Jared." The man nodded.

"Susie, Dad, this is Elizabeth Oliver, my caregiver."

Elizabeth stood and shook hands. She saw where Willy got his looks and stature. He was an exact image of Paul. Susie was almost as tall as Paul but very slender with reddish-blonde hair. She looked to be a few years younger than him.

"Come in and talk while we put the groceries away," Susie said, leading the way into the house.

Elizabeth and Jared followed the two into the kitchen. Susie began removing the groceries from the bags and putting them away. Paul opened the fridge, took out a beer and sat at the table.

"So what brings you out this way, Jared?" Susie asked. "We haven't seen you in about three months."

Willy had come back into the house and was standing by the door, his arms crossed. Jared glanced at Willy and then took the photograph from his pocket. He looked down at it a moment before handing it to Paul.

Nothing like getting right to it, Elizabeth thought.

Paul looked at it but never said anything. Susie looked over his shoulder and then went back to her unpacking.

"Look on the back," Willy instructed gruffly.

Paul turned it over and his jaw dropped. "What's the meaning of this?" he demanded, looking at Jared.

"I don't know," Jared said. "I received it in the mail."

Paul threw the photo on the table. "What kind of a sick mind would send something like that?"

Susie picked up the photo and turned it over. She gasped and quickly dropped it. She looked from Paul to Jared. "Someone sent this to you?"

Jared nodded.

"Why?"

"I don't know."

"What are you going to do about it?" Willy asked.

Elizabeth didn't like the way he was putting Jared on the spot. He knew what Jared wanted to do. Why didn't he let Jared tell their father in his own way?

Jared picked up the photograph and stared at the gravestone. "This grave is all I have of my mother," he said softly. "It's bothered me my whole life that she decided to leave me. I want so much to believe that she may have desired to see me grow up. If her choice was taken away from her, then I want to know. I want … no, I need to know that she would have stayed with me, if she'd been given the chance."

Elizabeth's heart went out to Jared as she suddenly understood what he was going through. Losing a mother as an adult was hard, losing a mother's love as a child must have been devastating.

"So you're going to try to find who sent this?" Paul asked. He finished his beer and went for another one.

Did he sound worried? Elizabeth wondered. She could feel the uneasiness building in the air.

"I want to find out if what they put on the back is true," Jared said.

"And how do you plan to do that?" Willy asked scornfully.

Elizabeth wondered what type of childhood Jared had had with a father who didn't show any emotion towards him and a half-brother who seemed so rude.

"I'm not sure," Jared said. If his brother's mockery bothered him, he didn't show it.

"Is that why you're here now?" Paul asked. His voice was tight.

"Yes."

Elizabeth was caught by surprise when Paul turned to her. "Did you know about this?" His eyes were narrow and furious. She could only nod her head.

"And you still agreed to come?"

"I think he has a right to know what happened to her." What else could she say?

Susie, who had been quiet until now, said, "I think he does too. She was his mother, and if someone took her away from him, then he should be able to find out who did it."

"Thank you," Jared said to her. She smiled at him.

"Will you be staying for supper tonight?"

That broke the tension in the room. Jared looked at Elizabeth, and she inclined her head. This was his decision.

"Yes," Jared replied.

"Grandma showed me Mom's suicide note," Jared said when they were eating dessert.

"What did she do that for?" Paul yelled angrily. He banged his beer bottle on the table. He and Willy had drank a lot of beer during the meal. Elizabeth wondered if this was a regular occurrence.

"Because with this message, her death can be looked at differently. She might not have committed suicide," Jared said. "Maybe she was in fear for her life and that's why she wrote it."

Elizabeth noticed he was using her words.

Paul snorted. "That's stupid," he said derisively. "She was a farm wife. No one wanted to kill her."

"According to her mother, you beat Anna," Elizabeth said. This man was irritating her, and it was time to bring him down a bit.

At least he had the grace to redden and look away. He didn't answer.

"Did you, Dad?" Jared asked.

"You don't know anything about what was happening back then," Paul said, his voice suddenly quiet. "Why don't you just leave things alone?"

"I can't," Jared said, just as softly. He wheeled away from the table towards the door. Elizabeth quickly stood and followed.

They went outside to the van. The only one who came with them was Willy. He leaned on the window as Jared locked his wheelchair into place.

"You know, things in our family were fine until you were born."

"What do you mean?" Jared asked, shocked.

"I mean Dad was a nice guy until you came along, then he changed. He was angry all the time, and he began to drink a lot."

"Are you saying that was my fault?"

"I'm saying that something happened to him after you were born." He turned and headed back to the house.

"That was a terrible thing to say," Elizabeth said quickly. "I don't think he meant it like he said."

Jared stared at his hands resting on the wheel. "Oh, I'm sure he did."

"But why would he say that? It's almost like he is trying to hurt you."

Jared nodded. "And I can't blame him. After all, this is a terrible thing that I'm dumping on them."

"It's a terrible thing that's been dumped on you," Elizabeth said quietly.

At the B and B, Brandon was welcoming more guests as they entered the house. Too bad, Elizabeth thought. She would have liked to talk to him about the house and the trees. But they were there for a few days; she might get a chance later.

There really wasn't much to do in the way of helping Jared get ready for bed. He could look after his own evening rituals, like brushing his teeth and putting on his upper pyjamas. He had brought along his lifting system, which consisted of a metal bar and a triangle. Elizabeth had attached it to the hook in the tracking on the ceiling and then locked it in place.

Jared positioned his chair in front of the bed and put on the brakes. Using the armrests, he pushed himself into a standing position, then when he was balanced properly, he quickly placed one hand on the bed for support. When both hands were on the bed, he pulled himself forward and twisted to get his bottom on. He rolled on to his back. While he grabbed the triangle to pull himself to the pillow, Elizabeth raised his legs on to the bed.

It was once he was in bed that Elizabeth felt awkward. She had watched Sally, and as his caregiver, Sally had been impartial and clinical while putting an adult product on Jared for the night. But as Elizabeth was romantically involved with him, it was a little more difficult for her to remain detached.

She rolled Jared to the far side and pulled down his pants and underwear. She pushed half of the adult product under him. Then she rolled him towards her to pull it out the other side and to remove his clothes.

However, in her effort to keep everything on an emotionally neutral level, she had laid out the product backwards so that the do-up tabs were in the front instead of the back. What a newbie thing to do! She apologized profusely as she rolled Jared off of it, turned it around and lay it down again. He laughed heartily while she did it up and drew his covers over him.

Did he realize that she was flustered because of the effect he had on her, or did he think she was incompetent? She wasn't sure which one she preferred.

Once Jared was settled, Chevy jumped up beside him. Elizabeth went to sit in the overstuffed chair, wondering how to get past this embarrassing moment. There were lots of things she still wanted to know about him. Maybe she could divert his attention.

"Tell me more about wheelchair basketball," she said. "I played basketball in school and, judging from that practice I saw, there is quite a difference."

Jared pulled the second pillow on the bed so that it was behind his head and smiled at her.

"Well, as you saw, there are five players per side, and the purpose of the game is the same: to score points in the opponents' net. The size of the court and the height of the baskets are identical."

"It must be harder to score since the basket is so much higher for the players."

"As in a regular game, it's a matter of hand-eye coordination, but we do need strong arm muscles."

"How are the rules different?" He didn't seem to mind all of her questions.

"There isn't too much difference. Travelling in wheelchair basketball is when a player touches his or her wheels three times after catching or dribbling the ball. The athlete must pass, dribble or shoot the ball after pushing their wheels twice to prevent being called."

"How did you get into it?"

"Well, I was always active, so after I'd adjusted to the fact that I wouldn't walk again, I began looking around for something to do. Everyone knows about Rick Hansen, and I used him as inspiration. It's only my legs that don't work. There's nothing wrong with the rest of me. So I joined a team and it went from there."

"Sally said you've been in a couple of Paralympics. That must have been exciting."

Jared brightened. "It was. And now I'm hoping that some of my students will have the same experience."

"I noticed that there were varying degrees of movement in the players. How does that work?" This was beginning to sound like an interrogation but she was finding it very interesting.

"There is a classification system for the players. The most disabled is a 0.5 and the most highly functional is 4.5. At any one time during play, the total point value of the members of each team mustn't be higher than fifteen."

"How does this classification work?"

"It takes into consideration the player's ability to perform certain skills, such as dribbling, shooting, rebounding and passing. Players range from Class 1, where the player needs both arms to raise their torso after leaning forward and they cannot rotate their trunk to catch an over-the-shoulder pass, to Class 4 athletes, who can move their trunk in all directions and lean forward and side to side without difficulty."

"Am I boring you with too many facts?"

Elizabeth shook her head. "No, carry on. I've seen clips of wheelchair basketball on television, but it was never explained."

"Class 4 is different from class 4.5 because they cannot lean equally in both directions and return to the upright position, due to a lack of leg power. I'm a 4. My leg power is not very good." He stopped.

"My turn to ask a question," Jared said. "How many countries have wheelchair basketball teams?"

Elizabeth didn't have a clue. She shrugged her shoulders. "Twenty, thirty?"

"Seventy-seven."

"Seventy-seven? Wow, that's a lot," Elizabeth said, impressed. She looked at her watch. There was more that she wanted to know, but she needed to take Chevy out again.

She kissed Jared goodnight. This time their kiss lasted longer than usual, and she could feel it throughout her body. She had the hots for Jared, and she knew it. She reluctantly pulled back. With his politeness and upbringing she wasn't sure how he would act if she threw herself at him. "I'll see you in the morning," she said.

As she headed outside with Chevy she suddenly realized she was tired. She just wanted to crawl into bed. Sometimes it seemed as if she was walking her dog all the time. But she didn't really mind. She loved him, and he was worth any work she had to do. On the way back, she called her father to let him know she was okay.

When she got to her room, she read one brochure to appease the research gods. She wrote some notes for her article before getting ready to turn in for the night.

Chapter 10

The next morning, Elizabeth rose at six o'clock to get ready for her first tour. She had all her equipment together along with extra batteries. She wasn't stopping for breakfast. Jared had said he wanted to get up early also, so after loading Chevy and her things into her Tracker she went and knocked gently on his door.

"Come in."

Jared had his head propped up on the two pillows and was reading his new book of poetry. He set it aside and smiled at her. Her heart lurched. Damn, she had it bad. After last night, she was glad that Brandon was getting Jared up and giving him his shower.

"You do like to rise early," Elizabeth said.

"Well, to tell the truth, I haven't been sleeping very well since receiving the photo. I spend a lot of time thinking about my childhood with my mom. And it's amazing how much stuff is surfacing, considering I was only four when she died."

"Like what?" Elizabeth asked with interest. His conversations about his upbringing had been mostly about school. She thought it would be nice to learn something from his early childhood.

"Mom built me a tree fort. We found some old lumber and went to the largest tree we had and nailed it up. It was just a platform, but when it came time for me to climb up onto it I got scared and refused. It seemed so high. So Mom climbed up with me, and we sat and looked out over the yard."

"That's so sweet."

"Yes, we'd go up there when Mom had the time and play 'I spy.'" Jared turned away and wiped his eyes.

Elizabeth waited a few moments before asking, "What are you going to do today?"

"I thought I would work on my poetry and then take a drive around the area and see some of the places I used to go to when I was little."

When Elizabeth started to leave, Jared reached out and took her hand.

"I really hope you realize how much I appreciate what you are doing for me." He ran the tip of his tongue gently across her palm.

Elizabeth was at a loss for words. This little romantic show was what she'd been waiting for. They'd never discussed if he could be sexually active, and so she'd never made any advances. But with this, it was obvious that he was taking the first step in her seduction.

In the movies, the woman would have purred something like, "Honey, I'm sure I'll think of some way you could make it up to me," but in her startled state, she couldn't think of a smart comeback. She knew she was totally bungling the moment when all she could say was, "Okay." Oh, how embarrassing, she thought as she fled the room.

While she drove to the site of the oil derrick, her mind went over and over the scene, and each time she came up with a more appropriate response in her most sultry voice. "I'll hold you to that, big guy." "I'll definitely make sure you do, sweetheart." "I have lots of fun ideas, darling."

She wished she could do it over again.

Elizabeth had to stand back to get pictures of the tall derrick, then she walked around it. When she was ready to leave, she called to Chevy.

Elizabeth knew that there were going to be many villages and hamlets that wouldn't be mentioned in her article and not everything to see and do at each place would be in it. So at the beginning she was going to state that the article in no way claimed to cover all that there was to see and do along this route. What it was intended for was to get the reader out and exploring this part of the province.

The first communities missed would be those between Redwater and Smoky Lake along Highway 28. Instead of following the highway to Smoky Lake, she had decided to drive the old Victoria Trail to Fort Victoria and then carry on to Smoky Lake.

Elizabeth drove out of town to the Victoria Trail sign. She turned on to the gravel road as Jared had done the night before, looking into the yard as she drove past Paul's place. What secrets were hidden there? she wondered.

In her research, she'd learned that the Victoria Trail was almost sixty kilometres long and the final part of an overland route from Fort Garry, Winnipeg, to Edmonton dating from the 1820s. Although the road now didn't always follow the exact trail, as some of it had been ploughed under for farmland, it did head in the same direction using as much of the original trail as possible.

Anna's Story

"I want my supper," Paul bellowed as he came in the house.

Anna groaned. Couldn't he see she was tired? Yes, she answered silently, he could. She stood and went over to the counter, where she pressed the button to start the coffee pot. She sliced the potatoes left over from the night before into the frying pan. While his steak was searing, she put the bread and butter and salt and pepper on the table. She set the steak beside the potatoes on a plate and placed it in front of him.

She poured him a cup of coffee. He took a quick gulp, then another. When it was empty, he demanded more. She never understood how he could down the hot coffee without burning his mouth or insides.

While Paul ate, Anna took Jared's hand and led him to the bathroom for his evening bath. She ran the water, put in a bit of bubble bath and let him pick out his toys.

"Coffee!"

"I've got Jared in the tub," she called back.

"I don't give a rat's ass what you are doing. I want more coffee!"

Anna knew better than to argue with Paul when he was in this mood. He was angry about something and looking for a reason to fight. She rushed to the kitchen, seized his cup from the table and refilled it. She was so tempted to dump the hot coffee on his head.

"I want some dessert."

"Jared's in the tub by himself," she said, anxious to get back.

"Then you'd better hurry."

With a sigh she opened the fridge door and grabbed the apple pie she'd made earlier that day. She sliced him a generous portion and put it on a plate. It seemed to take so long.

"And ice cream," he growled.

She snatched the container out of the freezer, looked frantically for the scoop in the drawer, found it and scooped out the ice cream on to the pie. She dumped the plate in front of him and hurried back to the bathroom.

Relief filled her when she saw Jared playing with his plastic dinosaur in the bubbles.

"I'm going to town," Paul yelled.

Anna heard the chair scrape on the floor and then the kitchen door slam. She felt some relief; she had freedom for the evening. But, she thought grimly, that would only last until he came home.

Chapter 11

Elizabeth couldn't believe how quickly she was getting through her tour. She'd driven the Victoria Trail to Fort Victoria and saw the clerk's quarters, which had been constructed by the Hudson's Bay Company in 1864. It was supposed to be Alberta's oldest structure still on its original foundation. The quarters had been restored, and she'd seen where the Hudson's Bay employees had carved their initials on the inside walls.

She'd stopped in at Pumpkin Park in Smoky Lake to see the seven giant pumpkins made by volunteers from town. Then she'd gone to Vilna to find what were claimed to be the world's largest mushrooms. This is the land of big food, she thought, as she stared up at a mind-boggling six metres of mushroom. They had been built in honour of a traditional upscale mushroom used by the area's Ukrainian population in their cooking.

Continuing the big-food theme, her next stop was Glendon, which billed itself as the Perogy Capital of Alberta. And to prove it, there was a giant perogy on a fork in the town's Perogy Park. Elizabeth stared up at it. It was even bigger than the mushrooms. She decided she'd take pictures for her records and then take advantage of the café across from the park and have perogies for lunch. The only ones she'd ever had were store-bought, and she hadn't cared for them. Maybe authentic ones would be better.

She headed to the café and read the menu. There were so many different kinds to choose from. After discussing what was in each type with the person behind the counter, Elizabeth opted for the plain potato ones, with bacon, onions and sour cream on top. Somehow the sauerkraut, meat, cottage cheese and even the Chinese ones didn't appeal to her, though that didn't appear to be the case for others. While she waited, a man came in and ordered two dozen sauerkraut perogies to go.

Elizabeth went outside to share her lunch with Chevy. He sniffed the pieces she gave him, then sat and stared at her.

"Okay," she acquiesced. "I'll get your food." She poured some dog food in his bowl and gave him some water too.

"You're welcome," she said, as he gobbled it down.

"You don't know what you're missing," Elizabeth said, after taking a bite. These were certainly much better than the store-bought ones. She dipped another bacon- and onion-covered piece in the sour cream and ate it. Yummy. She wondered if Jared liked perogies.

Dombroski could be a Ukrainian name, she thought. Maybe his grandmother made perogies. She'd have to wrangle an invite for supper.

At the beginning of her article, where she mentioned what to bring along on the trip, she would tell her readers that there were plenty of options for food if they didn't feel like packing a picnic lunch.

Wayne's Story

Wayne had first really noticed Christine in high school. He'd been in grade twelve, and she'd just started grade ten. He had known her around the community before, but she had been just a kid. It seemed that over one summer she'd grown into a beautiful young woman. Her hair was shoulder-length, blonde and turned up at the ends. Her skin was porcelain, her lips full and red. She was almost the exact image of Marilyn Monroe, the young movie star. He'd fallen in love with her as did just about every other boy in the school.

But his love was deep and serious, not a crush. He'd asked her out, and because he was a senior, she was awed and had accepted immediately. He had monopolized her time after that, taking her to dances, movies and every event that happened at school and in town. When another boy tried to date her, he would have a little chat with him, telling him to back off. Most of them listened, but one boy ignored him and asked her to a baseball game. Unfortunately, that boy broke his leg and couldn't make the game. After that, the other boys left her alone.

After he graduated, he continued to see her, and when she graduated, he asked her to marry him. By then, he'd worked a deal with his parents to buy the farm from them. His father had a heart problem and needed to get away from the heavy work. He and Christine married and began their life on the farm. And after Graham was born, his life was complete.

Christine's beauty had enhanced as she matured, and so had his jealousy. He had seen men look at her when they thought he didn't notice. He'd had more than one private talk with guys who made advances towards her. If they still pestered her, then he stepped up his measures a little until they learned.

But it was not only her beauty that he loved, she was just a wonderful person, a wonderful wife. She was loving, considerate, kind, helpful and a great mother. What more could you want for a life partner?

Their first big argument had been when she decided she wanted to get a job in town. He hadn't wanted to let her go. He enjoyed her company and liked going out to milk the cows with her, having breakfast and lunch with her and doing farmwork with her. He tried to talk her out of it, but she said they needed the extra money in case Graham wanted to go to university and also this way they would be able to pay off the farm faster. He couldn't argue with that, but he didn't like the idea of Christine being among all the men in town. He knew they would make passes at her, and she probably wouldn't tell him about them. What if she met a man at work she grew to like? He didn't like her spending as much time with others as she did with him.

His jealousy had been so strong that he went with her the first day to meet the people at the accounting office. There were three men and two other women. One man was older with graying hair, but the other two were in their late thirties. They were all very friendly. One man even said, "Don't worry. We'll look after her."

That was what he'd been afraid of. So for the first month he'd followed her to work and sat outside watching the accounting office. He wanted to see who she went with for lunch. Usually it was with one of the women, but occasionally one of the men joined them. One day she'd caught him, and after a major argument about him trusting her, he stayed home during the day. But his jealousy never really left him and he told her, "If you ever decide to have an affair, make it with someone you don't like, because I will kill him."

She'd given an exasperated sigh and asked, "Will you please stop with that? I'm getting so tired of hearing it."

Chapter 12

Elizabeth had wanted to include Bonnyville and Cold Lake in this trip but decided it would make for too long a day. She'd lived in Cold Lake for a few years when she was younger and still remembered how it lived up to its name, even in the middle of summer.

So instead she headed south to St. Paul. Elizabeth already knew she was going to begin this section saying, "As you drive into St. Paul, watch for unidentified flying objects hovering overhead, waiting for an opportunity to land on the world's first man-made UFO landing pad." She thought the kids would get a kick out of that.

In town she drove to the circular platform where provincial and territorial flags flew overhead. She got out and walked around it, discovering that not only was there a time capsule inside the pad, but the town of St. Paul had actually designated the site international territory. She chuckled to herself when she saw the number for a hotline the town operated: 1-888-SEE-UFOS. There's one for the article, she thought, as she headed back to the car.

On the way to gas up her vehicle, she thought about Jared again. Maybe it was a good thing that all these memories of his mother were surfacing. Maybe this was a way for his adult psyche to finally heal itself from the trauma of her death. She thought about suggesting that he ask his father to talk about her. But would Paul? It didn't sound as if he had valued Anna or their marriage.

She realized that she missed Jared. Maybe she would see if he wanted to come with her on one of her trips. They could make a day of it. Actually, that wasn't a bad idea. That way she could include mention of wheelchair accessibility in her article. She'd go through the other two routes this evening and see which one would be the best. She smiled. So much for being adamant that she worked best when she travelled alone.

Gas tank full, she set out on the road to Elk Point. She particularly wanted to visit the Peter Fidler Peace Park there, as it was part of the Peace Parks Across Canada project implemented on Canada's 125th anniversary of confederation. When she got there, she took a picture of the tall, wooden statue of Peter Fidler, who had been an early factor—a high-ranking trader—of the Hudson's Bay Company.

Her next stop was the Buckingham House–Fort George site. She took some quick notes on the history of the locale, and then she and Chevy followed the short interpretive trail to the actual sites of the forts above the North Saskatchewan River. She was tingling at the thought that over two hundred years ago, fur traders were lugging goods from their canoes up the hill to the forts or loading furs into the canoes.

The remainder of the trip took her to a couple of parks and the Historical Village and Pioneer Museum at a place called Shandro. Of course, in keeping with the theme of oversized attractions, she made a point of driving by and photographing the giant mallard duck in Andrew before her final stop at the Skaro Shrine, a popular local pilgrimage destination since the 1920s. After noting the details of when the annual pilgrimages took place, Elizabeth breathed a sigh of relief.

"You are now finished this section of Alberta and can head home," she recorded, then closed her laptop and put it away. She continued on to Redwater, wondering if her trip was done so quickly because she was getting better at finding places and doing her research or because she wanted to get back to Jared.

As she pulled into the B and B yard, she was glad to see his van in the parking lot. Chevy jumped out of the vehicle and bounced around while Elizabeth gathered her paraphernalia. Back in their room, she set her stuff down and tried to figure out how to approach Jared about the morning's romantic disaster. Just thinking of it made her squirm. She'd gone over it many times while driving and still hadn't been able to come up with a good way to let him know that she'd just been struck dumb and that was why she had dashed out of the room. She wanted him to know that, given a second chance, she would conduct herself in a more imaginative way. But how to mention it without making more of a fool of herself?

His door was open when she got there, and she knocked on the frame. He looked up from his laptop and smiled.

"How did your day go?" he asked.

"Better than I expected. I found all the places I was looking for, and I learned a lot about them that I didn't know. How about yours?"

Jared shrugged. "It was kind of sad driving around memory lane, but it got my poetic energies revved up, and I spent the afternoon writing poetry."

"Oh, may I read it?" Elizabeth asked. There was an awkward split second of silence before she added hurriedly, "Sometime, I mean," realizing he might want to keep it private. After all, she didn't like anyone to read her articles until they were completed the way she wanted.

To get off the subject, she asked, "Do you want to go for a hamburger, or have you eaten already?"

"No, I've been waiting for you," Jared replied.

"Okay. Where's a good place?"

"Get in my van, and I will take you there."

Jared pulled up in front of a restaurant, and they got out, leaving Chevy on the seat.

"My friends and I used to come here when I was in high school. At the time, they made the best burgers in town. I can't guarantee that now."

"Well, we'll find out, won't we," Elizabeth said and went to hold the door open for him to wheel through.

Once inside, Jared ordered a double cheeseburger, and Elizabeth ordered a mushroom burger. After the waitress left, Jared looked at his hands a moment.

"You know, I haven't had many girlfriends since I've been in this chair. And that's okay," he added quickly. "I understand that it's hard on a relationship because of my limitations. Some women don't like that I can't go skating with them in the winter or curling or backpacking or spelunking or a lot of things that they want to do."

Elizabeth's first instinct was to comfort him, but she knew the statement was true. And it was no one's fault.

He took her hand. "I've felt something from that first day we met," he continued. "And I've hoped that you have too. But then after this morning, I was afraid that I'd moved too fast or that maybe I'd read something into your actions that wasn't there."

Elizabeth tried to speak, but he held up his hand. "Please, I've been rehearsing this all day. We've only known each other a couple of months, and I shouldn't have said what I did to you this morning."

"I'm so embarrassed about that," Elizabeth moaned. "I acted like such an idiot."

"I did too," Jared said. "I shouldn't have licked your palm like that."

"But I'm glad you did." Elizabeth smiled shyly.

Jared's face brightened. "You are? Oh, I'm so relieved. I didn't want to scare you away."

Elizabeth's sultry voice kicked in. "It would take more than that to scare me away, buster," she drawled slowly, then leaned over the table and kissed him. This felt so good, so right.

While they ate their burgers, Jared told her that he'd been doing some thinking about what Willy had said to him the night before.

"I'm not sure if he was just trying to be mean, or if there is something behind it," he said. "Did Dad really change after I was born and if so, why? What caused the transformation? Was it really me or something else that happened at the same time?"

"Do you want to go back to the farm and ask him?" Elizabeth asked. "It might give you a better idea of what your parents' marriage was like."

"I've thought of doing that."

"I also wondered if we'd be able to get your dad to talk about your mother. That might help sort out your memories for you."

"I was discouraged from asking questions about Mom when I was young. Even as an adult I've been rebuffed when I brought the subject up. So, if he wouldn't before, I doubt that he will now."

Jared pulled the photograph of his mother from his wallet. "I carried this with me the first couple of years after Grandma gave it to me, but then I put it away in my drawer when it began to wear. I got it laminated last week, and I've gone back to keeping it with me."

He stared down at it, and pushed his hamburger aside, half-eaten. "There are so many questions that I've asked over the years. Like, how different would my life have been if she'd lived? How would she look today? And the worst one, why did she leave me? Now I have added two more. If she didn't die voluntarily, then who killed her? And why?"

"Maybe, before we're finished, we'll get those answered." Elizabeth was happy that Jared trusted her enough to be sharing these thoughts with her, and she hoped with all her heart that they would find the right answers to his questions.

"And there are so many other things I have to know. Like, where were my parents married? What was their wedding date? For that matter, how did Dad and Susie meet? I've never been told. She was at the farm one time when I visited, and he just introduced her as his new wife and that was that, no further discussion from him, and I never had the nerve to ask Susie." Jared looked up at her. "Let's pay the bill and get out to Dad's," he said decisively. "It's time to get some answers."

Elizabeth shared in Jared's disappointment when they only found Susie at the farm. She was sitting on the steps in the evening sunshine, shelling peas from her garden.

"Your dad and Willy are out in the fields," she replied, when he asked.

Elizabeth watched him hesitate. Could he ask her? Would he ask her?

"You didn't have a very good reception last evening, did you," Susie said, giving him an opening.

"It's not Dad's fault. I know I was astonished when I saw the photograph. He must have been too."

Susie nodded. "Even I was appalled that someone would send that, especially to her son. Why not send it to the police?"

"I feel like I'm going behind Dad's back, but may I ask you some questions?" Jared reached into the pail and grabbed a handful of peas to help her. Elizabeth followed suit.

"I know nothing about your mom's death, but ask away."

"How did you and Dad meet? When were you married? Why wasn't I invited?"

"Your Dad and I met through a mutual friend," Susie began. "I was living in Calgary then and working in a department store. We fell in love. I was tired of my job so I quit and moved out here."

"That must have been a big step."

"Not really. I was raised on a ranch south of Calgary. I was glad to get out of the city and back to the country. As for you not being invited to the wedding, well," she paused, frowning, "there hasn't been one yet."

"You mean you and Dad aren't married?" He looked at Elizabeth, disbelief on his face.

"No, although we tell everyone we are. I guess after all these years, we might as well be."

"Is there a reason why you didn't marry?" Jared popped some peas into his mouth.

"Not really. Once I moved in here, we just never got around to it."

"Did Dad tell you anything about my mother?"

Would a man talk about a previous wife to a potential one? Elizabeth wondered.

"Only that she was pregnant and committed suicide."

"He didn't describe her, tell you anything about her?"

"No, I'm sorry." Susie sounded regretful. "Do you mind me asking what was in the letter to your grandmother?"

"Mom was basically saying goodbye to them. She asked them to keep in touch with me."

"Saying goodbye as in, I'm taking my life?"

"I don't know. The police thought so, but Elizabeth pointed out that she could have been afraid of someone."

Susie nodded. "Those would be the only two reasons I could think of for saying goodbye in a letter."

"Do you know when Dad married my mom?" Jared asked.

Susie shook her head. "There's a box in the basement that has been there since I moved here. I asked your dad once what was in it, and he said it was just old stuff. Maybe there will be something in it that will give you some answers."

They went into the house, and Susie put the bowl of peas on the counter. She opened a door beside the refrigerator and headed down into the basement. Elizabeth sat in the same chair as the day before. Susie soon returned with a dusty cardboard box from the basement. It was sealed with tape.

"Do you think we should be opening this?" Jared asked. "It belongs to Dad."

"I don't see why not." Susie blew off some of the dust. "It might help you and maybe him. He drank more last night than he ever has since we've been together." Susie found a knife and cut through the tape. She opened the flaps, and they both peered in.

Elizabeth stayed seated. This had nothing to do with her.

"Looks like school report cards and pictures," Susie said, taking some out. "These are your and Willy's school photographs." She looked at them with a smile. "You boys sure don't look alike."

Jared pulled out a few report cards. "These are Willy's." He read some. "Wow, look, he was an honour student." He shuffled through a few more of Willy's report cards and a frown came over his face. "This is like night and day. One year he's an honour student, the next he's failing. He even had to repeat a grade. And then his marks pick up again for his final two years of high school." He looked from Susie to Elizabeth, his face stricken. "The bad years were the ones when Mom was here."

"Oh, I'm sorry," Susie said. As much as she wanted to give an appropriate response, Elizabeth could not think of one.

They dug all the way down to the bottom of the box without finding anything about Anna in it.

"I guess Dad was telling the truth when he said he was throwing all Mom's stuff out." Jared sounded disheartened.

They packed everything back up, and then Elizabeth and Jared said goodbye to Susie.

"Do come again if you have some more questions," she said. "And don't be afraid of your dad. I'll help you get through to him."

"We didn't get much accomplished," Jared said, as they drove away.

"Well, you know more about Susie than you did before."

"Yes, and it's about time. I feel kind of stupid now that I didn't have the guts to ask her before. I guess it goes back to being discouraged from asking questions when I was a child."

"And I think she's on your side," Elizabeth added.

"Well, she's always been the one to invite me to come out for holidays. She remembers my birthday, and she phones me occasionally. Actually, she's the closest thing I have to a mother."

"I think we should call it a night," Elizabeth said. "It's been a long day and tomorrow will even be longer."

Chapter 13

Elizabeth went to Jared's room to help him into bed. Once he was comfortable, she said, "I've decided to take tomorrow off from my research so we can visit one or two other people on the list." She sat in the chair.

"Sounds good to me, as long as you feel you can do that."

"Well, when you look at it, I should only be on the road two more days. The rest of the week I had set aside to work on my article."

"And will you still be able to do it? I don't want to be the cause of you not making your deadline."

Elizabeth was touched that Jared was so worried. "Yes. If my writing takes up a couple of my camping days, it won't be too bad."

"So you think we can resolve this that fast?" Jared sounded hopeful.

She hated to dash his hopes, but she thought she should be realistic. "I think if we haven't learned anything concrete in a week, then you should consider letting it go."

"Only a week?" He sounded disappointed.

Elizabeth knew she would exceed that if they were learning something, but she didn't say it. A week was all she was going to give it if they weren't.

"I'm thinking we'll start with Sarah Munter and Nick Thompson tomorrow, then Meredith Warren and, if we have enough time, Wayne Dearden."

"Okay, that works for me."

"You said that Meredith's poetry was about her and Ben's life," Elizabeth said to get on to another topic. "Could I look at one of her books just to get a sense of her before I meet her?"

"Go ahead. They're on my suitcase. And could you hand me my new one? I want to see what happened next. It's almost like she's writing a combination memoir/mystery novel through her poetry."

She handed him the book and helped him add the other pillow behind his head to prop him up.

Elizabeth wasn't much on poetry. She'd always had a hard time grasping the obscure meaning in most of what she'd had to read in her literature classes at school, so she hoped she could understand these. She randomly opened the first book and stared at the page. This wasn't the usual type of poetry she'd taken in high school. She looked up and saw Jared grinning at her.

"What is this?" she asked.

"Meredith calls it script poetry," Jared answered. "At the book reading and signing I went to, she told us that she'd taken a scriptwriting course many years ago but didn't do much with it. When she got in to poetry, she found that she could set up the scene and the tone for the poem and give some background for the narrative by using a script layout. She said it makes the whole poem more visual and that way she could get right to the meat of what she wanted to say."

Elizabeth read with interest.

Act One
Fade In
Interior–Farmhouse–Night
The lights are on in the living room. There is a couch against one wall, two overstuffed chairs with a table between them along another and a long row of windows make up the third. A woman is sitting in one of the chairs watching the television set, which is recessed in a cabinet between two doorways along the fourth wall. She is knitting a sweater. Periodically, she glances at the clock above the television.

You are a good son.
You go into town to help your
father run his hotel and bar.
I sometimes go and watch you
laughing with the women,
discussing farming with the men.
Everyone enjoys their evening
with you around.
Sometimes you stay late to

help clean up and spend time
with your father.
Or so you tell me.

Fade Out
End Act One

Act Two
Fade In
Interior–Farmhouse–Night
The woman hears a vehicle drive into the yard. She smiles and sets down her knitting. She goes through the kitchen to the back door and opens it, waiting for her husband to enter. He comes into the light and looks surprised to see her.

"What are you doing up?" you demand.
I am startled, stunned.
The smile on my lips and the
happy greeting for you both die.
What have I done wrong?
You walk past me into the house and
to the cupboard with the bottles of liquor.
You pour yourself a rum and Coke.
"You have been drinking a lot lately,"
I say to you as you down it.
"Quit nagging," you answer, as
you stare at the empty glass in your hand.

Fade Out
End Act Two

Act Three
Fade In
Interior–Farmhouse–Night
The man is sitting at the kitchen table with the bottle of rum in front of him. He finishes the drink in his hand and pours himself another. The woman hovers nervously. The clock in the living room chimes three times.

"Is something bothering you?" I ask,
wondering what has happened tonight.
You look at me, anger in your eyes.
"Who does Christine think she is?" you burst out.
"Not considering anyone's feelings."
"That is between Wayne and her," I say.
"Does love not count?" you ask.
"She does not love Wayne anymore."
"She is not leaving just Wayne,
she is leaving everyone who ever loved her."
"She has a right to her own life," I say.
"But he loves her," you cry.

Fade Out
End Act Three

Elizabeth was amazed. "I like this type of poetry," she told Jared. "The words mean what they are supposed to. There is no ambiguity in the sentences."

"She has won many awards with these books," Jared said. "Read what the critics wrote on the back of that book's jacket cover."

Elizabeth turned it over. "Meredith Warren's poems have an innovative, revolutionary style that is shaking the foundations of the conventionally staid poetry community." She looked at the next comment. "These poems from newcomer Meredith Warren are insightful and powerful. Her script poetry will remain popular for a very long time."

"Those are great quotes," Elizabeth said.

"Yes," Jared agreed. "I wonder how long it will be before others copy her style."

"Imitation is the best form of flattery, or something like that," Elizabeth said, laughing. She read another poem.

Act One
Fade In
Interior–Community Hall–Evening
A wedding has taken place. The reception is over and the dance is winding down. A band onstage is playing a waltz. Two couples are dancing but most are sitting at the tables around the dance floor. One couple is standing near the bar.

You are drunk when you say to me,
"I saw you and Wayne talking.
You two seemed pretty cozy."
"We were just talking about their problem."
You lean towards me, alcohol heavy on your breath.
"Well, do not get too close. A man in that situation
might turn to another woman for comfort."
I feel giddy. After all these years you are jealous.
Oh, how I love you then,
my heart overflowing with happiness.
In my innocence, my trusting,
I believe my man, my husband, loves me still.

Fade Out
End Act One

Act Two
Fade In
Interior–Community Hall–Evening
Onstage, the band is putting away their instruments. A woman is cleaning up the dirty paper plates off the tables. A man begins to take down the decorations. The couple is now sitting at one of the tables.

"Where is Wayne and Christine?" you ask.
"They left a while ago," I answer.
"She did not want to dance with me tonight."
Your voice sounds so very depressed.
I did not understand why.
"I do not blame her," I say.
"No one wants to dance with a drunk."
"I was not drunk." Your head slumps on to the table.
You are now, I think.
"What has gotten into him?" someone asks.
"I guess he is celebrating that his haying is done."
That is the only reason I can think of.

Fade Out
End Act Two

Act Three
Fade In
Exterior–Farmyard–Night
A truck pulls into the farmyard. It is a warm autumn evening. The woman driver climbs out then goes around to help her husband out of the passenger's side. He almost falls when he gets out. She supports him as they walk to the house.

You are drunk, far drunker than
I have ever seen you.
I wonder if it is because you are happy
that our farm is doing so well, that
our lives are so good.
Or is it because you are sad
for our friends whose marriage is dying?
"Why does she have to end it?"
you ask. "Why does she want to leave?"
I do not know if you want an answer.
I help you into the house and to bed.
You turn your back to me. You are crying.

Fade Out
End Act Three

"What do you think of them?" Jared asked.

"They're kind of melancholy," Elizabeth answered. "It sounds like she loved him and really thought he loved her."

"That's why I wanted to buy this one. Although I know the outcome, I want to know how she found out about Ben and Christine."

"You're right. It's like she's writing a memoir in poetry and yet giving us clues to something else."

"She's writing in script poetry," Jared corrected.

"Right. Script poetry."

Elizabeth looked at the poem in front of her. "I'm surprised she used the people's real names."

"I've done some reading on how to write a memoir, and it says that the memoir is your life as you saw it. You have a right to include everyone's names. If they don't like it, they can write their own version."

"Are you thinking of writing one?"

"Yes." Jared smiled sheepishly. "I thought I'd write about my life in a wheelchair. It would be for those who are already there, and it will give those who aren't a look at what it's really like."

Elizabeth nodded. "I think that's a great idea. There are so many people who still think that someone is different just because they are in a wheelchair."

"Right. I want them to know that I am still the same person I was before my accident; I just can't do all the things I did before. And I want them to understand that my chair is an extension of me, that when they touch it they are touching me. And like other people, I don't like to be touched by strangers. I have a friend who has cerebral palsy and she never grew very big. She is in her twenties but still looks like a child. She says that people come up to her and hug and kiss her as if she were a child, and she hates it."

"Isn't a memoir the same as an autobiography?"

"Not really. A memoir isn't about the person's whole life chronologically like an autobiography. It's about a specific time or experience or relationship."

"Like Meredith's life with her husband or your life in a wheelchair."

"Right. The protagonist in a memoir must lead the reader on a journey. But, like fiction, the writer must make the story interesting by setting up the obstacles he had to overcome in his life. He must build tension and suspense, must make the reader want to read on."

"Well, Meredith is certainly making me want to read on. Have you started your memoir?"

"I'm just organizing all the information and how I want to present it."

"Well, I don't have any experience with memoirs, but if there's anything I can do to help you with it, let me know."

"Thanks."

Elizabeth went back to her reading, but her mind was on something else. Since Jared wanted to be a writer and so did Sally, maybe the three of them could form a little writers' group.

Chapter 14

Anna's Story

It was another hot day. Even with both doors and all the windows open, Anna found the heat in the house oppressive as she stood over the stove stirring cheese into cooked macaroni. The heat had always bothered her, and now being pregnant, her energy was sapped. She waved at the flies as she served Paul his lunch of macaroni, brown beans and carrot salad, and then she went and sat in a chair. She was too hot to eat. She fanned herself with a paper.

"What's the matter with this food?" Paul asked.

"What?"

"Did you put poison in it? Is that why you are not eating it?" Paul laughed at his own joke, as he shovelled a forkful of macaroni in his mouth.

Anna leaned her head against the back of the armchair. Sometimes she wished she had the guts to poison him.

"I'd like roast chicken for supper tonight."

Anna lifted her head and looked at him. "I don't feel very good," she said. "I've already cooked potatoes for a salad and was going to serve leftover beef from last night."

Paul thought about that for a minute. "No, I still want chicken," he said. "It's time we tried the new ones."

Why, in this sweltering heat, did he want hot food? Roasting a chicken in the oven would just add to the discomfort in the house. Of course, after supper he would go out in the field until dark, when it will have cooled off somewhat. Only she and the boys would be putting up with the heat.

She fought back the tears. It was times like this when she succumbed to her loneliness. She had only one friend in the area, Meredith. She was about 20 years older and didn't have children, but at least she took the time to stop in occasionally and visit. Anna sometimes made a quick trip to see Meredith on her way shopping. She would only be there a few minutes, but it felt good to have that little bit of freedom. During the winter, when there was less outside work to do, they talked on the phone. But the conversations had to be short so that they were finished before Paul returned from doing chores.

Other than Meredith, she had no one who cared if she lived or died. Her parents were in Edmonton and long distance calls to them were out of the question. Not that it mattered. When she'd found out she was pregnant again, she did make a phone call to her parents. The response was not what she'd hoped for. She'd actually been optimistic that giving her parents a second grandchild would change their attitude. But her father hadn't sounded very enthusiastic about the idea. And that made it harder for her to ask if she could move in with them.

"If I could just stay until I can get a job or some training," she pleaded, "I could take some courses before the baby is born and the rest after."

"And then what?" her father asked.

"Then I could get a place of my own."

"How are you going to look after two children?" His voice was so scornful.

"I'll find a babysitter." She tried to sound confident. "I could do it if you would just let me stay there for a while."

"I don't think so."

She began to cry even before she hung up, only remembering afterwards that her father had never asked when the baby was due or how Jared was.

Sometimes it was just hard to keep going. The only one who showed any appreciation of her was Jared and that was because she was his mother and the only one who seemed to care about him.

When Paul had finished eating, he washed and put on a clean shirt.

"I'm going to the auction market," he said, coming into the kitchen.

"Can you buy some cereal while you're in town?" Anna asked. "I didn't have enough money last week to buy it."

"What makes you think I have time to go shopping?" Paul turned on her angrily. "If you'd shop properly, you'd have money left over."

Anna saw Jared staring at his father from the hall doorway. He then ran to his mother and tried to climb on her lap. Anna was discouraged to see that, even at his young age, he had already learned to fear his father's bad moods.

Paul walked out and slammed the door.

An afternoon of respite, Anna thought. She wouldn't have to worry about him coming home until supper, if then. He'd been known to head for the bar for a few drinks after a hard day of watching animals being bought and sold.

The door opened again and Paul stuck in his head. "Don't forget my chicken," he said.

When he was finally gone, Anna roused herself out of the chair and cleaned the dirty dishes off the table. As she trudged in the hot sun to the garage for a hatchet, she thought about Nick's new wife, Sarah, and what Anna had said to her when she first saw her. Maybe she should invite her over one day soon and tell her all about the man she had just married.

She went to the chicken pen and opened the gate. She entered the yard where the chickens clucked and scratched at the ground. They had bought chicks in the spring, and the birds were now big enough to eat. She reached down and grabbed the legs of one of the larger ones. She pushed open the gate and carried the chicken upside down to the piece of wood used as a chopping block. The chicken squawked and flapped its wings, as if it sensed its impending death. She held the chicken so its head was on the block, and lifting the axe above her, brought it down, neatly severing the head from the body.

"There, you lucky bird," she said. "Your miserable life is over."

She let it go and watched its wings whack the ground as its legs launched the body first in one direction, then another. It flopped and thrust in the throes of the death dance before lodging against the fence.

Chapter 15

The next morning, Elizabeth went with Jared to the dining room for breakfast. Although she was taking the day off from travelling, she did want to learn more about the B and B.

The dining room was large with ten tables. Did that mean they had ten rooms to rent? If so, the place was more like a hotel than a cozy, intimate home where you could spend time with your hosts.

Most of the tables were full. Jared directed Elizabeth to the buffet table in the centre of the room. It had a spread like she had never seen at a B and B. Sausages, bacon, ham, three different egg dishes, homemade hash browns, pancakes, toast, waffles, muffins.

"Wow," Elizabeth said, amazed. "Was it like this yesterday?"

"No," Jared replied, picking up a plate and setting it on his lap. "Today they have a conference taking place in their meeting room."

"I wondered about all the tables." Elizabeth loaded up her plate and followed Jared to a table with three chairs. He pushed himself into the fourth spot.

"So did you take a look around the building?" Elizabeth asked, as they ate.

"A bit. Their ground floor has the kitchen, dining room, meeting room, a gift shop and my bedroom. Brandon said that the upstairs is all bedrooms, including his parents' and his."

So it wasn't like a hotel. They'd just diversified.

Once they were finished, Elizabeth said she wanted to look at the gift shop. It was small but full of locally produced items, like wind chimes, stained glass ornaments, paintings and wooden toys. It was also on the honour system. There was no salesperson or cash register. A sign stated that if you wished to purchase something, just leave a note at the front counter. The item would be wrapped and given to you at the time of your checkout, and the price included on your bill. What a different way of doing things, she thought.

On their way to Jared's van, Elizabeth saw Brandon snipping some protruding branches from the elephant tree.

"I have to ask him about those trees," Elizabeth said to Jared. She headed over to him, Chevy at her heels. Jared wheeled beside her.

"Hi, Brandon," Elizabeth said. "Those are quite the shapes. Did your parents do them?"

Brandon stopped his cutting. "No, actually there was a guy in southern Alberta who had been working on them in his yard for years. Then he died, and his family sold the property. The new owners offered them for sale, and Dad bought them. It took quite a bit of work to get them dug up and transplanted here."

"How long have you had them?" Jared asked.

"About three years." Brandon returned to his trimming.

"Well, I don't feel so bad. I grew up in the area, and I was wondering why I hadn't heard of them before."

"What can you tell me about the house?" Elizabeth asked. "Is it an old barn or was it built new to look like a barn?"

"Half and half," Brandon replied. "It was built as a barn by my grandfather in the 1950s. As it began to fall apart he just left it. When Mom and Dad bought five acres with the house and barn off of him, they began to restore the barn, thinking it would make an unusual B and B."

"And it does," Elizabeth agreed. She looked around the property. "Where is the house?"

"Well, really it was an older mobile home, so they just sold it to a farmer who's using it as a bunkhouse for his hired help."

That answered all her questions.

In the van, Elizabeth pulled out the list of names Jared had given her. Jared used his cellphone to call the number for Nick Thompson and Sarah Munter and received the okay to visit.

At their farm, Elizabeth climbed out of the van and waited while Jared unloaded himself. The morning was already getting warm. She watched a very large woman in a red dress and a tall, slim man come out of the house. They descended the steps; the woman moved slowly, holding the rail.

"Hello, you must be Elizabeth Oliver," the woman said, holding out one hand. In the other she carried a small towel. "I'm Sarah Munter, and this is my husband, Nick Thompson."

Elizabeth shook his hand while Sarah looked down at Jared. "Hello, Jared. It's so good to see you again."

"Ms. Munter," Jared said. "Mr. Thompson."

"Call us Sarah and Nick," she said. "We're all adults now."

"We have a gazebo around back where we can talk," Nick announced.

Elizabeth and Jared followed the couple into the backyard. Jared had to work hard to move the wheelchair in the grass, but Elizabeth didn't offer to help. If he needed it he would ask.

The air smelled of freshly mowed grass. There was a tall elm and a weeping willow in the yard, and a hedge of lilac bushes blocked off the area from the barn and sheds.

The floor of the gazebo was even with the ground, and there were two doorways opposite each other. Sarah and Nick settled on one bench while Elizabeth took the one across from them. Jared stopped just inside the doorway.

"So do you want to tell us what this is all about?" Sarah asked Jared. "On the phone you mentioned it had to do with your mother and it was important. I must admit that you have our curiosity aroused."

Jared took his time. Elizabeth had to bite her tongue not to say something.

"I'm not really convinced that my mother committed suicide," Jared said.

Nick looked startled, then glanced at Sarah. Elizabeth wasn't sure if Sarah was blushing or if it was the heat.

"It was ruled a suicide," Sarah said. "The police concluded she threw herself down the well."

Jared took the photograph out of his pocket and handed it to Nick. Sarah grabbed it instead.

"I received this in the mail a while ago," Jared explained.

Sarah looked at it while Nick craned his neck to see. "That's your mother's grave," she said. "I always thought it was awful of Paul to have put that on her marker."

"Turn it over," Jared instructed.

Elizabeth watched their reactions. This was where she had expected them to be shocked, but instead, Nick's face tightened while Sarah's remained impassive.

"That's all you've got?" Sarah asked dismissively, as she handed the photograph back to Jared. "I don't see how you can base your opinion on three words taped to that."

Jared looked down at the words. He touched them with his fingers.

"If that person knew this was true, he or she would have gone to the police," Sarah continued. "If you want my opinion, I think someone is playing a not-very-funny joke on you."

"Can you tell us something about Anna?" Elizabeth asked. She sensed Jared's disappointment that they weren't taking this seriously and decided to conduct the questioning until he recovered. "Maybe how you met her, how long you knew her."

Sarah laughed. "I remember our first meeting well. Her words to me were, 'Get away from here! Move back to the city!' When I just stood and stared at her, she hissed at me, 'I mean it. Get out.'"

"Why did she say that to you?" Jared looked up.

Sarah shrugged. "I asked her that when we met at a community dance about two months later, and she said that she was just trying to protect me."

"Protect you from what?"

"From learning the hard way how tough farming can be on a city girl."

"When did she tell you to leave?" Elizabeth asked.

"My third week here. We'd just come back from buying groceries when Paul and Anna drove up." She looked at Jared. "You were with them, and she was pregnant. They didn't get out of the truck. Paul started talking to Nick, so I went around to introduce myself. But I didn't get a chance to say anything. She just had time to give me that warning, and they drove away. It wasn't until after they left that Nick told me who they were."

"So you had just moved here," Elizabeth said. "Where did you come from?"

"I was born and raised in Regina." She didn't give Elizabeth time to ask anything more. It seemed she had a story to tell. "I met Nick at a party put on by one of my college friends. He was a friend of her older brother. He was twenty-seven and a tall, lean farm boy who had been working in the city. We dated all winter and on my twenty-first birthday he asked me to marry him."

Elizabeth noticed that Nick was taking furtive glances at Jared. It upset her that able-bodied people stared at physically challenged people like they were an oddity.

"So how did you end up here?" Jared asked. He looked at Nick, but Sarah seemed to be the one who did the talking in the family.

"Soon after we announced our engagement, Nick inherited the farm." Sarah wiped the sweat off her face with the towel and continued. "I expected him to sell it, but he wanted to move back and become a farmer. Until then, our plans had been centred around living in the city. I must admit I was hesitant at the idea of moving away from my family and my life and so suggested that we have a long engagement while he decided if he wanted to farm. But Nick assured me that I would love living on the farm that had been in his family for three generations, and because I loved Nick ..." Here she looked at Nick, but Elizabeth did not see love in her eyes. "I finally agreed to a wedding in late June. After that, we saw little of each other. Nick quit his job and moved here, where he worked the fields and started to put in the crop."

Sarah stopped for a breath. She looked at Nick again and saw him glance at Jared. She turned back to Jared and Elizabeth.

"Would you like some iced tea or lemonade?" she asked.

"Thank you, that would be nice," Elizabeth said. The morning was getting hotter.

Jared nodded.

"Nick, get us some lemonade."

Elizabeth saw the glare Nick gave Sarah before getting up and heading to the house.

"Can you tell us about some of Anna's neighbours?" Elizabeth asked. She slapped at a mosquito on her arm.

"The farm you passed as you came from the highway is where Ben and Meredith lived," Sarah said, wiping her face again. "Now you want to talk about a murder, there was one. Ben was killed by Christine, who was married to Wayne, and they lived further down this road."

"When did that happen?" Elizabeth asked. It was obvious that Sarah liked to talk. They could probably learn a lot from her if they were patient.

"It was the winter before Anna died, or was murdered," she corrected herself, although Elizabeth noticed she didn't sound convinced.

"I didn't know it was that close to Mom's death," Jared said.

"It was," Sarah confirmed.

"Two unnatural deaths in this community in such a short time," Elizabeth said, astounded.

"The two people who died lived within two kilometres of each other."

"Wasn't that a little suspicious?" Elizabeth asked. She knew she would certainly think so.

"There was some talk, but the police never thought they were connected. That was mainly because Ben was killed in Redwater."

"Why there?"

"Because Christine had left Wayne and was living in town."

"Did you think there was a link between the two deaths?"

Sarah shrugged her shoulders. "I couldn't see one."

"Why not?" It didn't take much to keep her talking.

"Well, Ben was dead, and as far as I know, Christine had no reason to kill Anna."

"Were Christine and Anna friends?"

"Not that I know of. You've got to remember that I had just moved here. I didn't know anyone."

"Why did Christine kill Ben?" Elizabeth remembered Jared saying something about them seeing each other.

"It sounds as though they were having an affair and she wanted to end it."

"So she killed him?" Did Sarah notice that she was the one asking the questions instead of Jared? She hoped he would step into the conversation soon, or Sarah might start to wonder why.

"I guess he was terrorizing her, and she used the knife to protect herself."

"Did she go to jail?"

Sarah shook her head. "The jury believed her story and let her go."

"What was her story?" It didn't sound like Sarah believed it.

"That she'd stabbed him once and then was hit on the head by someone else who finished him off by stabbing him the other four times."

"Where is she now?" Maybe they should talk to her.

"She lives in Edmonton."

Nick returned with a tray of glasses and a pitcher of lemonade in time to hear the last of the conversation. "Who were you talking about?" he asked, as he handed each of them a glass and poured the lemonade.

"Christine," Sarah answered him curtly and then continued. "Wayne still lives on the farm but has become a hermit. He only goes to town for the mail and groceries. Other than that he just milks his cows and puts up hay."

"How well did you get to know Anna?" Elizabeth asked.

"Not very. We only had a couple of months before she died."

They sipped their lemonade in silence. Elizabeth tried to think of something else to ask, but she drew a blank. "So, you obviously grew to like the farm," she finally said.

"Well, I got off to a rocky start." Sarah smiled, but there was a touch of bitterness to her voice. "And being from the city I was certainly told about it. Right, Nick?"

Nick didn't answer her.

"I couldn't do anything right. I didn't know how to make scrambled eggs the right way. I was a farm woman so therefore I wasn't supposed to go anywhere. I was supposed to raise a large garden. I was supposed to know how to milk cows. My life was not easy."

Her statement left an awkward silence. Elizabeth wasn't sure if she should agree with her or not. Either way it may offend one of them.

"I'm sure it was hard to adjust to a new way of life," Elizabeth remarked. She'd run out of questions. She looked at Jared, wondering if he had anything to ask.

"Thank you for seeing us," he said.

Elizabeth stood and also thanked them.

"Feel free to come and talk again," Sarah said.

"I'm sorry." Jared glanced at Elizabeth glumly as they drove away. "I just couldn't think of anything to ask once Sarah basically told me my idea was stupid."

"That's okay," Elizabeth said. "It isn't easy, but I'm sure you'll catch on."

"So, what did you think?"

"It sounds like they believe your mom killed herself."

Jared nodded.

"They don't seem like a happy couple, do they?" Elizabeth mused.

"I got the impression that she doesn't love Nick anymore, and yet she's still on the farm with him."

"Let's grab something to eat and then go see Meredith," Elizabeth said.

Anna's Story

"I'm leaving," Willy declared, entering the kitchen with a backpack.

"Leaving?" Anna asked, looking up from rolling the perogy dough on the table. "Going where?"

"I'm going to stay with friends in town."

"Why?"

"To get away from you," he said harshly.

Anna slowly sank into a chair. She wasn't sure if she was glad or not. He did do a lot around here, but she was tired of his anger. She got enough from Paul; she didn't need it from Willy too.

"Your father won't be happy."

"He hasn't been happy since you moved here."

"Where are you staying?"

"I'm not telling you."

"Are you going now?"

"Yes, while Dad's gone."

"Where are you going, Willy?" Jared asked, coming into the kitchen.

"I'm going far away."

"Can I come too?"

"You're too young," Willy said, bending down to give him a hug. "But you can come when you get bigger," he added quickly, when he saw the crestfallen face.

"I'll be big soon."

"Yes, you will." Willy stood.

Anna was touched by Willy's treatment of Jared. Although he hated her, he did seem to care about his half-brother.

"I'm sorry," she said. "I didn't know it would turn out like this."

"You should be leaving, not me," Willy growled, stalking out of the house.

It was early afternoon when Paul came home. Anna busied herself getting his lunch, dreading what would happen when he found out. Should she mention it immediately or wait until he noticed?

Paul was seated at the table when Jared came in from the living room.

"Willy's gone away," he said to his father.

"What?" Paul looked at Anna.

"Willy's gone away," Jared repeated. "And he said I can go too when I'm bigger."

Paul stood. "Where's Willy?" he demanded.

"He left," she whispered, fear engulfing her.

"So you finally managed to drive him away."

Anna didn't answer.

"Where did he go?"

"I don't know."

Paul glared at her a few seconds, then rushed to the boys' bedroom. Anna could hear him pulling out the dresser drawers and slamming the closet door.

"When did he go?" Paul stood in the doorway.

"This morning."

"Where's he headed?" He lifted his hand.

"Into town to stay with friends." Anna hated that she said that, but she had to protect herself and the baby.

"I'm going to look for him," he growled. "He's too young to be out on his own."

Anna sank into a chair, her heart pounding. Now what did she do? Paul blamed her for Willy leaving.

"Mommy?" Jared tried to climb into her lap. "Why was Daddy mad at you because Willy left?"

"Because he didn't want Willy to leave," Anna said, hugging him.

"Will he be mad when I leave?"

"I don't know."

It was late afternoon when Paul returned with Willy. The tall, muscular teenager glared at her as he walked by her. "I'll get you for this," he said fiercely.

Chapter 16

Jared parked in front of the small house where Meredith Warren lived. The fenced front yard was full of flowers and bushes, and the lawn was newly mowed. Elizabeth held open the gate for Jared as he wheeled through. She climbed the steps and knocked on the door.

The woman who answered was short and stocky. Her hair was gray and her face lined. She looked to be in her late sixties, and Elizabeth noted that she had sorrowful eyes.

"I'm Elizabeth Oliver," she said. "Jared phoned you about us coming over."

"Yes. We'll go around to the backyard, where we can sit on the patio."

She came out the door and down the steps. "Nice to see you again, Jared. I enjoyed your haiku poems. Have you done any more work on your chapbook?"

"It's going slowly right now," Jared said. "I've got other things on my mind."

The backyard was a profusion of colour with more flowers, plus there was a water fountain and a vegetable garden.

"You must like gardening," Elizabeth observed, once they were seated under the umbrella at the patio table. On the table was a pitcher of water with ice in it and three glasses.

"I used to love it when I lived on the farm. But now that I have nothing else to do with my time but that and write poetry, it's lost its appeal," Meredith answered.

"I've just bought your latest book," Jared said. "And I'd like you to sign it."

Elizabeth reached into his backpack, pulled the book and a pen out and handed them to him.

"Now I have all three," he said, as he watched Meredith write her name. "When is the fourth one coming out?"

"I'm working on the poems now." She gave him the book. "I'd like you to look at some of them when they are completed."

"Okay. Just email them to me. I've got my laptop, so I can look at them whenever."

"Thank you. I will."

There were a few moments of silence, and then Jared cleared his throat.

"We're here because I think my mother may have been murdered," he said quickly. He reddened as he looked at Elizabeth. She smiled encouragingly at him.

"Whatever gave you that idea?" Meredith asked, her voice incredulous.

"This." Jared passed the photograph over to her.

"What about it?"

"Look on the back."

Meredith had no reaction to the pasted words. "Who sent this to you?"

Elizabeth had the impression she was more curious than concerned.

"I don't know," Jared answered. "It came in an envelope with no return address on it, but it was mailed from here in Redwater."

"So why are you coming to see me? You think I sent it?" Meredith asked, raising one eyebrow at him as she handed the photograph back.

"No, no," said Jared hurriedly. "Just because you were one of Mom's friends, probably her only friend at the time she died."

Elizabeth was impressed with how much more confident Jared was getting with his questioning. He was either a fast learner, or it might be because he and Meredith were such good friends.

"So? Her death had nothing to do with me."

"I know. I'm trying to find out more about her, about her life." Jared paused. "You've told me a few things about your friendship with her over the years but you never told me about that letter you gave Grandma Dombroski. Why?"

"I figured it was up to your grandmother to tell you." Meredith poured them each a glass of water. "Did you learn anything new from reading it that you didn't know before?"

"No," Jared said quietly. "It does sound like a suicide note. And if I'd read it years ago, it would just have confirmed to me that she did take her own life."

"But in light of this photograph, it could be looked at as meaning something else," Elizabeth explained, taking a sip from her glass. "Since you knew her the best, do you think she would have committed suicide?"

"I don't think she was happy, if that's what you mean," Meredith said, her voice cautious.

"Why?" Jared leaned forward.

Meredith looked carefully at him.

"Go ahead," he urged. "You can tell me."

"Your father began to drink soon after their marriage and your birth." She looked away, then back. "Gossip was even going around that he may have had a girlfriend on the side."

That was the first they had heard of that, Elizabeth thought. It could add a different slant to everything. Anna may have committed suicide because of the other woman, or she may have been murdered because of her.

"Who was she, do you know?" Jared asked. Elizabeth noted that today he wasn't letting the answers stop him from getting his questions asked. "Where is she now?"

"This is only hearsay," Meredith said. She picked up her glass and drank. "I never saw him with anyone, but the woman I heard about moved away years ago."

Too bad, Elizabeth thought. It would be tough to ask Paul about her.

"How did Dad treat Mom?" Jared continued. He finally had a drink of water.

"Not very well. They had one vehicle, so the only time she went out on her own was to go grocery shopping, and that was when he was out in the field. Even then she had to hurry in case something broke down and he needed the truck to buy parts. Sometimes, she'd stop in for a quick visit on her way to town."

Jared seemed unable to think of anything more. Elizabeth looked around the yard. The vegetables in the garden were tall and bountiful. She could see the pea pods hanging on the vines, the lush potato plants and the tall corn stalks. It was obvious that in spite of Meredith's lack of enthusiasm about gardening, she had a green thumb.

"We just found out that your husband Ben died the winter before Anna," Elizabeth said, looking back at Meredith.

"Your point?"

"We just wondered if there was a connection."

"There wasn't," Meredith retorted. "Christine killed Ben, and Anna committed suicide. No connection."

That was probably true, Elizabeth thought. The mystery bug had taken over and she was looking for hidden implications where there weren't any.

"Did she love me?" Jared suddenly blurted out.

Meredith looked stunned. Even Elizabeth was caught off guard by the question.

"Why on Earth would you ask something like that?" Meredith asked.

"Because I was told that she committed suicide to get away from me."

Oh, you poor man, Elizabeth thought, her heart going out to him. What a way to have lived your life. If he'd believed that all his life then no wonder he was still in doubt even after reading Anna's note.

"Who told you that?" Meredith demanded.

Jared reddened and looked down. "Dad told me one day when I asked him why Mom had gone."

Elizabeth could not contain her gasp.

"What a terrible thing to tell a child!" Meredith cried. She reached out her hand to Jared. "Your dad was wrong. I know that Anna loved you."

"But how do you know?" Jared implored.

Elizabeth wondered how much of this trip was to find out if his mother had been murdered and how much was to find peace.

"Well, for example, the community held a Christmas party every year in the hall," Meredith began. "The parents were supposed to buy their children a present, wrap it and then Santa would give it out. You were about three. I heard that your dad didn't want to waste the money on buying something for you. Your mom tried to sell one of the necklaces her grandmother had left her so that she could buy you a present. It was only costume jewellery and wasn't worth much, but I gave her ten dollars for it. She was so happy, she couldn't wait to go to town and pick out something for her son."

Jared listened with a pleased look on his face.

"Thank you," he said when she had finished.

"It sounds like you were a very good friend," Elizabeth said gently.

"Kids have to have something at Christmastime," Meredith replied.

"Do you mind telling us something about Ben?" Elizabeth asked. For some reason, she couldn't stay away from the subject.

"Why?"

"Just in case there is a link between him and Anna."

"There isn't."

"Please?" Jared asked. "I want to learn as much as I can about what was happening in the area when Mom died. I need to know if she was murdered and if not, I'd like to find out why she committed suicide."

When Meredith didn't answer, Elizabeth prompted. "He and Christine Dearden had an affair. Do you know when it started and how it began?"

Meredith turned her head away. "It's all in my books," she said, her voice subdued.

"Do you want to tell me about what your father said to you?" Elizabeth asked. She'd wanted to ask ever since they had left Meredith's place, but he'd been so quiet that she hadn't wanted to disturb him.

Jared didn't answer for a while. "I guess he was getting tired of me pestering him about my mother. There was just so much that I couldn't understand at that age. Finally, he said that she had committed suicide to get away from me and to leave him alone."

"That really wasn't a nice thing to do to a child."

Jared nodded. "I've spent my life being plagued with the idea that somehow her suicide was my fault. But I just couldn't figure out what I had done wrong. At times I would be generous with myself, thinking that something else could have gone wrong in her world that would cause her to take her own life. Whatever it was must have been terrible enough that even her love for me and her wanting to watch me grow up wasn't a good enough reason to stick around."

"You know, Willy may have witnessed your father beat your mother. Maybe he thinks your dad killed your mother and that's why he wants you to quit asking questions. I wonder if you should ask him."

Jared was silent.

"What?" Elizabeth asked, inclining her head.

"I did have a memory that I've been trying to deal with." Jared spoke hesitantly.

"Do you want to tell me about it?"

Jared pulled over to the side of the road. He took a deep breath. "I remember Mom and Willy fighting. At first I thought it was Mom and Dad because to me Dad and Willy's voices sounded the same, but when I peeked around the corner, it was Mom and Willy."

"Do you know what they were arguing about?"

Jared shook his head. "I'm not sure, but Willy kept yelling 'Go! Just go!' When I looked, he had his fist raised in the air."

"Did he strike her?"

"No, but I think he wanted to."

"Maybe we should ask him about that too. We can go there now, if you like."

Jared nodded. "I guess we'd better get it over with."

Elizabeth and Jared headed to the farm. A tractor with a hay baler attached sat in the yard. Paul and Willy were leaning against the tractor, talking. They looked up when Jared parked the van.

"I hear you've been asking your questions," Paul said, when they reached the tractor.

Jared nodded. "And I'd like to ask you and Willy some more too."

"Is that a fact?" Paul folded his arms across his chest. He didn't look or sound like he was going to answer any of them.

This seemed to intimidate Jared and he began to stammer. "Well … I really need …"

Elizabeth was not daunted, and she stepped in. "We've heard certain stories about both of you, and we'd like to clear them up."

Neither one said anything. Elizabeth took that as a good sign and pressed on. "Paul, we've heard that Anna was unhappy and that she basically was stuck on the farm since you only had one vehicle."

"So?"

"So, in your opinion, was she despondent enough to take her own life?"

"She must have been, because that's what she did."

"Did you try to make her happy, to find out what was wrong and correct it?"

"Look, obviously you don't know much about farming. There really isn't time to spend discussing feelings and having heart-to-heart talks. There is a lot of work to do."

"Willy, did you fight with Anna?" Elizabeth turned to him.

Willy looked startled for a moment. "Yeah, we had a few arguments. What stepmother and stepson don't?"

"Did you ever hit her?"

"No way!" He stepped back as if he'd been slapped. "Where did you hear that? Who is spreading those lies about me?"

Elizabeth wasn't going to admit anything, but Jared answered.

"I remember seeing you raise your fist to Mom," he said. "And you kept telling her to 'go.' Where was she supposed to go?"

Willy shook his head. "I just wanted her to leave so that Dad and I could get our life back the way it was before they married."

"Before I was born," Jared said quietly.

Elizabeth saw Willy blush under his tan. "I'm sorry I said that," he mumbled.

And you should be, Elizabeth thought.

"How did you change after Jared was born, Paul?" she asked. "What were you like before?"

Paul looked uncomfortable. He glanced at his watch. "I have to get the haying done," he said and began to climb into the tractor's cab.

"Dad, please," Jared pleaded. "I need some answers. What was wrong with me that you changed and Mom would rather take her life than see me grow up?"

"It wasn't your fault, Jared," Paul said, as he settled in the tractor seat. "It just wasn't your fault."

"But you told me it was when I was a kid."

"What?"

"You told me that Mom committed suicide to get away from me and to quit asking you about it."

Paul stared at Jared as if trying to remember. He shook his head. "If I did, then I was wrong about that and to have said that to you." He closed the cab door.

Elizabeth wasn't sure, but that sounded almost like an apology.

The others backed up when he started the tractor and drove away.

"I really wish you would leave this alone," Willy said.

"Is that because you think your father killed Anna?" Elizabeth asked.

Willy glared at her, then turned and walked away.

"Is that a yes or a no?" she called out but received no answer.

"Well, we didn't learn much this time," Elizabeth said, as they climbed back in the van. "I noticed you didn't mention the possible girlfriend."

"I don't know how to approach that, but when I do it will be just Dad and me."

"Tell me about your relationship with your father."

"Well, there isn't much to tell. I remember him yelling a lot when I was a kid. Then after Mom died, it's like he softened. He quit yelling at me, but at the same time he never told me he loved me."

"So basically, he provided you with a home and food and not much more."

Jared nodded. "He did the best he could."

"What about Willy? How was their relationship?"

"About the same, although Dad put his arm around him occasionally and laughed more with him."

"And how did you and Willy get along?"

"I don't remember much before Mom died. But afterwards he was a typical older brother, teasing me one day, taking me places the next. It's like he took over the role of my mother. He went to my Christmas pageants and cheered for me at my track meets. One time, he actually went with my class on a day trip to Edmonton."

Of the two, Willy was the one who acted guilty, who acted like he was seeking redemption. Elizabeth didn't say what was on her mind.

But Jared must have been thinking the same. "It sounds like he was trying to make something up to me, doesn't it?"

"We'll have to keep going back until we find out what they're hiding," Elizabeth said.

Jared nodded. "Maybe they'll get used to the fact that I need to know what took place. Plus, I hate that I'm thinking that my dad, or even Willy, may have killed my mom. I have to find out the truth."

Elizabeth looked at her watch. "Do you want to go see Wayne Dearden?"

Chapter 17

"I wanted to build another barn and expand our dairy herd," Wayne Dearden said. "Our son Graham had left home, and I felt it was time for Christine to quit work and for us to spend more time together. We had worked hard, me on the farm and she in an accounting office in town, and we had paid off the mortgage. I thought it was time for us to relax and enjoy the farm. It's ironic, but I wanted us to be like Ben and Meredith, who farmed together. But she had other ideas."

"What were those?" Jared asked.

They were sitting in Wayne's carport, since it was the only area out of the sun that would accommodate Jared's wheelchair. It had a cement floor and a flat roof, which was used as a deck from the upstairs patio doors. The structure, with its faded paint and slight list, looked old, and Elizabeth worried that it might fall down on them if a wind came up. After checking out the yard, Chevy came and lay at Elizabeth's feet.

They'd asked Wayne about Anna, but he'd stated that he'd probably only had five or six conversations with her in the time she'd been married to Paul. However, when they'd mentioned Christine and Ben, he'd opened right up.

"Christine told me she wanted us to sell the farm and move to Vancouver."

"Why?"

"That's what I wondered at the time. Her explanation was that she wanted to experience life, travel and do other things. But after she killed Ben, I found out that she'd wanted to break the affair off with him. I guess she also wanted to end our marriage but couldn't tell me outright. So she told me that she wanted me to sell our farm and move away. She knew I wouldn't do it."

"Why would she have known that?"

"Because this has been my home for all of my life," Wayne said intently. "I've never wanted to leave it, and I never will. I'm going to die here."

"So when you wouldn't agree, she moved into town," Elizabeth prodded. It seemed like the logical explanation, since she was living in Redwater when she killed Ben.

"Yes. It was just after our son, Graham, had returned home."

Elizabeth wondered if there was any significance to that, or if that was just a time marker for this older man with the lined face and stooped shoulders. Since it didn't seem to bother Wayne that she was asking questions along with Jared, she continued. "Why did he come back?"

"He'd gone to Calgary to get a job and to look at going to the Southern Alberta Institute of Technology to become an electrician, but after working for a year, he'd decided that farming was what he wanted to do. So he returned to help us."

"Where is he now?" She looked around the neglected yard, with its patchy grass full of tall dandelions. There was only one other vehicle besides Jared's in the yard. Maybe he was in town.

Wayne grimaced. "He's living in Edmonton with Christine."

That left Elizabeth unable to think of how to ask all the questions that statement had raised.

Jared jumped in. "How did that happen?"

"Christine moved back in here for a while before her trial. Then she decided to go to Edmonton. After a while Graham moved there too. When I asked him why, he said that she needed him. They came back for the trial, and the jury ruled she was not guilty because her lawyer had shown that someone could have hit her and then killed Ben. They returned to Edmonton, and she finished her course to become a certified general accountant. Graham went to the Northern Alberta Institute of Technology this time for his electrician's certificate." Wayne shook his head. "I couldn't understand it. After all I did for him, he went to her and left me to farm alone."

"Did you and Christine visit with Anna and Paul at all?" Elizabeth thought they'd try again.

"No. With Christine working all day, she was tired most evenings and didn't feel like going anywhere. And on weekends she cleaned house and worked in her garden."

"We never came here to see you?" Jared asked.

Wayne shook his head.

"So you don't know much about their lives." Elizabeth noticed that Jared was looking around the yard.

"I know Anna was a good cook." Wayne smiled for the first time. "Ben, Nick's dad, Joseph; Paul and I would get together to do a lot of our farmwork, such as seeding and haying. We would eat our lunches and suppers at whichever farm we were working that day." He looked at Jared. "Your mom always put on the best spread—homemade bread, pies, and her perogies were the best I've ever tasted."

As heartwarming as it was to know that she was remembered for something, that bit of information didn't help them.

"It seems strange that two people in the region would die within a few months of each other, and yet neither death was from natural or accidental causes."

"Are you saying they are somehow associated with each other?" Wayne asked.

"What do you think?"

"I think that's a dumb idea."

Well, that ended that line of questioning, Elizabeth thought.

"Besides, it was thirty years ago," Wayne continued. "If it is true that your mother was murdered, Jared, that photograph would have been sent a long time ago."

"Do you have an address and phone number for Christine?" Elizabeth asked.

"Why?"

"Well, we'd like to talk to her."

Wayne went and found his address book. It was old and tattered. He read out the information while Elizabeth copied it down.

As they drove away, Elizabeth looked at the rundown old house and the dilapidated barn, both of which were in dire need of repair and paint. It seemed that Wayne hadn't accomplished his desired expansion nor, for that matter, had he done much at all since his wife and son left.

Wayne's Story

Wayne was peeling potatoes when the phone rang. He knew even before answering it that it was Christine. She usually phoned at that time if she had to work late.

"Wayne, I won't be there for a couple of hours yet."

"Okay." He felt the familiar disappointment, but he had long ago given up trying to persuade her to stick to regular hours. His good news could keep until she showed up.

When Christine arrived home, he had the potatoes mashed and was waiting to fry up the pork chops. The astonishment on her face made him smile.

"How was your day?" he asked, putting the chops into the frying pan.

"Good," she answered, looking at the set table, the lettuce-and-onion salad, the wineglasses. "You've never done this before. What's it all about?"

He told her he had something important to tell her, but she would have to wait until after supper. He poured her some wine and they sat.

"You're not going to tell me, are you?" she said.

"Not until after we eat," he answered, though he wanted so badly to blurt out his plans. But he was enjoying the thrill of anticipation. He even cleaned off the table and loaded the dishwasher before they went into the living room.

"I've been thinking about the farm," he said.

"I have too," Christine revealed, which had excited him. That made it easier.

"I was thinking we should build another barn and increase our herd. Graham is out working, and we have enough money set aside in case he decides to continue his education. You can quit your job now, and we can run the farm together."

He watched her face, looking for the elation, the joy he had so often pictured her having at his announcement. But she didn't laugh and throw her arms around his neck. She didn't say she was glad to be able to quit her terrible job. Instead, she just sat gazing at her glass. He quickly realized that that wasn't what she'd been thinking. After a few moments, he asked her what she had in mind.

"I was thinking we could sell the farm and move to some place different, like Vancouver. We could get jobs, have weekends free for whatever we wanted to do and travel to exotic places on our holidays."

He just stared at her. She wanted to sell and travel? How silly was that? They'd decided years ago to wait until retirement to do that.

When he asked her why she wanted to sell, she said, "We could get enough to buy a house near the ocean, and with jobs we would have the money and time to travel."

He tried not to laugh out loud. What a ludicrous statement! He didn't want to work nine to five for someone else, and he had no desire to see the world right then. That was for when he was too old to work. And except for milking twice a day and fieldwork in the summer and fall, as far as he was concerned, they had plenty of time to do whatever they wanted. It was her job that stopped them.

"But we don't have time to do anything," she said, her voice pleading. "We always have to be home to milk the cows. We can't go to the city for a weekend; we seldom get to a wedding ceremony, the reception and the dance. We always miss one or two of them because we have to come back home to milk the cows. We can only go to the lake for a few hours during the day because we have to get home to milk the cows. We've never taken a holiday." Her voice rose in anger. "We don't own those cows, they own us."

"Is that how you see it?" Wayne couldn't believe it. After all these years, where was this coming from? Who had planted such an idiotic thought in her head?

"Yes. We've been doing the same thing every day since we were married. That's the real reason I went to work. I couldn't take the boredom of it week after week, year after year. And now that Graham has left home, I thought we could get a jump on our retirement plans."

He was at a loss. How she'd come up with such a ridiculous notion he had no idea. His first response was to tell her how absurd the plan was, but he knew that would get him nowhere.

"I really have to go somewhere and think about this," he said. He went out and checked on the cows. They were kept in a corral by the barn overnight so that they'd be close for the morning milking.

Maybe she was going through the change. He'd heard that some women got strange ideas during that time. He decided he would listen patiently to what she had to say and try reasoning with her. Eventually, she'd realize how stupid she sounded, and she'd soon see it his way.

He returned and headed to the bedroom, where she was reading a book in bed.

"Can we talk?" he asked, sitting on the side of the bed.

She looked up at him.

"I have to know how serious you are about me selling the farm."

She paused for a moment then said, "Very serious. There is more to life than what we have."

"I know, but I thought we had decided we were going to wait until we were older to travel."

"No, you decided that."

"And you didn't argue."

"There was nothing to argue about. At the time, Graham was still at home, and I wasn't sure what I wanted."

"I thought you liked the farm."

"I did. I do, but I've lived my whole life on a farm. I can't see living in the same house, in the same yard, in the same community for the remainder of my life. I want more than the small world we've created here. It's so restrictive."

She looked earnestly at him. "Remember the history we took in school: the Parthenon in Rome, the pyramids in Egypt, the amphitheatre at Pompeii. Or the places they show on television, like Bavarian cities, Buckingham Palace or the site of the Blarney Stone. Don't you want to visit them now while you're still young? Don't you just want to get away from here and try something new?"

So many questions ran through his mind. What made her think he would want to "get away," as she put it? There was no way he wanted to sell his farm just so he could go visit those places. What did they have to offer him? They were just old buildings from the past, and who wanted to kiss a rock? Home and family were the most important things in life.

"This farm is my home, our home," he began impatiently, then stopped. He had to humour her. "Go on."

"What about going to see the Grand Canyon or the Statue of Liberty or the Eiffel Tower or even down east to the Maritimes? Can you say you have never wanted to pack up and take off?"

"No, I've never had the urge. I'll see those places when I retire."

"By then we will be a couple of old cripples, hardly able to get around. How much will we be able to see and do then?"

"Why are you suddenly so insistent that we sell and move?"

Christine looked at him, then away. "I just need a change."

"Well, I'm proposing a change."

"That's not what I want. And why have you never said anything about it before?"

"I wanted to surprise you. I thought you would look forward to us working together on the farm, that you would be glad to quit your job."

"Well, the only way I'll quit my job is if I'm moving away." She sighed. "This is our first discussion, and we are at an impasse. Maybe we should leave the subject alone for a while longer."

Wayne quickly agreed. He was positive that if Christine had more time to think about his plans, she would agree with them. After all, he loved her. That's really all she needed.

"Yes, it will give us a chance to consider each other's vision."

Christine nodded and opened her book.

Chapter 18

"Well, that was just plain strange," Jared said when they left Wayne Dearden's farm.

"What was?" Elizabeth turned towards him.

"I had a feeling of déjà vu at one point. It was like I'd been at that farm before."

"You may have been there as a child."

"Not according to Wayne."

"Yeah, that's right. Can you think of what it was that gave you that feeling? An object you saw, a word?"

Jared shook his head.

"Maybe you'll remember eventually."

Jared glanced at her and smiled. "Maybe."

"I'm going to do my next tour tomorrow," Elizabeth said when they were back at the B and B. "I'll be ending up in St. Albert, so if I finish in time, I thought I'd go have a chat with Christine Dearden. I'm not sure when I'll be back tomorrow night, but I've checked with Brandon, and he'll be able to help you tomorrow evening. I'll let him know we're back so that he can come to your room to learn your routine."

"I think I'll go visit with Meredith tomorrow," Jared said. "I'm having some trouble with a couple of poems for my chapbook. And maybe she can tell me more things about Mom. Then I'll go see Dad. Maybe he will have cooled off and be willing to talk with me."

When Brandon came to Jared's room, they showed him what needed to be done to take care of Jared.

"Do you look after all the challenged clients who stay here?" Elizabeth asked, impressed by the young man's ability and thoughtfulness.

"If they want it, yes," Brandon said, as he helped Jared into bed.

"Have you had any training?"

"No, but I did take care of my grandmother when she broke her hip last year. She told me that I should check into the health care field, not only because I am good at it, but with the baby boomers aging, I would never have to worry about being out of a job."

"She's right," Elizabeth agreed. "Are you going to?"

Brandon grinned. "I've already registered for a fall course in Edmonton."

"Well, if you need a job or a reference, just let me know," Jared said.

"Thank you," Brandon said as he left the room.

Elizabeth looked at her watch. She'd hoped to do some transcribing this evening, but it was getting late. Time just seemed to disappear when she was with Jared.

"May I borrow Meredith's second book?" Elizabeth asked. "I'd like to read some more of her poems. I'm impressed with the way the poetry is written. It flows, and I don't have to go back and reread it to understand it. Plus, it's like you said, it's kind of a mystery unfolding. And I do like those."

Jared handed her the book. "So I won't see you until sometime tomorrow night."

"I'll probably be quite late. I'll see you the next morning."

Jared shook his head. "Come here when you get back. I'll be awake and I'll want to know what Christine had to say."

"Okay." She bent over the bed and kissed Jared.

He put his hand around her head and held her lips on his. "Have a good day tomorrow," he said when he let her go.

Elizabeth nodded numbly, wishing she wasn't going. She wanted to spend as much time with Jared as she could. She hurried to her room and, once settled in bed, opened the book to take her mind off of him. She didn't read the poems in order. Instead, she started them from the back of the book to the front, just like she read the newspaper.

Act One
Fade In
Exterior–Farmhouse–Night

There is snow on the ground. Stars twinkle in the clear night sky. A vehicle pulls into the yard and a woman climbs out. She stares at the house then takes a deep breath. She releases it in a vapour. With slow tread, she climbs up the steps and enters the darkened house. Inside, she stops and listens.

There is no noise in my house; it is dark and silent.
Today, I threw soil on your casket; I buried you.
Is this what it is like in your grave,
total quiet, total darkness?
I flip on the light and wander the house
looking at the possessions that were supposed to
symbolize our life, a life that I have learned
never existed, except in my own mind.
This has been our home for nineteen years,
but it now feels alien to me.
Because from today on, I know that mine
will be the only shadow in the house.

Fade Out
End Act One

Act Two
Fade In
Interior–Farmhouse–Night
All the lights are on in the house. The woman is in the kitchen. She pushes over the shelving holding plant seedlings and pots. She heads to the dining room and goes to a china cabinet with no doors. All the shelves hold figurines and dishes and knick-knacks. They crash to the floor with a sweep of her hand. The ones that don't break disintegrate under her foot.

"Damn you, Ben. Damn you to hell!" I yell.
I want you to hear. I want you to know
the sorrow and the pain you have brought me.
I go from room to room, expunging.
I spray your shaving cream on the walls.
I dump your aftershave in the tub.

I grab a knife and shred your clothes.
Finally, there is nothing of yours left.
I feel some satisfaction.
You destroyed my life and now I have
destroyed everything that represented yours.
"There, you bastard," I say. "Rot in hell."

Fade Out
End Act Two

Act Three
Fade In
Interior–Farmhouse–Night
The woman is standing in front of a picture on the living room wall. The furniture and floor are littered with debris. She takes the picture off the hook and stares at it a long time.

I find our wedding photograph on the wall.
I had had it enlarged for our tenth anniversary
as my loving gift to you.
Were you as pleased as you said you were
or was that just a sham?
I smash the glass against the corner of the table.
I cut my finger removing the shards.
I look at you smiling back at me.
Were you an impostor in our marriage?
For now I wonder, how many other
women did you see over our nineteen years?
I slash the picture with the knife. How symbolic.

Fade Out
End Act Three

Elizabeth read a couple more then set the book aside. She should get on with her own writing. She opened a new file and began to enter what she had learned so far about Anna's life and death.

Wayne's Story

Wayne heard the car before it turned in the driveway. He looked out the window and saw the white, 1969 Camaro.

Graham! Elated, he rushed out the door.

"Graham, what a wonderful surprise." He grabbed him in a big hug. "Why didn't you call and let us know you were coming?"

"It was kind of a spur-of-the-moment thing," Graham said. He pulled two large suitcases out of the back seat and lugged them into the house. "I'll just put these down in my room."

Wayne noticed that they were the same two suitcases Graham had left with.

"Looks like you're here for more than the weekend," Wayne said, when Graham returned to the kitchen. "Or did you bring your laundry home to be washed?"

"I quit my job."

"What? Why?" He held his breath. He'd tried to talk Graham out of leaving the farm, telling him that he wouldn't find a better way to make a living. But Christine had encouraged him to go and see what else there was to life. Ever since Graham had left, he'd prayed that he would come back home. Was his wish going to come true?

"I couldn't handle it anymore. I don't like the city, and I don't like pumping gas, so I quit. I decided to come home and work on the farm with you until I can buy my own land."

Wayne was delighted to hear that. He'd missed his son so much when he'd moved away. And now to have him say he was back and wanting to farm. There was just no measure to his happiness. The three of them were together again. Then he felt a twinge of apprehension. He and Christine hadn't told him about their problem. Maybe Graham's return home would put an end to that.

"Mom working late tonight?" Graham asked.

"I don't think so. She's going to be glad to see you."

Graham grinned. "I hope she's not disappointed that I came back. She was always after me to try something other than farming."

Yes, and now Wayne knew why. "She wanted you to know that you had other options."

"Well, I've seen some of them, and I like the choice I've made."

Graham helped Wayne with the milking, and they had just returned to the house when Christine drove in the yard. She shrieked and hugged Graham when she saw him.

"How long are you visiting?" she asked, taking off her coat.

Graham looked down at the floor, then over at Wayne. "I quit my job. I've been thinking about it for a long time, and I want to get some land of my own and start farming."

"Oh." Christine sounded perplexed. Then she said "oh" again, as if something had been clarified. "Your father will like that. Did he tell you about his plans?"

"No, he never said anything." Graham turned to Wayne. "What plans are these?"

Before Wayne could answer, Christine said, "He wants to expand the herd and build another barn." She shooed them out of the kitchen. "You two go into the living room and discuss it while I make supper."

At supper, most of the conversation revolved around Graham's life in the city and his decision to move back. If Graham noticed the distance between his parents, he didn't say anything. When they were done, Wayne and Graham went back into the living room to watch television while Christine cleared the table. Wayne's spirits had risen tremendously. He now had Graham on his side. Surely hearing his first-hand account of how he hated living and working in the city and how much he preferred living on the farm would make Christine realize how wrong she was. She would see that it wasn't the life for her.

He looked fondly at Graham and ruffled his hair as he had done when Graham was younger. "Good to have you back, son."

Chapter 19

Because the beginning of the Gibbons–Smoky Lake–St. Paul loop deviated off Highway 28 at Redwater to follow the Victoria Trail, Elizabeth decided to have the second route continue along Highway 28 from Redwater to Highway 36, then go north to Lac La Biche.

I would offer alternative routing for some of the overlap, she reasoned, so they could choose pavement or gravel roads. She hoped to get today's tour done as fast as the first one. She was itching to talk with Christine.

She stopped for gas, then began recording as she left town. "From Redwater, you continue along Highway 28 to Radway."

Radway was a tiny little hamlet whose claim to fame was a world-renowned bible school. She'd read that it accepted only twenty-one students each year. While most students applied for entry themselves, some were recommended by the Vatican. They came from as far away as Germany, Zambia, Ireland and Kuwait. Elizabeth looked around the hamlet, trying to imagine it from the perspective of one of these visitors. Would they have been able to see much of Alberta or Canada during their stay or was their time taken up with their studies?

For the next couple of hours Elizabeth focused on the natural beauty of the region. At her first stop in Waskatenau, she let Chevy run free along the asphalt nature trail while she recorded notes on the local wildlife and plants from the interpretive signs along the trail. Then they hopped back into the Tracker and drove the pretty stretch of highway past Smoky Lake to Highway 36 and then north to the Continental Divide.

In her research, she'd learned that a narrow height of land between Lac La Biche Lake and Beaver Lake separated the Hudson's Bay and Arctic Ocean drainage systems. She was disappointed that there really wasn't much to see. She'd pictured a height of land with views of valleys and rivers, but there were just trees on both sides of the highway.

After a quick stop for brochures and maps at the tourist information centre in Lac La Biche, Elizabeth headed out to Sir Winston Churchill Provincial Park, an island park accessed via a man-made causeway. To her delight, there was a flock of thirty or forty bright white pelicans bobbing about in the water by the causeway. She couldn't resist stopping the car to take pictures of the odd-looking birds with their giant bills. Startled by the loud honk of a car horn, she waved in quick apology, jumped back into her Tracker and continued across the causeway to check out the beaches at the campground and the birdwatching at Pelican Point. There was even a telescope she could peer through at a tiny island populated with pelicans and cormorants. What an amazing place for a camping holiday, she thought, and chuckled as she found herself wondering how wheelchair-friendly the area would be.

After finally tearing herself away from the island park, Elizabeth headed back through town towards Old Mission Road, where she found the old convent built in 1892 at the Lac La Biche Mission. It was a three-storey-tall white building, and she stood staring at it, wondering how such a large building could have survived the tornado in 1921 while the nearby church was destroyed. Inside, the artifact that she took the most pictures of was an old wood-fuelled heater. When Elizabeth looked at that heater and thought about the cold Alberta winters, she wondered how well it could have worked to keep the pioneers warm. It made her shiver just thinking about it.

She went to the gift shop and saw a silver necklace with a pendant of an eagle in flight. Should she buy it for Jared? How would she explain it? She shrugged. What the heck, she didn't need a reason to give him a gift. She paid for it, and then let Chevy out to wander through the old cemetery across the road. Elizabeth leaned close, trying to make out the lettering on the time-worn headstones. The grave of a little baby who died in 1885 really gave her a sense of the realities of a time when almost every mother could expect to lose an infant or two.

Anna's Story

Anna had a roast in the oven and was quickly peeling potatoes. The chocolate cake she had made was cooling on the counter. Jared was playing with a truck on the kitchen floor. She felt a tightening in her chest. There was just too much to do, and she always felt so tired.

Anna held on to the edge of the counter, trying to calm her nerves.

"Just remember that when our haying is over, Paul will be gone every day for a week," she kept telling herself, trying to picture some good to the pressure now. "He won't be here to shout or to make a mess or to slap anyone. Life will be quiet and peaceful."

She took a deep breath and finished the potatoes. Once they were on the stove, she took a few minutes to sit. She fanned herself with one hand and rubbed her belly with the other. It was near the middle of August, and the day was a scorcher. It was made even hotter by having to cook the meal, but sandwiches wouldn't do for a haying crew. If only it would rain to cool down the temperature. She longed to go out to the well for some cold water, but the men would be here soon.

She took three plates from the cupboard. There were some changes to the crew this summer. Nick was taking his father's place and Ben wouldn't be here. She wondered if they would find a fourth neighbour to replace Ben. After all, the work went easier with more men.

When they arrived, Paul ignored her, and Nick looked the other way as he mumbled a hello. Wayne nodded. It was her turn to look away. She didn't like Wayne and was actually scared of him. She'd heard the stories about his jealousy of Christine. When she'd dated Graham in high school, Wayne had been very surly towards her. Graham even told her that his father didn't want him to see her. He'd laughed at that and then invited her to the movies. But at the time Anna had worried that Wayne might try to discourage her the same way he discouraged men from flirting with or even just talking to Christine.

After they'd washed up and were sitting at the table, Paul growled, "Get us some beer."

Anna quickly took three beer cans from the fridge and set them in front of him. While she dished up the mashed potatoes, carrots, meat and gravy, the men talked about how well the morning had gone.

"I should have enough hay this year to feed about one hundred calves over the winter," Paul said. He slid a piece of beef off the platter on to his plate.

"Yes," Nick said, scooping up a spoonful of potatoes. "I was thinking about going to the bank and asking for a loan to buy calves. My problem is that I don't know if they will lend me the money, this being my first year of farming."

"Sure they will," Wayne said. "The calves are the collateral. When you sell them in the spring you pay the loan and pocket the profits."

"If there are any profits to be had," Paul added, around a mouthful of beef. "Some years the price of beef is so low that I've just barely paid the loan."

"When are you going to the market?" Nick asked.

"The farmers want to put as much weight on their animals as they can to increase their sale value, so they don't start bringing the calves in until late October, early November."

"I'll check at the bank and let you know."

Wayne smiled. "I'm glad I'm strictly in dairy. I don't have to worry about buying and selling anything."

When the men had finished the meal, eaten their dessert and drank their coffee, they hurried back to the fields. They would return for a snack at about four and then come in for supper when the evening dampness put a stop to the haying.

Anna put some food on a plate for Willy and washed the rest of the dishes. She was in the middle of making another cake, this time white, as there wasn't enough of the chocolate one left from the lunch, when Willy entered the house. His face was dirty from summer fallowing one of the fields. He went to the bathroom and washed, then came back and sat at the table. He hardly spoke to her anymore. She set his microwaved plate of food in front of him.

As she worked, she kept one eye on him. It wasn't that she was really frightened of him; it was just that a few times she'd caught him staring at her. She wasn't sure if that was just his way of trying to scare her, or if it was a veiled threat, but she wasn't taking any chances. After all, he was as big as his father.

Chapter 20

Elizabeth got back on Highway 55 and headed to Athabasca, which would be about an hour's drive. Along the way, she went over the questions she wanted to ask Christine. How well did she know Anna? What were her thoughts about Anna's suicide? Did she know of anyone who may have wanted her dead? And of course there were many questions about Ben. Elizabeth found that she was as curious about his death as she was about Anna's, though she couldn't explain why exactly. Her instincts told her they were somehow related.

As she neared Athabasca, she drove through Amber Valley, where two hundred African-Americans from Oklahoma had settled. She looked to see if there was any sign of their settlement but only saw open farmland. One question that came to her mind was, Did they suffer from prejudice once they'd moved here?

Once in Athabasca, Elizabeth visited the Union Hotel, the Canadian National Railway Station and the United Church, all built in the early twentieth century. As Elizabeth took pictures of the church, she found it hard to believe that when it was constructed it was one of the tallest buildings in the West. It sure wasn't so now, one hundred years later.

Elizabeth headed south out of Athabasca on Highway 2. Remembering what she had read in a brochure, Elizabeth recorded some thoughts about the area.

"When this highway was built, it bypassed Perryvale, Rochester and Tawatinaw, three hamlets that were along the original Athabasca Landing Trail. The Hudson's Bay Company developed the trail following the original

Aboriginal trail between the North Saskatchewan and Athabasca Rivers. For years it was used for hauling freight and furs."

Elizabeth pulled off of Highway 2 to go into Perryvale. She drove the section of the Athabasca Landing Trail from Perryvale to Rochester, and then to Tawatinaw, a Cree word for "river which divides the hills." There wasn't much to see in the three places, but Elizabeth enjoyed the feeling of being on the historic trail. After Tawatinaw, she pulled back on to Highway 2.

She glanced at her watch. She was doing very well for time. She thought about phoning Christine, but did she really want to warn her that she was coming? She decided not to. Elizabeth wondered if Wayne had called her about Jared's search for information surrounding his mother's death.

She photographed some of the village of Legal's large collection of wall murals that showed the contribution of the Francophones to Western Canada, and then stopped in at Morinville to see St. Jean Baptiste Roman Catholic Church, completed in the early twentieth century.

"St. Albert is south of Morinville," Elizabeth recorded. She drove straight to Father Lacombe's chapel, which she was surprised to see was a small log building.

"Stroll behind the St. Albert Parish Church and view the crypt, where the body of Father Lacombe lies in honour," she recorded as she walked. She then stood and looked at the crypt. The man inside there had spent his life helping to build the west. He'd given Alberta its first sawmill, bridge and horse-drawn grist mill. What a legacy.

As she drove out of St. Albert and into Edmonton, Elizabeth recorded another tidbit to continue the food theme from the day before. "If it's Saturday, go to St. Anne Street, which is the site of what is known as Western Canada's largest outdoor farmer's market. The market is held from July through September. Here you can buy meats and vegetables for barbecuing and dessert to take home with you."

Wayne's Story

"Are we still going to Charlie's wedding tomorrow?" Wayne asked. It was Friday night, a few days after Graham had returned. They were at the table drinking their coffee after supper. Graham had gone into town to see his friends.

"Yes, of course," Christine said. "Why wouldn't I?"

"I'm just not sure what you want. Since you seem to hate it here, I thought maybe you wouldn't want to attend community events anymore."

Christine sighed with exasperation. "It's not that I hate it here. I just want a different life."

"Well, supposing I sold the farm and we moved to Vancouver, what would I work at?" Wayne was not even considering the sale, but he hoped Christine would see that her idea was not the best for them.

"Graham got a job when he moved to Calgary, so you should be able to."

"At what, pumping gas like him?" He really couldn't believe what he was hearing. "I'm a bit old for that, and the pay wouldn't be enough to support us."

"I'll be making good money as soon as I get my accounting certificate."

"You're not looking after me!" he yelled, pounding the table. "How can you even think that I would consider something like that? My wife supporting me."

Christine was silent for a while. "You know about machinery, you could go to school and get a heavy duty mechanic's license."

Wayne could feel himself losing control of his anger. And rather than say or do something he'd regret, he stomped out the door. He went to the barn, the barn that housed the cows that were their livelihood. Two of the barn cats came up to him. He kicked at one, sending it flying against the wall. It let out a howl and ran to hide. The other slinked away. He looked for something to throw, something to hit. He needed to get rid of his anger. He took the fork and began to clean the stalls. He threw the straw from them into a pile in the centre of the barn. Then he got his tractor and pushed the pile out the door.

When he went back in the house, Christine was watching television.

"You really aren't going to think about it, are you?" She looked at him quizzically.

It was about time she realized that. "This is what I've worked for over the past twenty-five years. This is where I want to be, and I thought this was where you wanted to be too. I thought we were both working towards the same thing."

"At one time we were, but sometimes people change, outgrow the life they're living. I guess that's what I've done."

"You wouldn't have if you hadn't taken a job outside the farm."

"That's not true."

"What if we build that addition to the house you've always wanted?" He would do anything. "You could have your dining room with the oak china cabinet and table."

Christine shook her head. "No, that won't do now. I'm beyond wanting an oak china cabinet."

"What if we compromise? We keep the farm, and you take a trip every year to these places you want to see so badly. That way we'd both be happy."

"You don't understand, do you? A quick two-week trip is not what I want. That would leave me fifty weeks of still living here. I want to live a different life, not visit it."

"Well, I don't know what we're going to do," Wayne said.

"I do. I'll have to leave by myself."

"That won't happen," Wayne stated, furiously. "I won't let that happen."

"You don't have any say in it."

"Oh, yes I do." Wayne waved his arms. "You're my wife. I have lots of say in what you do."

"I've already found a place to live in Redwater, and I'm moving out the beginning of November."

Chapter 21

It was later than Elizabeth expected when she left Chevy in the vehicle and rang the doorbell. A woman opened the inside door and peered out.

"Christine Dearden?" Elizabeth asked, through the screen door. The woman must have been a beauty when she was younger. Elizabeth knew she had to be in her mid-seventies, but her face was virtually unlined. Her hair was a steel-toned gray and styled professionally. She had an air of elegance about her.

"Yes," she answered. "And whatever you're selling, I don't want any." She began to close the door.

"I'm Elizabeth Oliver, a friend of Jared Jones."

Christine looked puzzled. "Jared Jones? Why would a friend of his be visiting me?"

Elizabeth held out the photograph of Anna's gravesite. Christine stared at it but didn't open the screen to take it.

"I've seen that stone," she said.

Elizabeth showed her what was pasted on the back. Christine looked shocked. She swallowed and asked, "Was she really?"

"That's what Jared and I are trying to find out." Apparently no one had contacted her about this. Good.

Christine unlatched the door and opened it. "Come in."

Elizabeth stepped into the living room and closed the door behind her.

"I'm just brewing a pot of green tea," Christine said. "Would you like some?"

"Please," Elizabeth replied, following Christine into the kitchen. She took a seat at the small, square table.

"How did you get my address?" Christine asked. She lifted the lid of the teapot to see if the tea had brewed.

"Jared and I were at Wayne's place yesterday, and he gave it to us." Then Elizabeth explained who she was and why she was there instead of Jared. She concluded, saying, "Wayne said that you two weren't really friends with Paul and Anna."

Christine shook her head. "We weren't. Wayne and the other men worked together helping each other with the haying and harvesting, but I never really saw much of Anna. I think that's mainly because she was much younger than me, she and Graham weren't close after high school and I worked."

"So you don't know much about her and Paul's marriage."

"Only the gossip."

"And what was that?" It never paid to say you already knew something.

"That he drank, beat her and fooled around on her." Christine set a cup and saucer in front of Elizabeth.

"That's a lot of gossip."

"I know, and I don't know what was true and what wasn't, so I can't say any more."

Well, that was quick, Elizabeth thought. On to the next subject.

"There's been some speculation that Ben's and Anna's deaths were connected." She didn't add that she was the one doing the speculating.

"I didn't kill Anna, if that's what you're implying."

"I'm not. It just seems strange to have two people from the same community die unexpectedly within such a short time of each other."

Christine looked at Elizabeth shrewdly. "You know, over the years many people have called on me to ask about my affair with Ben and about that night. University students, police working on cold cases, true-crime writers; they were all trying to make a name for themselves by solving the mystery of who had hit me and finished him off. Is this your way of getting me to 'spill the beans,' as they say?"

Elizabeth was stuck for an answer. She had decided it wouldn't be fair to Jared to write a true-crime article about his mother's death, even if they could prove it was a murder, but she hadn't thought about Ben's murder.

"I'm trying to help Jared find out what really happened to his mother. The only reason I'm asking about Ben's murder is they happened so close together that Jared is wondering if there is a connection. If they are related somehow, then the more we learn about Ben's death, the more we might learn about Anna's also."

"Jared's in a wheelchair now, isn't he?"

"Yes," Elizabeth answered slowly, wondering where this was leading.

"I remember him as a shy little boy. I used to feel sorry for him when I saw him at the community events. He always seemed a bit frightened, jumping at sudden noises." Christine paused. "He hasn't had much of a life, with his mother dying when he was young and then having his accident. And now to receive this message, it must be stirring it all up again for him."

"Yes, it has been hard for him," Elizabeth agreed. She would go the sympathy route if she had to.

"I know there is no association between the two deaths, but if it will make Jared feel any better I will help if I can."

"Wayne told us about him wanting to expand the farm and you wanting to sell it and possibly move to Vancouver." Elizabeth wasn't going to give this woman a chance to change her mind.

"Yes. He probably also told you the reason was I wanted to get away from Ben." She poured them each a cup of tea.

"Yes. And that you didn't love him anymore."

Christine nodded. "I was tired of farming and of our marriage. I felt there was more to life. I knew he would never leave the farm, so rather than tell him I didn't love him, I said I wanted to sell. When he wouldn't even consider that, I had a reason to move out."

"I got the impression that Wayne didn't take it very well."

"That's an understatement," Christine said, with a grim smile.

"Now you've got my curiosity aroused." Elizabeth leaned forward. "Would you care to elaborate?"

Few of the people she'd talked to knew anything about Anna's life and death. Most of them, however, knew and were willing to talk about Christine and Ben's affair and Ben's death.

"I was hoping to stay in the house until I'd finished my course," Christine said. "But we were having so many arguments that I found a place to live in town. Graham, our son, had moved back in with us. Did Wayne tell you about him?"

Elizabeth nodded.

"On November first, while they were out milking the cows, I got the furniture from the spare bedroom ready to move. I'd already put a deposit on a used couch and a dining set in the second-hand store, and I wanted to pick them up that day also. I packed some clothes and toiletries into a suitcase. All the while I was hoping Wayne would understand my decision and maybe even help me move."

"Did he know you were leaving?" Elizabeth asked.

Christine nodded her head. "I had told him, but I don't know if he believed me. So I was really worried and scared. I didn't know how he would react when I actually did it. My stomach was churning as I waited for them to come in. I hated doing this in front of Graham, but at the same time I hoped that, with him there, Wayne wouldn't cause too big a scene."

"You were moving to Redwater?"

"Yes. I had my job there, but once I had my CGA certificate I was on my way to Vancouver. I had to get as far away from Ben as possible."

"Why?" Elizabeth asked.

"I'd been so wrapped up in the thrill of the affair, in having some excitement in my life, that I didn't realize I didn't love him." Christine went to the cupboard and took out a bag of cookies. She placed some on a plate and set it on the table. "When I figured that out, I wanted to end it. Wayne was a possessive man, but Ben was almost as bad. He didn't like Meredith even looking at another man, even though he himself was having an affair. And he certainly didn't want his lover to drop him."

"And how did Wayne react to your actual move?" Elizabeth took a cookie.

"He stared at the stuff that I'd piled by the door, then looked at me. 'I'm serious about wanting a different life,' I said to him. Well, after arguing and pleading and even some tears, he realized I was really leaving. He was furious and refused to help. He even tried to stop me from using our truck. I said I would rent a truck in town and was headed for the door when Graham agreed to help me. We loaded everything into the back of the truck, and he drove it while I drove my car. Wayne didn't even say goodbye."

"How did he take Graham helping you?"

"Not very well. Graham said it was over a week before Wayne even talked to him. I'd given Graham my phone number, which he must have passed on to Wayne because Wayne phoned me the next morning wondering how I was doing."

"What did Ben do?"

"He actually thought I'd moved out so that we would have more freedom to see each other." She sipped her tea.

"So what actually happened that night Ben died?"

"That's a long story," Christine said. "Both Wayne and Ben began coming to see me. I was so afraid Wayne would see Ben's truck there, but it never happened that I know of. They always seemed to miss each other. Graham even came a few times."

It was getting late, and she wanted to get back to Jared at the B and B, but Elizabeth realized that Christine could not be hurried in her storytelling. Maybe, now that she had started, she needed to tell it all. Elizabeth knew she wasn't going to get away soon. She had another cookie.

"Did Wayne visit you a lot?"

"Yes, to the point that one evening when he came I ignored the knocking. I was just getting so tired of having the same conversation over and over with him. But he wouldn't go away. He began pounding, and that made me angry enough that I opened the door.

"'What do you want this time?' I demanded. I'd given up trying to be nice anymore. It was cold, but Wayne just stood on the step and stared at me, seemingly oblivious to the wind that whipped the snow around him. He said he wanted to talk. I told him that unless he had come to tell me he had a buyer for the farm, there was nothing more to say. When he wanted to come in I quickly rejected the idea and tried to shut the door. But his hand shot out, knocking the door from my grasp and against the wall. He barged into the kitchen, pushing me back."

"That must have scared you," Elizabeth remarked.

"It did." Christine nodded. "I told him I would call the police. 'I don't think you'd better,' he said, his voice menacing. 'Sit down.' I complied, and he said, 'I'm not going to hurt you. I could never hurt you.' Well, at the moment I didn't believe him, but I nodded anyway."

"Self-preservation," Elizabeth said.

"Right," Christine agreed, smiling slightly. "So he began telling me we could work it out. I could move back home, and with Graham there to look after the cows we could do some travelling. I told him that I knew he didn't want to travel at that time, and he said he would to save our marriage."

"It really sounds like he loved you."

"I know, and believe me, my guilt was immense. I pointed out that if he decided he didn't like travelling, that he would rather be with his cows, then we would be back in the same situation. He disagreed, citing that once I was back, I would realize that I really wanted to stay on the farm." Christine shook her head. "He just couldn't get it. I tried telling him again that I didn't like farming. I actually told him that I didn't love him anymore, but I'm not even sure he heard me. I was tempted to tell him about my affair with Ben. I thought maybe he'd get the message then, but I still had Meredith to consider. Plus, I know Wayne would have beaten Ben up or maybe killed him if he found out."

"Really?" Could Wayne have been the person who hit Christine on the head and then stabbed Ben? Elizabeth couldn't see him letting Christine take the blame for it all these years, though. Not if he'd loved her as he claimed.

"Oh, yes. Wayne had a terrible jealous streak. He broke the leg of a boy who asked me out in high school. He beat up guys who paid any kind of attention to me. Everyone knew that. Anyway, he finally asked what he could do to change my mind, and I told him nothing would. You can imagine my relief when he stood and left.

"It was after midnight when the pounding began again. I peeked out the window and there was Wayne, but this time he was swaying on the porch. I hollered at him to go away, and he yelled back that we had to talk again. His words were slurred badly. 'We've talked enough,' I said, as harshly as I could. 'It's over. Now go home.' He started pounding again. I quickly opened the door and gave him a shove. He staggered off the porch and fell into the snow. 'Go away!' I yelled and slammed the door. I don't know how long he lay in the snow before getting up and going home because I went back to bed. In the morning he was gone."

"What about Ben?' Elizabeth prompted.

"His visits were almost the same. He wanted us to get back together, and I didn't. He threatened to tell Wayne. I told him to go ahead, my marriage was over anyway. Like Wayne, he'd go away and then come back a day or two later. Sometimes it was just after Wayne had left, so I know he'd been sitting outside waiting.

"That last day was really busy. Meredith came to see me, and she'd just left when Graham arrived for a visit. He had barely left the yard when Ben banged on the door. I was really glad that they had missed each other. I could tell Ben was drunk. I didn't know what to do because by this time I'd had a few complaints from my neighbours about the noise, and I was afraid they could call the police. He began running at the door with his shoulder, and eventually the frame broke and he got in. I tried to run, but he lunged at me and grabbed me by the hair. I actually thought I was going to die. I thought he was going to kill me. I grabbed a knife and stabbed him."

Elizabeth knew that this was where the story took a different turn. "And then what?" She leaned forward eagerly.

"That I still don't know. I woke later, and there were paramedics and police in my kitchen. I had a terrible headache, and Ben was on the floor covered in blood. I told the police that someone must have hit me on the head and then killed him. Even though I had a bump on the back of my skull, they didn't believe me, and I was arrested for his murder."

"But you don't recall what took place after that first stabbing?"

Christine shook her head. "The police decided I'd stabbed him another four times, then fainted and banged my head."

"Did the police look for someone who may have knocked you out before finishing Ben off?"

"They tried, but they never found any hard evidence of another person on the scene after the first stabbing. However, because of the lump on my head, my lawyer was able to show that someone could have done just that, so there was reasonable doubt. That's why I was found not guilty."

"Do you know who that person could have been?" Elizabeth asked.

"No."

"If Graham had just left, do you think he may have seen Ben enter? He could have come back in and seen what was happening. In anger, he might have stabbed Ben after you tripped and fell or something like that?"

"Look, there's no point speculating," Christine said adamantly. "Like I told you, I remember stabbing him once and then nothing else until I woke up and the paramedics were there."

"Did Graham say anything to you?"

"What's the matter with you? I don't like what you're insinuating, and I never invited you in for an interrogation!" This time she stood. "Tea time's over. I think you'd better go."

That was fine with Elizabeth. It had been a long day, and she was tired.

Clearly, she wasn't going to find out anything more from Christine. Maybe if she talked with Graham.

"Where's Graham?" Elizabeth asked, as she opened the door. "I thought he lived with you."

"He knows nothing about it." Christine closed the door.

Christine's Story

Once she and Graham had unloaded the furniture and Graham had left, Christine went to the bedroom to put the bed together and make it up. She'd taken the first step to begin her new life, but somehow the elation she thought she would feel was not there. In its place was sadness for the life she had had to leave, and for the first time she realized it was not going to be easy to step from her old life into her new one. She went to bed without eating because she had no food. That was one thing she'd forgotten about.

The next morning, Christine arose feeling just as tired as she had the night before. She hadn't slept. She wasn't used to the noise of vehicles driving by during the night, of people walking and talking at all hours. Plus her mind kept her awake, going over and over the decision she had made and remembering the fun times of the past twenty-five years: the excitement of Graham's birth, the happiness of paying off the farm. They had worked hard to make their farm a success.

But over the years she had gone through some changes, done a lot of thinking. She had discovered that farming wasn't what she wanted to do for the rest of her life and she had questioned her love for Wayne. She really was getting tired of his jealousy. She wanted to be able to talk normally with men without worrying about his reaction. She knew that when she suggested he sell the farm and go away with her, his first reaction would be to refuse.

The phone rang just as she was putting on her coat. The only one who knew her phone number was Graham.

"Hello?"

"Christine," Wayne said. "I was just wondering if you wanted to have breakfast here when you get the rest of your things."

Christine wasn't sure how she should answer that. "No. I'll stop and have some toast and coffee at a restaurant."

"But you're coming here anyway."

"Okay." It was easier to agree than start another fight. "I'm leaving now."

"I'll have it ready."

Christine had to smile. The only other time Wayne had voluntarily cooked a meal for her was the night he had sprung his plans on her.

At work on Monday, Christine gave her change of address to one of the secretaries.

"What happened?"

"Just a parting of the ways." Christine shrugged. She really didn't want to talk about it.

Later, Tony, one of her bosses, stepped up to her desk and said, "I hear you're now free to go out with me."

Christine looked up. "No, I'm not."

"But you're separated. There's nothing stopping you."

Christine knew she had to be careful. "I'm still married."

"If you really thought that, then you would be living at home."

"I'm not interested in jumping out of the pan and into the fire."

Tony leaned on her desk and looked down at her. "Well, this fire won't be extinguished until you agree to go out with me."

"Maybe later, when things have settled down with Wayne."

"Okay, I'll give you some time, but don't take too long."

What was it with men? Why did they think they could direct her life?

Chapter 22

As she drove away, Elizabeth wondered if Christine thought Graham may have had something to do with Ben's murder. That may explain why Graham had moved to Edmonton to be with her. They shared a terrible secret. Maybe it had played out as she had said, but instead of someone unknown, it was Graham who came back, saw what was happening and stabbed Ben to protect his mother. They could have concocted the story about her stabbing him then passing out. Graham could even have hit her on the head to give her the bump.

Elizabeth shook her head. She must be tired to have come up with that wild scenario.

By the time she reached the B and B, she was drained. But she didn't think she could sleep. She wondered if Jared was awake. He'd said he'd been having a hard time sleeping since he'd received the photograph, and he'd also said he would be awake when she got back. She hated the idea of checking. What if he'd just managed to get to sleep and was having the first good sleep in days? She let Chevy visit a few bushes in the yard, then picked him up and carried him quietly into the house. She went to Jared's door and tapped lightly.

"Who's there?" he called softly.

Good, she hadn't woken him. "It's Elizabeth," she whispered.

"Come in."

He smiled when he saw her, and her heart melted. She went over and kissed him.

Jared set the book aside that he had been reading and removed his glasses, which he placed under the edge of his pillow. He patted the bed beside him. She lay down and placed her head on his shoulder. He put his arm around her. Chevy jumped on the bed and settled at Jared's feet.

Jared began stroking her hair. She snuggled closer. This felt good lying here with him.

"Do you want to come under the covers with me?" he asked.

Boy, did she ever! To heck with telling him about her visit to Christine. That could wait until tomorrow.

The next morning, Elizabeth stretched luxuriously and looked over at Jared sleeping beside her. What a night they'd had. She looked at her watch. It was late. Chevy jumped off the bed and went to the door.

"Okay," she whispered, getting dressed. She opened the door softly and peeked out. No one. Feeling like a naughty teenager, she snuck down the hall and out the door. She knew she wasn't going on her third trip today, and she didn't even mind. When she and Chevy got back to Jared's room, Chevy immediately jumped up on the bed and walked over to Jared's face.

"Well, do come and say hi." Jared laughed, as he reached out and scratched Chevy's ears. "I'm glad you brought your owner back with you." He smiled up at Elizabeth.

She bent over and kissed him. "That's not all I am," she purred.

Jared lifted the covers for the second time in the last few hours. "You left here so fast that you missed breakfast."

"Do you serve brunch?" Elizabeth asked, sliding in beside him.

"I serve anything, anytime."

To save time, they showered together. When Jared was dressed, Elizabeth donned a clean pair of his shorts and a shirt and ran to her room.

"I'll meet you for a real breakfast," Jared said.

They just barely made it under the eleven o'clock cut-off for the meal.

"So tell me about what you learned yesterday from Christine," Jared said, while they were eating.

"It wasn't very productive," Elizabeth began. "She didn't know your mother very well, and she doesn't think Ben's death and your mother's death have anything in common."

"So she couldn't tell us any more than what we already know?"

Elizabeth shook her head. "Like everyone else, though, she was very willing to talk about Ben's death. It must have been quite an event for people to still be talking about it."

"I talked with Meredith about it yesterday, and she said that the place was swarming with reporters after the killing and during the trial. They were making it out to be the romantic triangle of the century."

"Christine told me that she broke it off with Ben and was leaving Wayne and the farm. Wayne would show up at her place drunk, trying to get her to come home, and Ben would show up drunk, trying to get her to patch up their affair."

"Sounds like a fiasco."

Elizabeth nodded. "And the night of the killing, Meredith visited her, then left before Graham arrived, and he left before Ben showed up."

"Busy evening."

"Yes," Elizabeth agreed thoughtfully. "It's strange that with all his visits before, the only one who didn't go there that night was Wayne."

"What if he did and she's covering for him?"

"Or maybe Graham came back, and she could be protecting him."

"I wonder if Wayne knows more than he is saying," Jared mused.

"We could always go ask him." She stopped. "We're getting sidetracked from why we are really here."

"I know," Jared said, grinning. "But I can understand how you can get caught up in trying to solve crimes. It's like putting a puzzle together or trying to find the last word in a crossword. You just got to keep at it."

He took the picture of his mother out of his pocket and looked at it. "It seems so hard to learn anything about Mom."

"Not many people in the area really got to know her. She must have had a very lonely life," Elizabeth said. "Do you know who any of her friends were in that grad photo?"

Jared shook his head. "I'll ask Dad today."

"You didn't go yesterday?"

"I tried. I even got as far as the road in front of the farm. Although the house and the outbuildings and the yard look the same, I didn't feel as comfortable entering as I used to before receiving the photograph. The message on the back has raised too many questions, too many doubts about the people who live there, the people I call family."

"So you left?"

"Yes. I thought I'd try again today. I'm not sure what more I can learn, but I hope it's something that will settle my mind, quiet the fears growing inside me. But I don't want to go alone. Can you come with me?"

Elizabeth nodded. "I've already decided not to do any research today so yes, I can."

Jared breathed a sigh of relief. "Thank you."

Elizabeth reached into her pocket and pulled out the small bag that held yesterday's purchase at the mission.

"I bought this for you."

"For me?" Jared looked startled. "What is it?"

"Open it," Elizabeth urged, smiling.

Jared pulled the bag apart and held up the eagle on the silver chain. "It's beautiful," he breathed. He immediately hung it around his neck. "How does it look?"

Elizabeth felt a lump in her throat. It fit perfectly in the V of his shirt and stood out against his suntan.

Chapter 23

When they got to the farm, Paul, Willy and Susie had just sat down at the table.

"Would you like a roast beef sandwich?" Susie asked, heading for the cupboard.

"No, thank you," Jared said. "We just finished breakfast."

Susie looked from one to the other and smiled. "Then have a seat, Elizabeth."

Elizabeth noted that it was Susie who was making them feel welcome. The two men continued to eat.

"How's your little investigation going, Jared?" Paul finally addressed him.

"Not very well," Jared admitted. "Not many people knew Mom."

"Have you found that phantom link between her death and Ben's?" Willy asked.

Elizabeth couldn't tell if Willy was ridiculing him or not. She didn't need to ask how he knew about that. Gossip travelled fast around here.

"No." Jared turned to Paul. "Dad, what day did you and Mom get married?"

"Why do you want to know?"

"Because I never knew when your wedding anniversary was. I don't know how Mom was dressed. I don't even know if you were married in a church."

"We were married on May 21, 1976. Now, does that help you?"

Jared did a quick calculation on his head. "She was almost four months pregnant."

"Yes," Paul said gruffly.

"Did you know?"

"That's why I married her."

"What church were you married in?"

"We went to a local marriage commissioner."

Elizabeth noticed that Paul was not adding any more information than was asked for.

"Who all was there?"

"Just Willy and my mother."

"Why not Grandma and Grandpa Dombroski?"

"They wanted nothing to do with her once they found out she was pregnant. They moved away soon after because of it."

"Why didn't you put the dates of her birth and death on her gravestone, like everyone else has on theirs?"

Paul didn't answer.

"What do you want to know for?" Willy demanded.

"Because I've wondered about it for years, but I've never had the guts to ask."

"And today you do."

Jared lifted his chin. "Today, I do."

"It would have cost too much extra money," Paul said abruptly.

"What?" Jared asked.

"It would have cost more for them."

"Then why didn't you put them on instead of that horrible inscription?"

Elizabeth admired Jared for keeping his voice calm. She'd have been yelling by now.

"Because I didn't care if people knew when she was born or when she had died, but I definitely wanted everyone to know how she had died."

"You were that angry?"

"Yes." Paul's voice was becoming curt.

Elizabeth figured that he wouldn't take much more of this.

Jared pulled the photograph of his mother's graduation from his pocket. "Do you know any of these people with Mom?"

Paul glanced at it and threw it on the table. "No."

"But you hardly even looked at it," Jared protested. He picked it up and handed it back. "Please."

Paul grabbed it from his hand. He held it in front of his face, then again tossed it in Jared's direction. "There, you satisfied?"

"Paul, that wasn't very nice," Susie admonished.

"Well, how would you like it if someone came around insinuating that you are a killer?" Paul demanded.

Elizabeth noticed that Paul said "someone" not "son."

"Dad, I remember you hollering at Mom," Jared said, his voice steady. "I remember you slapping her across the face and her backing away with her hand on her cheek."

Paul slammed both hands on the table and stood angrily. "I didn't kill her!" he yelled.

Jared ducked reflexively and held up his hands in a defensive gesture, fear plain on his face. Elizabeth stood to defend him.

Paul opened his mouth to say something, but instead he turned and headed towards the door.

"Dad, I was hiding behind a chair when you hit her, and just thinking about it now, I can feel the same panic in my stomach."

Paul hesitated, and then pushed open the door and left.

"I keep telling you to leave it alone," Willy said.

Jared quickly wheeled himself out of the house and followed Paul to the barn. Elizabeth hurried along with him. For some reason, she didn't want to leave him alone with his father. Paul had just grabbed a fork to clean out the stalls when they entered.

"Dad, did you have a girlfriend?" Jared demanded.

Paul turned to him, fork in hand. Elizabeth stepped forward. Jared put his hand on her arm. Paul looked at her and threw the fork away.

"Did you?" Jared asked again.

"Where did you hear that?" he asked, his voice low and controlled.

"It seems to be common knowledge," Jared said.

Elizabeth restrained a smile. He'd learned a few things from her about questioning.

"She had nothing to do with your mother's death," Paul said.

Elizabeth's heart sank for Jared. So it was true.

"Why?" Jared asked, his voice croaking. "Why did you need a girlfriend?"

Paul shrugged. "It's not as if we had a marriage."

"She was pregnant. You had something."

"She had something."

"What do you mean by that?"

Paul waved his hand. "Nothing."

"No. You wouldn't have said it if it meant nothing."

Paul put his hands on Jared's armrests and leaned over until they were face to face. He looked Jared straight in the eye.

"Your mother was not murdered. She took her own life."

"Was that because you were seeing another woman?"

Paul threw his hands up in exasperation. "I give up. Okay, I had a girlfriend. We saw each other for about a year, and then we broke it off. She moved away. That's all there was to it."

"Did Mom know about it?"

"I really don't know, and I really don't care. That was a long time ago. Nothing that happened then can be changed, no matter how many questions you ask." Paul's voice dropped to a tight whisper. "And if you are not careful, you might learn some things that you wished you hadn't."

With that he turned and left the barn.

Christine's Story

She was finishing her course work one evening when there was a knock at the door. Christine went to the kitchen window and looked out. Wayne was standing on the porch. It had been a week since her move, and this was the first time he'd come to see her. He knocked again, louder. She opened the door.

"Hi," she said, standing back and letting him in.

Wayne stood just inside the door.

"Have a seat," Christine said. "I've just made some coffee."

Wayne sat at the kitchen table and accepted a cup. He still hadn't spoken.

"How's Graham?" Christine finally asked.

"He's okay, I guess," he said.

"Good."

"Is this still what you want?" Wayne asked.

"Yes," she replied, wishing she could explain everything to him. Then he would truly understand that their marriage was over. But since she couldn't, she had to continue her ruse.

"Why?"

Christine looked away. What could she say that she hadn't said before? She had grown to dislike the confines of the farm. She did want to travel and see more of the world. She did want to move to Vancouver. She did have to get away from here and from Ben and from him.

"I just have to," Christine said, knowing the words were too inadequate to explain the upheaval she had caused in his life.

"No," Wayne said emphatically. "You don't have to."

Yes, Christine said silently, I do.

"Can't all this wait until we retire?" he asked. "I promise I'll travel all over the world with you."

"When will that be? In thirty years?"

"Won't you change your mind?" Wayne asked.

"Won't you?" She knew he wouldn't. She was counting on the fact that he wouldn't. As much as he loved her, he wouldn't choose her over the farm.

"How can you throw away twenty-five years so easily?"

"Believe me, it isn't easy. It's been the hardest thing I've had to do in my life. I thought about it for a long time before I moved out."

"Do you know what everyone in Redwater is saying? They're saying you left me for another man."

Christine's breath caught. This was her opportunity. But she didn't want the resulting outburst, the anger, the possible fight between him and Ben. Her leaving him was one thing she thought he could handle. Knowing that she had been having an affair with one of his friends was something she didn't think he could.

"No, I didn't. I left because I wanted to."

Chapter 24

"You know," Jared began softly, as they drove away, "the man I've called my father all these years is rapidly becoming a stranger to me."

Elizabeth didn't know how Jared was managing to hold up under everything that he was learning. She wished she could do something to ease the pain that he must be feeling.

"I wanted to follow him and demand to know what those things were he was hinting at, but the way he said it, so quiet and cold, sent a shiver through me. For the first time, I'm afraid; afraid of the past, afraid of what I'm going to find out during my search."

He looked at her. "I know you warned me that I might not like what I learned. But for some reason, I was the one chosen to discover what really happened to my mother."

"Well, we certainly did learn some more about your mom," Elizabeth said.

"Yes, with Mom being almost four months pregnant with me, that could explain my grandfather's reaction to her and to me."

"It sure sounds like your grandfather was capable of holding a grudge. I wonder why your parents waited so long to get married. Surely she'd have known earlier that she was pregnant."

"I never thought to ask. There are so many things I didn't get to ask about."

"Well, we'll just have to keep going back until you get all your answers."

"Providing Dad lets us," Jared said ruefully. "Where do we go from here?"

"Let's head to the Munter-Thompson farm," Elizabeth said. "Sarah seems quite willing to talk with us."

"Well, I thought you'd be back," Sarah said, coming out of the house and looking down at them. "I'll get some juice, if you want to go to the gazebo."

"You're right," Jared said to Elizabeth, as he pushed himself around to the backyard. "She seems happy to see us."

They had just settled in the gazebo when Sarah arrived with glasses on a tray.

"I hope you like orange juice," she said. "That's all we have right now."

"It's fine with me," Elizabeth said, taking the glass offered to her.

"Nick has gone into town," Sarah explained, passing the juice to Jared. "I don't go much anymore. It's too hard on my legs to stand for very long."

"Do you two still farm?" Elizabeth asked, taking a sip.

"No. We rent out most of our land now. Nick's not feeling that good these days so he's had to slow down. But he keeps active by doing the gardening and mowing the lawn."

Sarah sat down on the bench. "Word has been circulating about you two," she said, changing the subject. "You're both creating quite a stir."

"What are people saying?"

"That you are trying to show a link between Ben's and Anna's deaths, that you are asking all sorts of questions about Anna's life. Christine even phoned Wayne and gave him shit for giving you her address."

Elizabeth wondered why. Christine had monopolized the conversation, telling her about that night. The only bad part had been at the end, when she'd asked about Graham.

"Seems that you implied that Graham had something to do with killing Ben," Sarah said, as if reading her thoughts.

"Well, he was there that evening," Elizabeth pointed out. "And so was Meredith."

"Oh, yes. There was a lot of speculation about that when it came out at the trial, especially once Christine's lawyer claimed that she had been hit on the head after she had stabbed Ben only once."

"Did the police look into that?"

"They did, but they concluded that she had killed Ben, and then passed out, hitting her head."

"When the jury found her not guilty, did the police try looking for someone else?"

"Not that I heard of. I think they figured that they had the right person, but just not enough evidence."

"We've been reading Meredith's books," Jared said. "She definitely loved Ben."

"That I wouldn't know, seeing as how he was killed the winter before I moved here." She grinned. "I can tell you about some of the stories I heard, though."

"Okay," Elizabeth agreed.

"Apparently, she and Wayne were having their own little affair."

"They were?" both Jared and Elizabeth asked at the same time.

"Yes." Sarah nodded. "They were spotted coming out of a hotel room one night and were seen having a good time at the auction market one day."

"Auction market?" Elizabeth asked.

"That's where some farmers take animals to sell and others go to buy. Auction day is the highlight of the week. Every farmer who can find the time attends the auction market. Some go because they're checking the price of cattle. Others want some piglets to raise or just one full-sized pig to butcher. In the fall, those who have enough hay put up go to buy calves that were born in the spring. They feed them over the winter and then sell them as yearlings the next spring. In the spring, those who have extra pasture go to buy the yearlings to put on the grass and fatten up for selling in the fall." Sarah paused for a breath. "But most farmers just go to see who is buying or selling and to visit."

"Doesn't sound like an exciting place to go on a date," Elizabeth said.

"It's not, but it is a good excuse to get together with someone without raising much suspicion."

"Except in this case, it made people suspicious. And yet, according to Christine, Wayne wanted her back," Elizabeth said.

"Well, Ben didn't want to break up with either Christine or Meredith," Sarah said. "It's too bad people don't stay with their marriages like Nick and I have. Sure we've had our differences, and we've learned a lot about each other that we didn't know before we were married, but you have to get past that. You have to decide what is important in your life. To me, my marriage is the most important thing in my life. I've worked hard at getting it the way I want it."

Christine's Story

Christine woke late Christmas morning, and it felt good. She had spent too many years baking apple and pumpkin pies the day before Christmas, and then getting up early the next morning to make the dressing and put the turkey in the oven. A quick breakfast, followed by opening presents, and then it was time to peel and cook the potatoes and carrots, make the salad and set the table for the relatives. She had never been able to enjoy Christmas Day like everyone else.

She'd been out to visit her parents and had explained what was happening between her and Wayne. Although they didn't give their outright approval, they did state that she had the right to do what she wanted with her life. So this season she hadn't extended any invitations nor had she accepted any sent her way.

Christine got up and started a pot of coffee. As it brewed, she showered, and then she sat at the table with a mug. She hadn't bothered to decorate a tree for Christmas, although she had put a string of lights around her window and a garland around her doorway. This was her first Christmas alone. She did have some presents for Graham and he was coming over later that day to pick them up and have Christmas supper with her. She had bought a ham instead of a turkey because she didn't want to have leftovers. Wayne had offered her one of the turkeys they had raised during the summer, but she refused. It would have meant going out to the farm, killing it, plucking it and cleaning it, all with Wayne beside her.

She wasn't going to do anything that would bring them together under any circumstances. She hadn't even bought him a gift.

After a light lunch, she began preparations for the evening meal. There wasn't much to do and for that she was thankful. For the meal, she peeled four potatoes and made a small salad to go with the peas and carrots. To celebrate being able to totally relax today, she'd bought a pumpkin pie at the store instead of baking one. She then curled up in her chair to read the newest bestseller she had given herself as a Christmas present.

The phone beside her rang. She hesitated, and it rang again. She grinned and grabbed it. He wouldn't call today. It must be Graham, letting her know he was on his way.

"Hello?"

No answer.

Christine's stomach did a flip. It was him again. This was the third time.

"Why don't you leave me alone?" she demanded angrily.

"How is your Christmas?" a voice rasped.

She didn't recognize the voice. Maybe it was disguised.

"Was Santa good to you?" the voice asked.

"Leave me alone!" she yelled, slamming the phone down on the receiver. She leaned against the back of the chair. "What have I gotten myself into?"

Christine jumped at the knock at the door, and then realized it would be Graham. She hurried over to answer it, forcing a smile when she saw her son standing on her porch.

Chapter 25

Elizabeth worked on her article for the rest of the afternoon, while Jared had a nap. When she grew tired of transcribing from her tape recorder she went to her Anna Jones crime file and added what she'd learned the past few days. She also opened a new file on Ben's death. It would be something if there was a link between them.

That evening after supper with Jared she again picked up Meredith's book of poems.

"Why don't you lie beside me while you are reading," Jared suggested, patting the bed.

"Okay," she said. She went to the closet, brought out two pillows for herself and snuggled up against his side.

After reading for a while, she found one poem that she read out to Jared. "She even admits that there was something between her and Wayne," Elizabeth said. "But nothing like the affair between Ben and Christine. Of course, history can be changed by the use of words."

"Yes, that's true."

"I'm doing my last tour tomorrow," Elizabeth said, putting the book down. "Do you want to come with me?"

"We'd have to take my van," Jared pointed out.

"That's fine. Actually, it would be more than fine." Elizabeth smiled. "I'd like to have a handsome chauffeur drive me about. It will free me up for recording."

Anna's Story

Paul returned from his trip into town and threw the mail on the table. Anna saw the family allowance envelope among the flyers. It was addressed to her, but if Paul planned on going to the bar on the day it arrived, he made her sign it so he could cash it at the hotel. She held her breath as he clomped around the kitchen, getting a drink of water and looking for his work gloves.

Anna found herself staring at the envelope, which held the means for her escape. She pulled her eyes away, afraid he would be able to read her mind, afraid he would guess what she was planning. She turned her back to the table and picked up Jared. She didn't want him to get in Paul's way.

"I'm going out to work the west field," Paul said.

"Okay." Anna didn't say more. She didn't want her tension to come through in her voice and give her away.

She heard the tractor start and then chug out of the yard. Even then she didn't pick up the envelope. He could have forgotten something and come back. She paced for ten minutes, and when he didn't return, she tore the envelope open and stuffed the cheque into her purse. Then, while Jared watched television she went into her bedroom and pulled the suitcase out from under her bed. She'd been afraid to pack before in case Jared accidentally said something to Paul about it.

Anna threw some of her and Jared's clothes into the suitcase. Fear clung to her like a wet sweater. She expected Paul to walk in the door at any moment, and every noise made her jump. When the suitcase was full, she pushed it back under the bed. She found the bit of money she'd been able to stash away over the past year. It wasn't much, but it would help. She made some sandwiches for them to eat.

Anna picked up the phone and dialled a number. Her mother answered.

No time to waste on preliminaries. "Mom, I can't take living with Paul anymore. He beats me, and I'm afraid he'll start hitting Jared, so I'm coming to the city on today's bus. Could you meet me at the bus depot?"

"Anna? Oh, Anna, I don't think your father ..."

"Mom, I'm coming. Can you meet me or not?"

"Your father is out right now. I'll ask him when he gets home."

Well, it wasn't a flat no. "I'm not sure what time the bus gets in so you'll have to phone the depot."

"Maybe you should wait until you can talk to your father."

Anna looked out the window. He could come back at any time. "I have to leave now."

Anna got the suitcase from under the bed and grabbed the sandwiches.

"Come on, Jared," she said. "We're going for a ride."

"Where?" Jared asked. He obediently followed her out of the house, leaving the television on.

"To Redwater."

"Are we going shopping?"

"Yes."

Anna continually watched for Paul as they left the yard. She knew he couldn't see their house from where he was in the field, but she couldn't shake her fear.

Her first stop was the bank. She hated to leave Jared in the truck, but it would be faster. She hurried into the bank and cashed her family allowance.

Anna had phoned the bus depot weeks ago to find out the schedule and then spent the time in between thinking about what could go wrong with her plans. On family allowance day, Paul might spend too much time having coffee in Redwater and arrive home too late for her to get into town for the bus. It might rain so he couldn't go to the fields. Equipment could break down, and he'd have to spend the day in the yard fixing it. There had been so many things that could go wrong that she had spent the past weeks with a knot in her stomach and a headache.

She climbed out of the vehicle. For the first time she thought about the second set of truck keys she was supposed to have brought with her.

"Oh, no," she said aloud.

"What's wrong, Mommy?" Jared asked, still sitting on the seat.

"Nothing, honey." She wiped the sweat from her upper lip. She'd planned to bring both sets so that even if Paul found the truck he wouldn't be able to follow her, for she had no illusions that he wouldn't find out where she was headed.

Anna pocketed the keys she had and helped Jared out of the truck. She grabbed her suitcase and, holding Jared's hand, walked into the depot. They were early and would have an hour's wait. An hour in which Paul could get a neighbour to drive him here. That would make him angrier. It wouldn't take long for word to get around that she'd left. She wondered if she would have the strength to fight him and get on the bus if he did show up.

"I thought we were going shopping," Jared said.

"I've decided to go see Grandma and Grandpa in Edmonton." She knew it would mean little to Jared, since he hardly ever heard their names mentioned.

She bought their tickets and sat on a bench. The hour passed so very slowly. She handed Jared a sandwich. She didn't have enough money to buy anything for the trip. She had to save the little left over from the tickets for the city bus, in case no one met her in Edmonton. As the time for departure got closer, the depot filled.

When the bus pulled in, she hurried over to it with the others going to the city. But they had to wait for the few passengers to get off and for the bus driver to give out the pieces of luggage from the compartment. Then he stood at the door and accepted the tickets. Anna set her suitcase near the compartment and waited in line. Her stomach churned. She had no doubt that Paul would find some way of getting into town and she listened for the screeching of tires. She kept waiting for his hand to clamp on her shoulder.

As each person got on the bus, the rest in line shuffled forward. Finally, she held out their tickets. The driver tore off the one side and handed the rest back to her. She helped Jared climb the three steps, and they walked down the aisle looking for two seats together. She found them near the back.

Jared took the one near the window and immediately knelt on the seat to look out. Anna sat down and leaned back with a sigh. She had made it this far.

The bus pulled out. Jared was mesmerized by the passing scenery. Anna felt so weary. She tilted the back of the seat as far as she could and closed her eyes. Her mind began to work on what would happen once she got to the city, and she willed it to stop. She didn't want to brood on whether her mother would be at the depot. She didn't want to wonder if her parents would take her in. She didn't want to think about what she would do if they didn't.

Anna could feel the bus slow down. She opened her eyes. Were they in Edmonton? No, just stopping to pick up someone waiting along the highway. The minutes used up for the stop meant minutes that Paul was making up. Her only hope was that she would have enough time to convince her parents to take in her and Jared, to protect them from him.

Christine's Story

Christine looked around, and then headed over to where a uniformed man stood behind a counter. He glanced up when she approached.

She smiled uncomfortably. She had never been inside a police station before and she hated being here now.

"May I help you?" the man asked.

Christine hesitated. "I've been getting these phone calls," she began.

"From whom?"

"I don't know. He never gives his name."

"I'm Constable Perry." He took a piece of paper from behind the counter and began filling it out. "May I have your name?"

"Christine Dearden."

He wrote that down. "Now tell me about these calls. When did they start, what does he say, when does he call, everything about them."

Christine couldn't remember when she'd received the first call. "They began before Christmas. He usually doesn't say anything. When he called me on Christmas Day, he asked if Santa had been good to me. He calls in the evening and sometimes during the night."

"When he talked, did you recognize the voice?"

"No, I think it's disguised."

"Are you sure it's a he?"

"No."

"Are you married?"

"My husband and I separated last fall."

"Do you think it's your husband calling you?"

Christine knew she would be asked this question, and she didn't know how to answer it. She didn't want to think that Wayne would be making these calls. She didn't want to even insinuate that he might be.

"I don't know." She didn't dare mention Ben

"Was your separation friendly?"

"We discussed it, if that's what you mean. Then I moved out."

"How did he take that?"

"He wants us to get back together."

"Is that what you want?"

"No."

"And yet you don't think he's making these calls?"

"I don't know."

"Where does he live?"

Christine explained how to get to the farm while he wrote down the directions.

"Can you do something to stop the calls?" she asked.

"We usually advise women in this situation to get an unlisted number and then not tell it to anyone."

Christine had a thought. "Is this happening to other women?"

"It could be. Sometimes a caller will phone a number of women but not all of them will contact us."

"Has anyone else complained recently?"

"No."

"So what will you do?"

"We'll go out and visit your husband, but we really have nothing to go on. If that person calls again, listen carefully to other noises on the phone. It might give you an idea of where he is calling from. And if he says anything that means something to you, let us know."

Christine thanked the officer and left. The first thing she did was to get an unlisted number. She didn't like the idea of the officer talking with Wayne, though. If he was making the calls, he certainly wouldn't admit it, and if he wasn't, then that would set him off.

It hadn't taken the police long to contact him or for him to respond with a visit to her.

The next day, she was on her way to work after eating her lunch at home.

"So, I hear you've been getting obscene phone calls," a voice said behind her.

Christine turned, startled to see him walking slightly behind her. She hadn't even heard his footsteps. She continued walking.

"And thank you very much for sending the police out to see me," Wayne said, striding beside her. "I really enjoy being questioned about my state of mind since the separation and being asked if I've ever made a crank call to my wife."

Christine could feel Wayne's anger, and she didn't blame him. She shouldn't have gone to the police. She should have thought of getting the unlisted number on her own.

Wayne suddenly grabbed her by the arm and swung her around to face him.

"Would you stop walking and talk to me?" he demanded.

She shook his hand off her arm. "Not here," she said, looking around to see how many people were watching them.

"Yes, here. I want to know about those calls and why you think it's me?"

"I don't think it's you. The police just asked about my husband, and I told them we were separated. They're the ones who went out to see you."

"What are they going to do about the calls?"

"They say there's nothing they can do, since I don't recognize the voice. They also said that it could be some guy who calls strange women and that I am the only one who has reported the calls so far."

"So it could be some loony who might decide to peek in your window next and then visit you some day."

"They didn't say that."

"Well, it makes sense. These guys like to scare women before they rape them."

"Are you trying to frighten me?" Christine resumed her walking. She was going to be late.

"No. I'm trying to make you see that you might not be safe here, that you should come back home."

Christine stopped and turned to Wayne. "Are you making those calls to frighten me into returning to the farm?"

Wayne's face flushed with anger.

"How could you think that of me?" He raised his hand, and she jumped back, shocked. Then, just as quickly, his anger left him.

"I'm sorry," he murmured, dropping his hand to his side. "I didn't mean to do that."

"I have to go now." Christine hurried the last half block to her office. She didn't look back.

Chapter 26

Elizabeth and Jared rose early to get ready to go on her Vegreville–Wainwright–Tofield loop. Breakfast began at seven o'clock, and Elizabeth had told Brandon that they would be there at that time. She let Chevy do his morning jaunt, and then she and Jared ate.

Elizabeth wasn't in any hurry this time. She had Jared with her. Chevy was curled up on the floor mat between them.

"Head east out of Edmonton on Highway 16," Elizabeth spoke into her laptop's built-in microphone while Jared drove. "When you turn into Elk Island National Park, watch for wildlife, especially buffalo, which roam freely through the park. If you see one, take your picture from inside your vehicle or just sit and admire it. Do not get out and approach the animal, and do not try to feed it."

She directed Jared where to turn, and soon they were at the parking lot of the visitor information centre. It wasn't open yet, so Jared suggested that she and Chevy hike the short trail to a Ukrainian pioneer home while he read some more of Meredith's poems. The inside of the home was blocked off to the public but she could see the plastered walls and thatched roof. A second trail led to a monument to the Plains buffalo, which provided food, clothing and weapons for the First Nations' people, and meat, for the making of pemmican, for the fur traders and explorers.

The information centre was open when Elizabeth returned. She found her brochures and went back to the van. While they carried on along the road in the park, Elizabeth read some of the brochures.

"Hey, listen to this," Elizabeth said to Jared. "At one time there used to be large herds of elk in Alberta." She looked at him. "Can you imagine how majestic they must have looked, thousands of them loping along with their huge antlers held high in the air?"

"That would have been a great picture," Jared agreed.

"This park was formed to protect the elk."

"So how come there are buffalo here?" Jared asked.

"Some buffalo were lodged here temporarily while Buffalo National Park was fenced for them at Wainwright. When they were moved, some got left behind."

"Oh, look," Jared exclaimed, braking. "Speaking of buffalo."

Elizabeth looked up as a large, shaggy buffalo crossed the road in front of them. While Chevy growled at the animal, she sat and stared at it, then grabbed her camera and leaned out her window to take a picture, remembering her own advice about not getting out of her vehicle.

Back on Highway 16, they soon reached the Ukrainian Cultural Heritage Village. Jared decided to get out too.

"This is part of my heritage, and I've never been here," he said.

"You have to stay here for this one," Elizabeth told Chevy, as she gathered up her camera and tape recorder.

"Yeah, she's taking me this time," Jared said.

Elizabeth patted Chevy on his head, then went and paid their entrance fee. They began their tour of the more than thirty old buildings that had been moved on to the grounds.

"So tell me what you learned in your research about this place," Jared said.

"This village was started by a group of Albertans to preserve their Ukrainian heritage, and the provincial government purchased the restored settlement a few years later. It's now one of Alberta's largest historical sites."

"Hey, this is great," Jared said, grinning. "I have my own personal tour guide."

They walked through the site and, at each building, talked with the interpreters who were dressed in period clothing that represented the time when the building was actually used. They also answered questions as though they were currently in that time period. In one building, the year represented was 1919, and the events of that year were discussed by the interpreters. If Elizabeth mentioned anything that took place later in history, they had no knowledge of it.

"This feels like we've taken a step back in time," Jared said.

For the most part, Jared was able to wheel everywhere, and Elizabeth made a note of that. She also noted that there was so much to see that she could spend the whole day exploring the place. The readers could determine if they wanted to make this place a day trip and then do the rest of the tour on another day at Mundare.

"We have to stop in and buy some sausage," Elizabeth urged, when they were on the road again. "I remember when Dad returned from a trip to Saskatchewan and brought home some Mundare sausage. We all loved it, and ever since, when one of the family is in the area, they bring back some sausage."

"Sounds good to me," Jared said. "I'm getting a little hungry."

They first stopped in at the Basilian Fathers Museum, where Elizabeth took pictures of some displays, and then they went into Stawinchy's Meat. At the small deli, Jared picked out some pepperoni while Elizabeth bought turkey sausage. They went out to share with Chevy, then Elizabeth took pictures of the world's largest sausage before leaving town.

"You know," Jared said, "I remember Mom making her own sausages."

"You do? That's so cool. How did she do it?"

Jared thought a moment. "She cut pieces of meat really small, mixed in some spices and then she'd dump a bunch into her hand grinder, which she bolted to the table. She put a length of sheep's gut on the nozzle, and while she cranked the handle, I held the sheep's gut for the sausage to come out into." Jared laughed. "When we had a couple of lengths, she'd fry them up for us to eat. They tasted so good."

Later, as they entered the town, Elizabeth asked Jared, "Have you seen the Pysanka at Vegreville?"

Jared shook his head. "I don't think so."

He followed Elizabeth's directions to where the giant Easter egg overlooked the Vegreville Elks/Kinsmen Community Park.

"I'll just go into the visitor information centre and gather what I can about the area while you get unloaded," Elizabeth said.

"Can't you find all this on the Internet?" Jared asked.

"Going on the Internet is okay, but I've learned that talking with people is the best way to find out the little things." Elizabeth smiled. "Except for the time I went in and asked what there was to see and do around this one town, and the young girl behind the counter replied, 'There's nothing to see and do around here.'"

Once Elizabeth had her information, she met Jared, and they headed over to the Pysanka suspended on its pedestal.

"You know," Jared said, "I have been here before."

"With your Mom?" Elizabeth asked.

"No, I think it was with Dad."

"Your Dad?" Elizabeth couldn't keep the astonishment from her voice.

"Doesn't sound like him, does it? But there were other people with us, so maybe we had company and he brought them here."

After stopping at the provincial park in Vermilion so that Elizabeth could walk some of the trails and Chevy could have a run, they headed to Wainwright. Elizabeth sat back in her seat as Jared pulled out of the parking area. Oh, it felt wonderful to have Jared along with her. If she'd realized how much fun it would be, she'd have invited him on the other two trips.

Chapter 27

Christine's Story

The longer Christine lived alone, the more she grew to like it. Her home was cozy and just the right size for her. She only had a five-minute walk to work instead of a twenty-minute drive. It didn't matter if it was snowing, blowing or raining, she didn't have to worry about being on the highway in bad weather conditions.

She also found she liked her solitude. She had wondered if she would, having married right out of high school and going from her parents' home to her and Wayne's home. And she had freedom. She only had to cook for one, do laundry for one, clean up after one and she didn't have to account to anyone for whatever she decided to do.

When Christine heard the knock at her door, her first reaction was to not answer it. She wanted to work on her course, had to work on it. She didn't have time for Wayne's visits, which were becoming more frequent. Sometimes he was waiting for her when she got home, sometimes he came knocking after supper. She'd lost count of how many pointless conversations they'd had by now.

Christine didn't want to invite him in. All the arguments, all the pleading were beginning to consume her energy, leaving little left over for her job or her course. She didn't want to talk with him anymore. She opened the door but kept the chain on.

"There's nothing to say."

"Yes, there is. There's lots to say. May I come in?"

Against her better judgment, Christine undid the chain and stood back. She would not offer him coffee, though.

"Did you find out who was making those phone calls?" Wayne asked, sitting at the table.

"Yes, one of the men at work asked what happened to my phone." Christine also sat. "Since he had never called me before, I knew it was him."

"Which one is he?" Wayne demanded. "I'll go have a chat with him."

"I already complained to my boss, and he was fired."

"You expect me to believe that?"

She shrugged in response.

"So you're not going to tell me?" he insisted.

Christine shook her head.

"I am just so miserable without you." Wayne reached out to take her hand.

"Nothing lasts forever." She pulled her hands back and set them on her lap.

He stared at her. "How can you be like this? So cold, so distant? What have I done that is so terrible to make you treat me this way?"

"You've done nothing wrong." She kept all emotion out of her voice.

"Then why are you treating me as if we're suddenly strangers? Didn't I mean anything to you over the years?"

I'm trying to make you see that I am not going to change my mind, Christine wanted to say. And if necessary I will try to make you hate me, so you will leave me alone.

"Yes, you did. You still do in a certain way."

"In what way?" Wayne's voice was suddenly bitter. "As the chump who supported you all these years? As the guy who busted his butt to pay off the farm, so you wouldn't have to work?"

"I worked hard for that farm too," Christine replied quietly.

"Are you comparing sitting at a desk to working in the field, hauling bales and feeding the cows in the winter?"

Christine didn't reply. She wasn't about to argue over that. It had no relevance to her leaving.

"Are you going for a divorce?" Wayne suddenly asked.

"I'm thinking of it."

"If you do, don't expect any money from me."

"I don't want your money; I've got money of my own." Since she'd started working, she'd been putting a little of her earnings into an account in her name only. At first she'd done it to save for the china cabinet she'd wanted, but over the years she'd realized it was for her future.

"And you don't get any of the farm."

"It's all yours."

Wayne suddenly looked confused, lost.

"I'm the man. I'm supposed to be in charge, to support you. You're my wife. You're supposed to stick by me and help me."

"I have for twenty-five years. How much more do you want?"

"I want you to be with me for the rest of my life."

"And what about my wants?"

"I always thought they were the same as mine."

"They used to be. They're not now."

Wayne shook his head. "Are you really going to walk away from me and the farm?"

"Yes."

"I don't understand it. I really don't understand it. How can you do it?"

"You know how strongly you want to farm, how deep your desire is to increase your herd. Well, that is how strong my desire is to travel and my need to leave here."

"But women aren't ..."

"Women aren't what? Aren't supposed to have desires, aren't supposed to want to do something different from their husbands?"

"My mother never wanted to leave the farm. She was content where she was."

"That was your mother. I'm me, and I want more."

Christine stood. This had gone on long enough. She was tired of explaining. "I think you'd better leave."

Wayne walked slowly to the door. He turned and looked at her. "I still don't understand."

It was after ten o'clock when Christine moved the curtain slightly and peeked out the living room window. The truck was still there, across the road, and she could see his outline in the driver's seat. He'd been sitting there for over an hour, watching her house.

Had he parked out there on other evenings? Had he spent hours watching her move around in her house until she closed the drapes before going to bed? This was the first time she'd noticed him but maybe not the first time he'd been there. She didn't know what to do. She'd thought about calling the police but decided against it. She knew what they would say. It was a free country, and he had a right to park wherever he wanted.

She let the curtain fall back in place and resumed the pacing she had begun when she first noticed him. How had this whole thing gotten so far out of control? How had it gone from her wanting to leave to phone calls and angry visits? All she had wanted to do was make a change in her life. She hadn't wanted to hurt anyone; in fact, part of the reason she was doing it was to prevent the people she loved from getting hurt.

Christine looked out again. In the glow of the streetlight, she could see exhaust coming out of the tailpipe. He'd started the truck. Maybe this time he would be going home instead of just warming the cab up. But no, he wasn't. The truck ran for a few minutes, and then he shut it off.

Christine walked away from the window. She wanted to go to bed but knew she wouldn't be able to sleep as long as he was out there. She made a pot of tea and sipped it during the late news on television, determined not to look out the window until the broadcast was over. But she didn't hear one word; her mind was on the man sitting outside.

When the news, weather and sports reports had ended, she finally stood and walked over to the curtains. After a moment's hesitation, she carefully pushed one aside and peered out. Ben was gone. Not believing, she looked up and down the street. He wasn't parked anywhere within her vision. She leaned her head against the wall in relief, and then went to bed, hoping she could get some sleep before the alarm went off in the morning.

Chapter 28

"So what's in Wainwright?" Jared asked, turning off the highway on to Main Street.

"Well, that there is Canada's largest buffalo," Elizabeth said, as they passed the statue. "And there's the Memorial Clock Tower, which is also a cenotaph."

Jared pulled up to a four-way stop sign and stared up at a tall rock structure with a clock at the top.

"Look at this, the tower is in the middle of the intersection. So which way would you go if you wanted to turn left?" Jared asked. "Do you go in front of the tower or around behind?"

"I really don't know," Elizabeth said. She looked in the mirror. "There's no one behind us, so let's wait and see what people do."

Three cars went through the intersection before one finally turned to its left. The driver went around the tower.

"There," Jared said, pointing. "Now we know."

Elizabeth toured the museum and the Wainwright Railway Preservation Society grounds. While she walked among the displays, she wondered if it had been a good idea after all to bring Jared. She'd noticed him repositioning himself in his chair. She knew he did that to keep from getting pressure sores, but he also lay down most afternoons. Since they'd arrived in Redwater, he hadn't had many of those rests.

Back on the highway, they drove through Fabyan and followed the signs to the Battle River Trestle, also called the Fabyan Trestle. At the viewpoint, Elizabeth let Chevy out for a run. Jared got out of the van, and they both looked down at the long railway trestle.

"You know," Jared said, "just from what I've seen today, there's a lot about this province that I don't know. I can understand why you like being a travel writer."

"It's very satisfying," Elizabeth said. "I've learned so much since I started this."

He grew serious for a moment. "Thank you for inviting me. I really needed to get away from thinking about Mom and what may have happened to her."

Elizabeth kissed him. "I'm really glad I invited you too. This is much more enjoyable than travelling alone." She didn't voice her concerns about his comfort. There really was nothing either of them could do until they were back at the B and B.

At the Viking Ribstones, Elizabeth and Chevy climbed a small hill, and she took pictures of the large, white rocks. Back in the van, she showed them to Jared.

"Wow, they do look like ribs," he exclaimed. "Who carved them?"

"The First Nations people. A number of sites like this have been found in Alberta. They made them as a monument to Old Man Buffalo, who was the protector of all the buffalo."

As they approached the town, Jared said, "I know what you can say about Viking. It's the home of the Sutters."

"Yes, I know. Brian, Darryl, Duane, Brent, Rich and Ron played in the NHL at the same time during the 1970s and 80s," Elizabeth recited smugly. "Darryl, Brian, Duane and Brent also went on to become coaches and general managers."

"Oh, you're a hockey fan."

"Yup. Terry, Sherry, Dad and I have season's tickets to the Oilers."

"That's better than me. I only buy a ticket once in a while, but I watch most of the games on television.

"Let's do a taste test," Elizabeth suggested. "Let's stop in to buy some Viking sausage at Viking Meats and compare it to the Mundare sausage."

Elizabeth ran in to buy the sausage. She was surprised to see that the Viking type was long and slim like a pepperoni, although lighter in color and not as wrinkled. She gave Jared and Chevy a piece, and then tried some herself. The taste was quite mild.

"I like it," she said.

"Me too," Jared agreed.

Elizabeth toured the Viking Museum and the Holden Museum, and then they headed west from Holden.

When she saw a tall grain elevator to their right, she told Jared, "The tiny community here is called Poe and is supposed to be named after the famous master of detective and horror stories, Edgar Allan Poe."

"That's news to me," Jared said. "I didn't even know we had a hamlet named Poe in the province. I'll bet Edgar Allan would be pleased to know that some place in the world has been named for him."

"Well, I don't know how true it is that it was named for him."

"Oh? Why?"

"Because I also read that in England, Poe is the name of the potty used to toilet-train children."

Jared laughed loudly. "I think I'd rather live in a place named after a famous writer than a place named after a kiddie's potty."

After visiting the Ryley Museum, she thought about making museums the theme of this tour. At Tofield, they stopped at the Beaverhill Lake Nature Centre and the Tofield Museum, all in one building. Inside she looked at the displays of Tofield's history as well as stuffed birds, pictures of birds, books on birds and information on Beaverhill Lake, one of the best places to see snow geese on their spring migrations.

"If you are a birdwatcher, you can pick up a pamphlet at the centre listing more than 250 documented bird species that have been sighted on or near the lake," she whispered into her recorder.

"You know," Elizabeth mused, when they were driving again, "when I was researching Tofield on the Internet, I found a site that mentioned the discovery of a partially decomposed body of a man in a septic tank near the town in 1977."

Jared glanced at her. "Are you serious?"

"Yes." Elizabeth nodded. "He was called Septic Tank Sam. Isn't it strange that just last summer I figured out how a skeleton ended up in a septic tank near Fort Macleod. My guy was dubbed Septic Stan by the media."

"Was the Septic Tank Sam murderer ever found?"

Elizabeth shook her head.

"Have you thought that maybe you should ...?" Jared left the sentence hanging.

"No way," she said loudly, startling Chevy out of his sleep. "Sorry," she murmured, rubbing his head.

Elizabeth directed Jared to her last stop.

"What's this?" he asked, as he pulled into the Waskehegan Staging Area parking lot.

"It's part of the Cooking Lake–Blackfoot Grazing, Wildlife and Recreation Area," Elizabeth said. "Coyote, elk, moose, deer and more than 200 varieties of birds live in the reserve, along with cattle. And there are more than 150 kilometres of trails for people to snowmobile, cross-country ski, hike, bicycle and ride horses."

"Whew, how do you remember all this stuff?"

"I read it over enough times when I'm working on my routes. I try to find the most interesting places."

"Well, you've done a great job on this route."

"Thank you. I'll take Chevy on one quick jaunt to see what the trails are like."

Chevy was excited about this new sniffing trail and made the most of the length of his leash. Elizabeth inhaled deeply of the fresh air. They didn't go far, Elizabeth remembering Jared's need to get to the B and B and lie down.

Back in the van, Elizabeth shut off her laptop.

"I'm finished my research," she said. "Let's go to the B and B."

"Could we find a place to eat first?" Jared asked. "I'm hungry."

Elizabeth looked at her watch. "Oh, sorry. I seldom get hungry when I'm working like this, and I always forget about the time."

"That's okay. I've managed to sustain Chevy and myself on the sausage we bought. But we both could use a good meal."

Chapter 29

Anna's Story

She felt a sense of security and promise when she saw the buildings of the city ahead of her. All she had to do was move in with her parents, apply for a student loan and enrol in a nursing course. Then she could find a place of her own and raise Jared without the fear he'd been experiencing all his life. Oh, if only her parents will agree ...

Anna woke Jared when they pulled into the bus depot. They disembarked and picked up their suitcase. She looked around warily as they walked into the building. She was relieved when she didn't see Paul and discouraged when she didn't see her parents. It doesn't matter, she told herself. She'd take a city bus to their place.

She went out to find a bus stop. She had never been to her folks' house in the city, but she had their address, which she gave to the bus driver. He told her the stop to watch for. Finally, after two transfers, she stepped off at a stop within two blocks of her parents' home.

When she found the right address, she looked around for Paul's truck. She didn't see it, so they walked up the front sidewalk to the door. Anna set the suitcase down and rang the bell. Her mother opened it.

"Oh, Anna," she exclaimed, her voice a mixture of joy and dismay.

"Hi," Anna said, as cheerfully as she could.

Her mother looked down at Jared.

"Mom, this is Jared, your grandson." She needed to try everything to get her parents on her side. "Jared, this is your grandma."

Her mother stepped aside and let them in. In the kitchen, she found her father sitting at the table. He didn't look up when she entered, and she feared she had lost her bid to save herself and her children.

Jared was hesitant, hiding behind her. These people were strangers to him. She took his hand and led him to the table

"Dad, this is Jared, your grandson," she said determinedly. "Jared, this is your grandpa."

Her father glanced at Jared, and then looked away. She saw her mother start to reach out her arms for Jared but draw back when her father shook his head.

"Paul called," her father said. "I told him you were on your way here."

"I can't go back to him," she whispered, her voice quivering.

"A woman's place is with her husband."

"Yes, but her husband isn't supposed to do this to her," Anna said, raising her lip to show her broken tooth. "He isn't supposed to beat her and threaten her children."

"You dated him against our wishes. You disgraced us by getting pregnant."

Anna couldn't believe her father still held that against her after five years.

"I made a mistake. I admit that. How long do I have to pay for it? How long do my children have to pay for it?"

Her father only shook his head.

She just wanted to sink to the floor, close her eyes and go into a deep sleep, never to waken.

The doorbell rang. Fear encompassed her. Paul was here already.

"Please, can we stay?" she begged, dropping to her knees in front of her father. "Please, for Jared." She put her hand on her belly. "And for this one."

Stone-faced, her father stood, walked around her and went down the hallway. She could hear him open the front door. She turned to her mother, who was now holding Jared.

"Please help me, Mom."

"I can't." There were tears in her eyes.

"Why can't you?" Her voice was weak with despair. "I'm your daughter. You heard what Paul is doing to me."

"You made the choice years ago." She leaned her cheek on Jared's head.

Anna heard the two sets of footsteps in the hallway. She hadn't had enough time.

Mustering what little strength she had left, she whispered quickly, "If something happens to me, will you check on Jared? Will you try to make sure Paul doesn't harm him?"

Before her mother could answer, the footsteps entered the kitchen. Anna covered her face and wept. She had failed, and she and her children would suffer for years because of her attempt at freedom.

"Time to come home," Paul said, pulling her to her feet by her arm. He didn't let go once she was standing.

She looked imploringly at her mother and saw her glance at her father. In that glance she saw thirty years of a wife's subservience to her husband, a subservience that could not be broken in one hour. Her mother looked down.

Paul picked up the suitcase with his other hand. "Come on, Jared."

Anna had expected an outburst from Paul as soon as they were in the truck, but he didn't say anything, which heightened her fear. His cold silence was worse than his tirades.

When they pulled into the farmyard, Paul spoke for the first time.

"I don't know how you thought you were going to get away with this. You've made a fool of me in front of our neighbours. You've cost us money and time in the field, and you can believe that you will pay for it. It won't be tonight, and it might not be tomorrow. You won't know where, and you won't know when, but," he spoke these last words very precisely, "you can be certain it's coming."

Christine's Story

There was a knocking on her door, but she had decided to ignore all unwanted visitors. If her neighbours complained, she would tell them to call the police. She didn't want to talk anymore about her leaving. She didn't want to have to listen to someone telling her she couldn't go, that she couldn't live her life the way she wanted.

The knocking continued, louder now. She moved the curtain enough to see who it was, then went back to her chair. Eventually he would leave.

But he wasn't to be put off. The noise increased until she couldn't concentrate. Maybe she should call the police. Maybe it was time she let them know what was happening. She hadn't in the past because she didn't want to feel guilty about the lives that might be upset.

Christine went to the door. "Go away!" she yelled through the little window.

"Let me in!" he hollered back.

"No. I want nothing more to do with you."

"I'll stay here until you open the door."

"I'll call the police."

"And what will they do? I'm your husband. I have a right to talk to you."

Christine dialled the police station. She gave her name and address.

"My husband is standing on my porch and pounding on my door," she explained. "He won't go away."

"Why don't you let him in?"

"We are separated, and this is my home. He lives on a farm."

"Is he threatening you?"

"No, he's just making a lot of noise."

"Okay, we'll send a car around."

Christine had to endure ten more minutes of Wayne beating on her door before the police car drove up in front. She pulled the curtain aside and watched as the officers talked to Wayne. He kept gesturing and pointing. Finally, one of the policemen knocked on her door. Christine went and unlocked it.

"Are you sure you don't want to talk to him?"

"Yes. I want you to make him leave me alone."

"Has he threatened you in any way?"

"No."

"Well, we can't stop him from coming here, and if he hasn't threatened you, then there is nothing we can do."

"You mean he can come here any time he wants."

"You can charge him with trespassing if you wish, or you could go to court and get a restraining order so he has to stay away from you. If he hits you, then you can charge him with assault."

Christine closed and locked the door. She watched as the three men talked some more, and then Wayne turned and headed for his truck. They had convinced him to go. She waited until he had driven away before making herself a cup of tea to soothe her nerves.

Chapter 30

"Did I tell you how much I liked yesterday?" Jared asked the next morning as they showered together.

"Yes, you did," Elizabeth replied, smiling. "Many times."

"Did I thank you properly?"

"Yes, you did that too. Many times."

"Well, that's good. Just so long as you know how I feel."

"I think I do. You've been very demonstrative."

Once they were dressed, they went for breakfast. Elizabeth felt very relaxed. Her research was done. Her worst fear had been that the mystery would eat up her time and she wouldn't get her travelling in. She didn't have to worry about that now. And her article was partially written. She just wished they'd been as successful with Jared's mission.

At their table, Elizabeth said, "I don't think we're getting anywhere with either death. And we're running out of time. I have to get back soon and finish my article."

"I know, and I just can't come up with anything new to do or say to anyone." Jared sounded disappointed.

"Well, after we eat, let's go see Meredith again. Maybe she can tell us something about Christine."

Jared nodded.

"Still looking for your mother's killer?" Meredith asked, when they were settled on the back deck.

"Yes," Jared admitted. "And we're not having very good luck."

"Can you tell us about your friendship with Christine?" Elizabeth asked.

"I thought you were here to find out about your mother's death. Why are you asking about Christine?"

"No one seems to know much about Mom, so we are trying to learn everything that happened during that time to see if it will give us some sort of clue."

"It was strange that we started our married lives the same, and yet we grew apart," Meredith began. "Ben and I had been friends with her and Wayne for years. We went to dances and parties, and Christine was always the life of the party. She had a great sense of humour and was willing to do anything for a laugh.

"Then she decided to go to work in Redwater, and she slowly changed. Her garden got smaller, she spent less time working on the farm and she quit coming to our farm to pick the extra raspberries I had. Over the years we still visited, but Christine and I had little in common to talk about. Christine told me about her job and I talked about my garden. Sometimes I thought it was just our husbands that kept us together. During the last year I noticed that Christine had become distracted, thoughtful, as if she had something important on her mind. But I never asked her. Maybe if I had ..."

"So why did Christine go to work in the first place?" Elizabeth asked

"I thought it was to earn money to pay the farm off, but she didn't quit even when it was paid up."

"When did she begin working?"

Meredith shrugged. "I don't remember. Graham was in his early teens."

"Did she find it hard to leave him and go to work?"

"I don't think so," Meredith said. "I couldn't understand why she would want to leave her home to work in town. I had never had the inclination, even though we didn't have any children. I liked my home, my farm. In fact, I seldom went anywhere, only making two or three trips to Edmonton a year to shop or visit. When we paid off our mortgage, Ben wanted to take winter holidays to Hawaii or Mexico. I went on two trips and then refused to go again. Lying on the beach or haggling with vendors was not my idea of a good time." She blushed. "He began calling me a stick-in-the-mud."

"Did you have other troubles in your marriage?" Jared asked.

Good. Elizabeth sat back and let him take over.

"Not that I knew of. I thought we had a comfortable, though quiet, marriage."

"We heard a rumour that you and Wayne were also having an affair."

Meredith looked a little startled, then asked, "Is that rumour still floating around after all these years?"

"We've heard it more than once," Jared said, nodding. "Plus you mention it in one of your poems."

"If you read the poem, then you know that we weren't having an affair."

Elizabeth allowed a look of skepticism to cross her face. "Some people saw you two at a hotel, and then later you were seen at the auction market together."

Meredith reddened. "We did go out one evening when Ben and Christine were at a concert in Calgary."

Elizabeth raised her eyebrows.

"Yes, I know. We were totally gullible. They wanted to go to see some popular band, and we didn't, so they went together and we stayed home."

"And spent the night at a hotel ..." Elizabeth prompted.

"No. I told you, it wasn't an affair. It was only one night when we were both a little drunk. And we were only in the hotel room a few minutes before we realized how stupid we were being."

"In one of your poems, you describe a visit from Wayne," Jared said.

"I've written so many poems," Meredith said.

Jared asked Elizabeth to get the book out of his backpack.

"This is the one I mean," he said, riffling through the book until he came to the right page.

Act Three
Fade In
Exterior–Farmyard–Night
The man opens the door and leaves the house. He is lurching a little. The woman follows him, also a bit unsteady. At the vehicle, she reaches out and pulls on his arm. He turns to her.

The whiskey has made me light-headed and dizzy.
I try to tell Wayne that
he is drunk, too drunk to drive.

"You better stay here for tonight," I say.
"No." He staggers. "I've got to tell her now."
He opens his truck door, and then turns to me.
"Thank you for listening."
"That's what friends are for," I say.
He drives out, barely missing my flower beds.
I wonder if I should phone Christine,
then decide against it. This is serious.
I don't need to make it worse.

Fade Out
End Act Three

"So why would Wayne come to see you?" Elizabeth asked. "Didn't he have someone else to go to, some male friend?"

"You just don't let go, do you? As I said, there was no more to our relationship than friendship," Meredith said tersely.

"It does sound like you two spent a lot of time together," Jared commented.

"I have work to do." Meredith stood.

"I'm sorry," Jared said. "I guess I'm just trying anything to learn the truth about Mom's death."

"Well, her death had nothing to do with Ben's."

"Do you think Christine may have heard the rumours about you and Wayne?" Elizabeth asked, hoping this was a more reasonable question.

"I did wonder but reasoned that if she did, she would have said something. Plus, then Ben would have known too."

"For not having had an affair, they did seem quite chummy," Jared said, as they drove away. "I wonder if we shouldn't try some of the other names on the list."

Elizabeth reached over Chevy, who was sitting on her lap, and pulled the list from Jared's pouch.

"Tylar and Brittany Heigh. Who did you say they were?"

"Brittany was Ben's sister. She and Tylar bought the farm from Meredith."

"Where did they live before that?"

"In town."

"So it isn't likely that they will know much about your mother."

"Probably not." Jared turned to her with a smile. "But they should know a lot about Ben."

Elizabeth grinned. "Okay, let's go see them."

She was enjoying this immensely and, for now, would rather be with Jared than working on her article.

As they pulled into the yard, Elizabeth wondered if the flowerbed by the driveway was the one in Meredith's poem. An older woman dressed in jeans and a plaid shirt was walking from the chicken coop with a basket of eggs in her hand. She came over as Jared lowered himself in the lift.

"You're Jared Jones, aren't you?"

"How did you know, Mrs. Heigh?" Jared asked.

"Oh, everyone in this community and half of the town of Redwater know about the man in a wheelchair who is going around trying to tie his mother's and my brother's deaths together."

"And this is Elizabeth Oliver, my caregiver," Jared said.

"Ah, yes. The caregiver who asks a lot of questions."

Elizabeth felt herself redden. Obviously, she hadn't been very subtle.

"What a cute dog." Brittany knelt down to let Chevy sniff her hand. "What's his name?" She rubbed his head.

"Chevy." When Brittany had stood again, Elizabeth put Chevy back in the van and closed the door. He immediately jumped up on the passenger seat and looked out the lowered window.

"So I imagine you're here to talk about Anna and Ben," Brittany said.

Elizabeth liked this woman immediately. She was direct, and her voice had a lilt to it that suggested a happy person.

"Yes, we are, Mrs. Heigh," Jared answered.

"Well, I don't know what I can tell you, but please come in." She led the way to the house, which had a ramp built beside the steps. "And call me Brittany."

Just as Elizabeth was wondering who in the family was in a wheelchair, Brittany explained, "This ramp was built for my aunt, who lived with us for a year before her death. We just never got around to removing it."

In the kitchen, Brittany poured them all an iced tea. "Tylar will be home soon. He's a part-time real estate agent, and he's showing a house right now."

"So you don't farm?" Jared asked.

"No, never have. You probably know we bought the farm from Meredith after Ben died. We sold the farmland, keeping five acres for us to live on."

"Then may I ask why you bought it?" Elizabeth asked.

"I was raised on a farm. Tylar was raised in town, and we lived there after we married. He sold real estate full-time then, and I worked in the hospital. But I always wanted to live in the country. So when Meredith approached Tylar about listing the farm with him, he bought it for me as a twenty-fifth wedding anniversary present."

Wow, she'd like to meet this Tylar. Where were all the men like him in her generation? She looked at Jared, and her heart warmed. Maybe she had found one.

"Did you know my mother at all?" Jared asked.

"She went to high school with our daughter, Fay, so she did come to the house a few times. But I never knew her as anyone other than Fay's friend."

The door opened, and a tall man with a thick head of gray hair entered. Brittany stood up and ran to greet him.

She was pretty spry for her age, Elizabeth thought.

They hugged, and then Brittany introduced her husband Tylar to Elizabeth and Jared.

"Yes, we've heard about you two," Tylar said, smiling. "So, it's our turn for the inquisition, is it?"

Elizabeth laughed. "Just let us get our tools ready."

Brittany laughed as she set some cupcakes on the table. "Ask away."

Jared began with the usual questions about his mother and her life. When he didn't get any better answers than they'd already heard, he pulled her graduation picture out of his wallet.

"Do you know these people with her?" he asked.

"Gee, that's a long time ago," Tylar said. "It brings back memories of Fay. She graduated in the same class, you know."

"Yes, I was just telling them that Anna had been to our home in town a few times as a teenager," Brittany explained, as she looked at the picture. "That's Penny Dixon, Graham Dearden, and Nick Thompson."

"Nick Thompson?" Both Elizabeth and Jared leaned over.

"Which one?" Jared asked.

"There, the boy with his arms around your mother's shoulders."

"Were they dating?" Elizabeth asked.

"Yes. Hasn't anyone told you that?"

Jared shook his head as he stared at the picture.

Elizabeth watched him. She knew what questions were going through his mind. Why hadn't Nick admitted to dating his mother? Why hadn't Paul said it was Nick in the picture?

"How long did they date?" Elizabeth asked.

"All through high school," Brittany answered. "Fay kept telling us about the crush Anna had on Nick. Apparently, she told everyone that she was in love with him and that they would marry when they finished school. Then after graduation, Nick moved away, and Anna began dating Paul." She shrugged. "That's about it."

"Do you know how long Paul and Anna dated before marrying?"

Tylar shook his head. "It wasn't very long. We were all surprised that they married so soon after meeting." He looked at Jared.

"That's okay. I know that she was pregnant with me."

Tylar nodded. "Then you should know that everyone wondered if you were Paul's child or Nick's."

There was a moment of dead silence. The statement hung in the air. Elizabeth looked at Jared. He was staring at Tylar, his mouth open.

"Are you suggesting that Jared isn't Paul's child?" Elizabeth asked.

"I'm just telling you what could have happened," Tylar said.

Chapter 31

Anna's Story

Why had Paul decided that they had to go to a dance tonight? Anna wondered. Did he want people to see that he had his wife back, that she hadn't left him? The dance was a fundraiser for a family whose house had burned down, but it wasn't as if they really knew the people who were burned out. They only saw them at the occasional community event.

"It doesn't matter how well we know them," Paul had said, when he told her they were going. "It's that they are part of the community, and we have to help them."

Where was your generosity last Christmas when I needed money for a gift for Jared from Santa at the hall, she wanted to ask, but she knew it would just lead to a fight.

Anna didn't have much in the way of fancy maternity clothes. Most were for around the house. Sorting through her closet, she'd found a pair of white pants that she seldom wore, even when she wasn't pregnant. She cut the front of them out for her belly, then hemmed the cut and sewed elastic to the sides of the waistband. Holding them up, she scrutinized her handiwork. Not bad. With a top covering it, no one would even know. And it might keep her cooler.

The hall was a large white building two kilometres from their farm. The parking lot was at the back, and Paul found a place among the other vehicles. They stepped out of the truck and were greeted by two couples who were standing to the side talking. One was Nick and Sarah, the other Tylar and Brittany Heigh, who had come out from town. Tylar knew some of the farmers because he had sold them their farms.

Nick made the introductions. "Sarah, this is Paul and Anna Jones."

It was an awkward moment for Anna. The last time they'd met, she'd told Sarah to go back to the city. Now they were face to face and she didn't know what to do. She was saved by Tylar asking Sarah, "So how do you like country life?"

"I really haven't been here long enough to judge yet."

"Oh, yes, well ..." Tylar stammered. "I guess we should get inside. Talk to you later, Nick."

"Well, that was really nice," Anna overheard Nick say.

"What?" Sarah asked.

"You could have shown a little more enthusiasm."

"About what?"

"About living here."

"Well, it's true. I haven't been here very long. And why did he assume that I'd like it better here than in the city?"

"Because it is better here."

Anna watched them walk away. Trouble in paradise? As she walked into the hall she wondered if tonight would be a good time to tell Sarah about Nick's past. Maybe she should first ask Nick if he'd already told her. She doubted it. He wouldn't admit it to himself, so why would he tell his young bride? There was a donation box set up just inside the door. Paul dropped a twenty-dollar bill in it.

Yellow and white streamers were strung from corner to corner, with yellow bells hanging where the streamers crossed in the middle. It looked almost like a wedding was taking place, Anna thought.

Lines of tables ran at an angle from the side walls, leaving the centre area open for the dance later. Some people were already seated, while others milled around talking. Children ran in and out the door and between the tables, playing hide-and-seek or tag. The band was tuning up their instruments.

Paul found a place for them to sit at a table, and then went to the bar for a drink. Anna encouraged Jared to go play with the other children. He hung back, watching them run up and down the floor. Finally, he went over and sat beside another boy about his age. Soon they were talking.

Anna watched the hall fill up. She knew most of the people but was friends with none. No one came over to talk with her. She didn't know if she should be embarrassed or disheartened by it. This was not the life she'd envisioned for herself.

She saw Meredith enter the hall and look around. No one went to greet her either. Anna had heard that in the months since Ben's death, she had been shunned by most people in the area. It was almost as if they blamed her in some way or weren't sure what to say to her. She'd also heard that she had sold the farm to Tylar and Brittany and was moving soon. Anna waved, and when Meredith saw her, she came over, limping on her right leg.

"Hi," Meredith said.

"What happened to your foot?" Anna looked down at the bandage.

"Oh, I slipped off a curb and sprained it two days ago."

"Shouldn't you have crutches?"

"I do," Meredith replied with a smirk. "But I hate using them."

"When are you moving?"

"The end of the month."

There was an awkward silence between them. Meredith glanced around the room.

"Quite a crowd," she noted.

"Yes. Looks like everyone in the community showed up."

"It's too bad about the Bakers," Meredith said. "But it was an old house."

"Did you know them well?" Anna asked.

"We saw each other occasionally when Ben was alive," Meredith said. "I haven't seen them since his death. In fact, I haven't seen many of my friends since then."

Anna almost said, "Well, I only have one friend," but she didn't. No use for the two of them to sit here feeling sorry for themselves.

"It was nice of you to come out for them," Anna said.

Meredith shrugged. "This is the first time I've gone anywhere since … well, you know what I mean."

Anna nodded. "I suppose you've heard about me going to Edmonton," she said.

Meredith nodded. "Everyone is talking about it. Paul never should have gotten Harvey to drive him to the bus depot. I heard that man was in the coffee shop two minutes after Paul pulled out of town." She put her hand on Anna's. "I'm sorry you didn't make it."

"I am too."

"Will you try again?"

"I don't know. Dad made it very plain that I wasn't welcome in his house, and there is no one else I can turn to."

Anna looked around for Paul. He was standing with a group of men near the bar. He wouldn't be back until it was time to leave. She saw Nick by the table with the coffee urn. Now would be a good chance to speak with him. She stood.

"Would you like a cup of coffee or a juice?" she asked Meredith.

"Oh, I can get it," Meredith said.

"You'll hurt your foot worse. I don't mind."

"Okay, coffee would be good. Cream, no sugar."

Anna headed to the table.

"Hi," she greeted Nick. He nodded.

"When are you and Sarah coming for a visit?" she asked, pouring Meredith's coffee.

He shrugged. "I don't know, we're kind of busy. Why?"

"I just thought Sarah should know about the type of man she married."

"What do you mean by that?" He looked around, as if to see if anyone was close enough to hear them.

"You mean you haven't told her about us, and how we used to make love in the hay fields and in the barn and in the schoolyard? And you haven't told her about your other girlfriends, girlfriends you had when we were going together?"

"What happened before I met her is none of her business."

"Then you haven't told her that you have a child with another woman."

Nick stepped close to her. "I don't have a child," he said, through clenched teeth. "And don't you dare spread that rumour around."

Anna smiled sweetly. "It's not a rumour," she said, walking away.

She put Meredith's cup in front of her and sat down. She was hot, and she really didn't know how Meredith could drink coffee in the heat. But other people were doing it too.

The band began to play. The lights were dimmed, and a few couples got up to dance.

Anna sat and fanned herself with a napkin. It wasn't working.

"I'm going outside to cool off," she said to Meredith.

"I'll come with you."

Others had the same idea, and the sidewalk in front of the hall was full. Anna saw Sarah standing by herself. "I'm going to talk to Sarah."

"Hello, Sarah," Anna said, checking to see if Nick was nearby.

"Anna." Sarah took a deep breath. "I've been hoping we would have some time together. I'd like to ask you why you said those words to me that first day?"

Anna thought about the best way to tell her. She'd only been married a short time, and there were many ways she could take the news. She looked away, then back at Sarah.

"How much has Nick told you about his past?"

"What about it?" Sarah asked.

"Nick's not the man you think he is," she said quietly.

"What do you mean?"

"Well, I'm just wondering if he told you about his girlfriends."

"We've decided not to discuss old boyfriends or girlfriends."

Anna smiled slightly. "Yes, I'll bet he would want an agreement like that. Whose idea was it, yours or his?"

"Both of ours," she said crisply. "And why are you asking?"

"I just thought you should know a few things about him."

Sarah hesitated, and then asked, "Such as?"

Anna had known that her curiosity would be aroused. Whose wouldn't be?

"Well, we were almost engaged to each other during high school. But he always thought he was a lady's man and was still seeing other girls behind my back."

"I'm sorry to hear that. What has that got to do with him today?"

"Well, he's the father of my son, and you might ask him about kissing me in his garage last spring."

Sarah gasped. "Are you saying Nick had an affair with you when he moved out here?"

"Sorry to have to be the one to tell you." Anna rubbed her belly, suggestively. "But I thought you should know."

"I don't need to listen to this." Sarah rushed away with tears in her eyes.

When Anna got back into the hall, the band was taking a break, and two of the fundraising organizers were on the stage making speeches. One held up the donation box and handed it to the Bakers, who cried when they received it.

"Thank you so much," Mrs. Baker said.

"We'll use this to help us rebuild," Mr. Baker added.

There were three Baker teenagers who stood self-consciously on the stage and hurried off when the speeches were finished.

People got up to stretch their legs. Some went outside, some visited friends at other tables. Once the band began to play again, the dance floor remained full for the rest of the evening.

Chapter 32

"I'm sorry you had to hear that Nick could be your father," Elizabeth said, when they were back in the van.

Jared stared straight ahead.

"You and Dad—or should I say, Paul—did warn me that I might find out things I didn't want to hear," he said softly. "And this is certainly one of them."

They were quiet as Jared drove.

"So now what do I do?" he finally asked.

"If you want to continue with this, we can go talk to Sarah and Nick. If you don't, we can pack up and go home to Edmonton."

Jared pulled over and stopped the van. He laid his head on his hands. Elizabeth reached out and rubbed his back. This was a tough decision. Jared looked up, his face grim.

"I've come too far. I've raised so many doubts about who I am that I can't quit now. I can't leave this hanging over me for the rest of my life."

He turned the van around, and they headed to see Nick and Sarah. Nick was in the garden.

"Sarah's lying down," he said. "The heat bothers her."

Elizabeth wasn't sure how to start; it was all so delicate. She decided the direct approach was the best.

"We've heard that you and Anna dated through high school," Elizabeth said.

Nick looked startled. "Yes, we did," he said, tentatively.

"Why didn't you tell us that when we were here before?"

"I've never talked about my old girlfriends in front of Sarah, and she's never talked about her old boyfriends. It's just an unspoken pact we've had."

"According to what we heard, Anna wanted to marry you."

"We did discuss marriage," Nick admitted. "But I wanted to get away from here, and she wanted to marry right out of high school."

Elizabeth had been comparing Nick and Jared, and there was some resemblance. If Jared could stand, he would be as tall as Nick. Both were slender. Nick's hair was mostly gray, so it was hard to tell what the original colour would have been. What would be a good way to ask him if he and Anna had had sex?

"Could you be my father?" Jared asked.

Nick blushed a deep red. He looked over their shoulders. "I don't think ..."

"Well, hello," Sarah called, coming up behind them on the grass.

How much had she heard? Elizabeth wondered.

"Nick, it's time to take your parents' anniversary gift to them."

"What ... oh, yes. Uh. Right." Nick looked at Jared, and then hurried away.

"We'll come back another time," Elizabeth said.

"You don't have to leave. I'm not going with him."

It was on the tip of Elizabeth's tongue to ask why not, but she restrained herself. Maybe there were some bad feelings between the in-laws. Then she remembered their previous conversation.

"Come and sit in the gazebo, out of the sun," Sarah said.

Elizabeth noticed that she didn't offer them lemonade.

"Now tell me what you want to know this time."

If she'd heard Jared ask Nick if he could be his father, she gave no indication of it. And while Jared could ask Nick outright, they couldn't do the same with Sarah. Elizabeth thought they might as well find out more about her life on the farm and see if they could find out more about how well she knew Anna.

Christine's Story

Christine climbed the steps of her porch. It had been a long day. It was the beginning of the tax season, and their customers were bringing in their boxes of receipts and other papers and wanting the office to complete their taxes immediately. Christine knew she would be working late most nights from now to the end of April. She was relieved to get home, knowing she could put her feet up and relax. She had just put her key in the lock of her door when a figure loomed beside her. She screamed in fright, and then stopped when she recognized who it was.

"Oh, God, you scared me." She leaned against the side of the porch, holding her chest where her heart threatened to beat itself to death.

"It's about time I got your attention." He reached over, turned the key in the lock, and opened the door for her.

When she had regained some of her composure, Christine stepped to her doorway, and then turned to block it.

"I don't want you in my house, Ben."

"Well, that's too bad," he said, lifting her and carrying her into the kitchen. He kicked the door shut with his foot.

"Put me down," Christine yelled, pushing her hands against his chest. "Can't you leave me alone?"

"That's not what you want, and you know it." Ben kissed her neck.

"Let me go." Christine struggled harder.

"Okay, okay." He removed his grip and held his hands up in front of him. "See, I let go."

"Now get out."

"Not until we've settled this."

"There is nothing to settle." Christine took off her coat and hung it up on a hook by the door. "I'm breaking all ties with this place and my life here. And that includes you. Why can't you understand that?"

"You can't do this," Ben said angrily. "We've meant something to each other for a long time. You can't just throw it away."

"Yes, I can and I have. Now go."

"No!" he yelled, shoving her against the wall. "You're not going to leave me. I won't let you."

Christine pulled herself away from the wall. "You have no say in the matter," she said, her voice low and angry. "It is my life and my decision."

"But it is affecting my life, and I don't like it."

"I really don't care anymore what you like."

"You used to care. You used to care a lot."

"Can't you understand?" Christine yelled. "It's over. It's over. It's over."

"No!" His hand shot out and slapped her across the face.

Christine's head snapped back, and she had to take a step to keep her balance. She stared at him as she raised her hand to her stinging cheek. She could feel the heat from the slap. No man had ever pushed her or hit her, not even her father.

He glared back at her, his face full of rage. For a few moments, she thought her life might be in danger. She had never seen him so furious. She hadn't known he had such a temper.

"I didn't think you'd ever do that," she said, looking up at him.

Suddenly, he was holding her, kissing her hair, her cheeks.

"I'm sorry," he said. "I'm so sorry. I didn't mean to do that. I don't know what came over me. It's just that I care for you so much, and I don't want you to break us up."

Christine shut her eyes to his kisses. She stood still, not wanting to say or do anything that would set him off again. She waited until he was finished, then pulled herself free of his arms.

"I've had a long day," she said, trying to keep her voice level. "I'm tired. Can we discuss this some other time when we are both in a better mood?"

"Why do you keep putting me off? Why can't you just stop and talk to me?"

"I have talked, and I'm tired of explaining over and over again. Why are you not listening to me? What combination of words can I use that will make you understand that I mean what I say?"

Should she call the police? Could she call the police without him knowing? The closest phone was in her bedroom, and there was no way she wanted to go in there."Would you please leave?" She had no energy to argue with him anymore.

He was prowling around the kitchen and living room, looking in cupboards, in drawers, turning on the television. He stopped and looked at her.

"What are you making us for supper?"

"Go home. Meredith will have supper ready for you."

"You're not very friendly."

"That's right, I'm not. Now will you go?"

He looked at his watch. "I'll leave if you'll agree to go out with me tomorrow night. I could take you to our favourite restaurant in Smoky Lake, and then maybe we can visit our favourite hotel afterwards."

At that moment, she was willing to agree to anything if it meant he would leave. "Fine."

"What time should I pick you up?"

"Call me at work. It's tax time, so I don't know when my day will end."

"Okay." He walked over to give her a kiss. She turned her head away.

"Don't be mad at me," he begged. "You're the one who's causing all the trouble."

Christine locked the door and leaned against it. He was gone. That was the second time she'd been scared for her life. She'd actually thought she would have to defend herself against an attack. She couldn't believe he'd acted like that, that he'd actually struck her.

There was no way she was going to make time tomorrow night to go out with him. She'd drive her vehicle to work, stay late and make sure no one was in her yard or around her house when she got home. And she couldn't call the police, couldn't charge him with assault. Too many questions would be asked and too many hurtful answers would be given.

But she had to do something. This was getting out of hand. She picked up the Vancouver paper. Maybe she should move there now. She had enough money to rent an apartment and to keep her going until she found a job, at least for a little while. She could send a change of address for her course. Yes, she decided with a nod of her head, that was what she would do. Get away from all this hassle.

Christine looked at the clock. It was nine-fifteen here, eight-fifteen in Vancouver. She looked up her cousin's number in her personal phone book and dialled. They had been close growing up, even though they'd only see each other in the summers. Brenda would come out to spend a week on the farm, and then Christine would spend a week in Vancouver. During the rest of the year, they wrote back and forth, telling each other about girlfriends and boyfriends and school and teachers.

Once they were grown, their letters had dwindled to Christmas cards, and their visits were once every two or three years. When she had written to Brenda asking for a copy of the paper, she had also told her about the separation and her plans.

"Hi, Brenda. It's me, Christine."

"Hi. Did you get the paper?"

"Yes, it's in front of me right now."

"So when are you moving here?"

"Well, it might be sooner than I thought. I'm having some trouble with

Wayne, and I need to move now instead of waiting until after getting my certificate."

"That's too bad. Is there anything I can do to help?"

"If I move now, would I be able to use your address for my mail?"

"Certainly. And why don't you stay here instead of finding an apartment?"

"Oh, I couldn't put you out like that."

"You wouldn't be. Tony has moved out, so his bedroom is free, and you can store your furniture in the garage."

"Oh, thank you." Christine could not keep the relief from her voice. She immediately began to make plans. "I'll have to give notice, pack and hire a moving van. It'll take about a week, so I'll call you then and let you know when I'll be there."

"Good. I'll be waiting. We can catch up on the past twenty-some years."

Christine put down the receiver. She felt elated, as if a burden had been lifted. She had set a deadline and was leaving, getting away from the horrible predicament she was in. All she had to do was get through the next week.

Chapter 33

"You said you had a hard time getting used to the farm life," Elizabeth said to Sarah.

"What does that have to do with Anna's or Ben's deaths?"

Good question. She needed a good answer. Unfortunately, she didn't have one.

"Nothing, I guess, but you had just moved here when Anna warned you to leave. I'm just wondering if you ever thought about going back to Regina."

"Oh, many times," Sarah admitted. "You wouldn't believe what I had to go through. Nick changed once we lived on the farm. He was always pointing out the differences between farmers and city people. Like the first time I saw Ben and Meredith's place. They had a small, park-like area beside their house. I said I liked it and could spend a lot of time there. 'Well, they don't get to use it very much,' Nick said. 'Farmers,' and he emphasized the word, 'don't have time to lie around.'"

Elizabeth attempted to say something, but Sarah kept talking.

"When we married, I had some money in a savings account. Can you believe that Nick expected me to just hand it over to him?

"I can remember standing on the verandah and watching Nick work on the hay mower. I had just started down the steps on my way to see if he needed any help when I heard a clang, saw a wrench fly through the air, followed by, 'God damn this piece of frigging junk.' I turned on my heels and headed for the garden.

"As I worked, I heard more banging and swearing. This was a new side of

Nick. I had never seen him lose his temper before, and he certainly hadn't sworn like that when we were dating."

Elizabeth didn't know what to say to that. "Yes," she said carefully, "a different environment can change people."

"Or maybe something in that environment changes them," Sarah spat out.

Again, Elizabeth was at a loss on how to keep up her end of the conversation. She looked uneasily at Jared. Sarah was getting worked up about the past. Maybe this wasn't such a good idea. But Sarah didn't care if anyone answered her or not.

"He wanted me to quit wearing red, and he hated pierced ears. For the first few months I went along with it, and then I decided I had a right to do what I wanted, so I went back to wearing red, putting on makeup and wearing my earrings again."

"Life must have been hard back then for you." Elizabeth tried to sound sympathetic.

"Hard is not the word for it. I was miserable much of the time. I just couldn't do anything right. I didn't know how to plant a garden or how to milk a cow. When people asked me how I liked the farm and I told them that I hadn't been here long enough to judge yet, Nick would get mad.

"'You could have shown a little more enthusiasm,' he'd say to me."

She was quiet for a few moments, a distant look in her eye. "I remember the first time I went to help Meredith and Brittany kill chickens. I went there so I could learn another part of farm life. I'd never seen a chicken killed before and didn't know what to expect. Meredith grabbed a chicken by its legs and carried it to the chopping block. She lifted the axe above her and brought it down, cutting off its head. As soon as the axe landed I lost all interest in the lesson. Blood spurted from the open neck, and when Meredith threw the chicken into the grass, its wings whacked the ground as its legs launched it first in one direction then another, as if frantically looking for its lost head. It hurled itself towards me, and before I could react, it bounced against my pant legs smearing them with blood. To me, a city girl, the slaughter was just horrid. I just made it to a small bush nearby before losing my breakfast."

"How did you manage to stick it out?" Elizabeth asked, genuinely curious.

"At first it was because I was in love," Sarah said ruefully.

When she didn't elaborate, Elizabeth pressed on. "Do you have children?"

Sarah shook her head. "No. Nick wanted some, but I wouldn't have any."

"Is there anything you can tell us about Mom?" Jared spoke for the first time.

Sarah looked at him, as if weighing whether she should say something. "No, we saw each other a couple of times and that is all."

"She didn't confide in you, tell you that she was unhappy and planned to commit suicide?"

"No."

"Well, we certainly didn't learn anything there today," said Jared, as they drove out of the yard.

"Oh, yes we did."

"We did?" Jared glanced at her.

"We know we can't trust Sarah." Elizabeth idly scratched Chevy's head.

"Why not?"

"Well, for one thing, on our first visit she said that Nick had inherited the farm, which to me means his parents are dead. Yet today she sent Nick to their place with a supposed anniversary gift."

"You're right. I'd forgotten about that conversation."

"I think she was getting rid of him because we were asking him about being your father. I wonder if that means that it's true, and she's trying to keep it secret?"

"And Nick went along with it," Jared pointed out. "So we also have to watch him."

"What I want to know is, What else has she or both of them lied about?"

"I guess we could come right out and ask her," Jared said.

"I doubt that we would get a straight answer," Elizabeth mused. "There has been a reversal of roles in that family. She made it sound like he was the dominant person in the marriage at the beginning, but we know that she is now. I wonder how and why that changed."

"Do you think Nick is my father?" Jared asked, suddenly stopping the van on the deserted road.

"I did some comparing before he left," Elizabeth admitted. "And there are some similarities."

"Such as?"

"You are both about the same height. You are both slender. Your noses and chins are almost the same. But I think it would take DNA testing to be sure. We could try to get Nick alone and talk to him," Elizabeth suggested.

Jared leaned his chin on the steering wheel and stared out the windshield. Again Elizabeth felt sorry for him. This was turning into a bad trip for him. She changed the subject.

"I wonder why Sarah said she wouldn't have children."

When Jared didn't answer, she added, "It just sounded strange the way she put it. Not that she didn't want any or couldn't have any, but that she wouldn't have any."

He continued to gaze out the windshield.

Christine's Story

Christine peeked through the window before opening her front door. They stood awkwardly, looking at each other, and then she smiled at Meredith.

"Come in," she said. "Let me take your coat." She held out her hand.

Meredith shrugged out of her parka and handed it to Christine, who carried it to the bedroom and laid it on her bed. She was curious as to why Meredith had called and wanted to come over. Did it have something to do with Ben? Her stomach was a mass of knots while she waited to find out.

"I've made some tea," she said, guiding Meredith into the kitchen.

They sat at the table with cups in front of them. Christine poured then passed the cream to Meredith.

When Meredith had called, the conversation had been formal and rigid, not the type expected between two women who had been friends for so many years. Although it was almost typical of the way they related to each other now.

Finally, Meredith spoke. "Christine, what's going on? Why are you moving?"

Christine relaxed a little. "Wayne's already told you."

"Yes, he has, but I can't believe you are planning to leave here completely."

"I am."

"But why? What made you decide to do this?"

"It's been a long process." She was getting so tired of explaining it.

"I thought you liked the farm," Meredith persisted. "You never complained about it."

"Not complaining and liking have two different meanings."

"We've been such good friends for so long," Meredith said. "I noticed a change in you, but I thought it was because of your job."

Christine looked at Meredith. She had been a good friend and she hated to say this.

"Maybe it's time for each of us to move on. Friendships don't always last forever."

Meredith looked hurt. "I always thought ours would."

Christine suddenly put her hand on Meredith's. "I've always valued our friendship, and it is something I'm really going to miss. I hope you can forgive me."

"Forgive you?" Meredith asked. "For what? You've done nothing to me that needs forgiving."

Christine was silent for a while. "By doing this, I'm running out on everyone who means the most to me. It's been a tough decision, but I have to do what is best for me. And, in a way, I'm trying to make up for my past mistakes."

"What do you mean? What have you done wrong?"

Oh, Meredith, if you only knew. Christine smiled humourlessly.

"I'm just hoping to leave without hurting too many people."

"Well, you're hurting Wayne," Meredith said, standing.

"I know. And that can't be helped." Christine got Meredith's coat.

She had just opened the door for Meredith when Graham appeared on the step.

"Hi, Mom." He turned to Meredith. "Are you coming or going?"

"I'm just leaving. Bye, Christine."

"Bye," Christine said and turned to Graham. "What brings you here?"

"We needed a few things, and Dad didn't feel like coming into town, so I came. I thought I'd bum a cup of coffee off of you."

Christine smiled at her son. "I'll even let you bum some cake."

Chapter 34

Elizabeth assisted Jared into bed. He didn't invite her to stay with him, to share his bed. In fact, he hadn't said more than five words since leaving Sarah and Nick's place. He'd refused to go out for supper, just wanting to go to his room. And she didn't blame him. He was discovering a lot about his mother that probably wasn't what he'd expected.

She went to her room and brought up her notes. She began to edit, working until Chevy wanted his walk. Afterwards, she drove into town and found a pizza parlour. She ordered a large pepperoni pizza with extra cheese and asked for a couple of paper plates and napkins. With it in hand, she went to Jared's room and listened at the door. She didn't hear anything. She could see under the door that there was a light on. Was he sleeping, reading or writing? She hated to think that he was just staring at a wall going over and over everything in his mind.

She knocked.

"Come in."

She opened the door, and Chevy immediately bounded over and jumped on the bed. He went up to Jared's face and licked it.

Jared laughed and held him off at arm's length.

"Oh, I'm so glad you're okay," Elizabeth said, relieved to hear him laugh.

"I'm sorry for the way I acted. I was on a pity trip for a while."

"I don't blame you." Elizabeth set the pizza carton on the bed. "I thought you'd be hungry, so I went and got this for us."

"Oh, you definitely are a girl after my heart. I was just lying here wondering why I'd been so stupid as to refuse going out with you tonight. I can't believe I was so sulky. It's not like me to act that way."

"You've had a lot of stuff thrown at you in the last few days. I think you're entitled to feel sorry for yourself a little." Elizabeth helped Jared prop himself on the pillows, and then handed him a plate with a piece of pizza on it.

"We haven't gone out for pizza yet, so I wasn't sure what kind you liked. I ordered the pepperoni because it doesn't have anything fancy on it."

"I love just about any topping except anchovies."

"Yuck, I hate those too."

"Do you like perogies?" Elizabeth asked, remembering that she'd wondered while eating the ones in Glendon.

"Of course. I think I'd be disowned by my Ukrainian ancestors if I didn't. Why do you ask?"

"I had some on my second day of travelling, and I realized then that we hadn't talked much about our food likes and dislikes."

After devouring the pizza, they began their discussion of what they'd learned during the day. It didn't take very long.

"The only really new thing we learned is that Nick and your Mom dated in high school. She was talking marriage, and he wasn't. She was pregnant when she married your dad, which could mean that Paul just might not be your father. She wouldn't be the first woman who got pregnant by one man but, for whatever reason, married another."

"If I was Nick's child," Jared said. "Why would Mom have married Dad, I mean, Paul?" He shook his head. "I don't know what to call him."

"I think Dad is good, at least until confirmed otherwise," Elizabeth said.

Jared nodded. "Yes, you're right."

"Didn't someone say that Nick moved away after graduation? Maybe he left before she knew she was pregnant. Maybe she was already seeing Paul when she found out and told him the child was his so he'd marry her. She might even have thought it was at the time."

"It sounds like she had a mixed-up life," Jared said.

"She certainly wasn't content," Elizabeth agreed. "But I've gotten the impression that whatever she did or tried, she was doing it for you."

"Thank you, Elizabeth," Jared said. "I always feel better after talking with you."

Christine's Story

What an evening, Christine thought, as she finally relaxed in her chair. First she'd worked late, then Meredith had wanted to come for a visit, and then Graham had popped in. He'd just left. She turned on the late news and began going over her plans for her move. She groaned at the rap at the door. She knew it had to be Ben. She'd told him this afternoon that she couldn't make it for their "date," as he termed it, and he hadn't sounded happy about it. She wished she was in Vancouver and away from all this.

Christine didn't even go to the door. Instead, she turned off the television and then walked through the house, shutting off all the lights.

"I know you're in there! Open the door!"

Christine went back into the living room, where she sat in her chair. The room was dimly lit by the shine from the streetlights reflecting off the snow. Outside, the night had a gloomy brightness. The pounding and yelling increased. She covered her ears to block out the noise. But she couldn't block out the sound of him kicking at the door. She stood and went to the kitchen entrance. It was darker in the kitchen, but she could see the wood of the door frame splinter when the lock gave way.

She screamed as the door flew back against the wall and he entered the house. She rushed through her bedroom door to the phone. She frantically grabbed the receiver and began dialling the police station, but he caught her from behind and knocked the phone from her hand. She screamed and kicked back, but he didn't let go.

"So you think you can give me the brush-off," he rasped in her ear. His breath stank of alcohol.

"Let me go!" she shrieked. "Let me go!"

"Not until you say you love me again."

Christine struggled, trying to get away from his imprisoning arms.

"Say it. Say you love me."

Christine suddenly stopped her kicking. She was so very scared. She could feel the panic rising in her, and she knew she had to contain it. Her life depended on it. Her breath was ragged as she tried to think calmly. She had to get out of his arms. He had them wrapped around so that she couldn't elbow him. Kicking him in the shins was doing no good. If only she could trip him somehow.

"I'm waiting."

"Please let me go. I won't call the police. You can go home and we'll pretend this never happened."

"It's too late."

"No, it's not. No one knows you're here. If neither of us tells, then you can continue with your life, and I can get on with mine."

"It won't work. I want you in my life too much to just let you go."

"But you're throwing everything you have worked for away, your life with Meredith."

"If you're leaving me, you're leaving this world too."

He dragged her backward out of the bedroom into the kitchen. She snaked her right foot behind his leg and pushed hard with her left. His backward movement, plus her foot and extra shove, tripped him, and they toppled over. He automatically let go of her as his arms flung back. She heard him bang his head against the table.

Christine scrambled to her feet, and in the dim light she grabbed a knife from the set on the counter. She held it in front of her as he slowly climbed to his feet. He rubbed the back of his head.

"Get out," she said, waving the knife at him. "Get out, or I'll use this."

He laughed and moved closer to her. "You wouldn't. You don't have the guts."

Christine took a step back. "Get out," she repeated. "I don't want to hurt you. I just want to be left alone."

He took another step towards her. "Give me the knife."

Her fear threatened to choke her. Her hand was unsteady. She fought to keep from falling in a quivering heap on the floor. She either had to use the knife or give it to him. And she was sure he would kill her if he had it.

Suddenly, anger welled up inside of her. He had no right to be here. This was her home, and he was an intruder. She was the one who had the rights in this house, and she had the right to defend herself.

She jabbed at him with the knife, trying to frighten him. Instead, he laughed.

"You don't scare me," he taunted.

She saw him raise his hand, and the memory of his slap flashed through her mind. Without thinking, she lunged forward and plunged the knife into his stomach.

"Uh," he grunted, doubling over and grasping his midsection with both hands.

Suddenly, she felt herself sliding to the kitchen floor. She lay there a few moments, wondering what had happened. Then she saw a shadow flit across the floor. She struggled to say something but slipped into unconsciousness.

Wayne's Story

Wayne watched the police car pull into the yard. What was Christine complaining about this time? The RCMP officer stepped out.

"Mr. Dearden?"

"Yes."

"I'm Constable Keeley from the Redwater RCMP detachment. We have your wife, Christine Dearden, at the station."

"Why? What's the matter? Is she okay?" He felt a chill sweep through him. Something had happened to Christine.

"She was attacked last night ..."

"Attacked! By whom? Was she hurt?"

"Ben Warren assaulted her in her home, and she stabbed him."

"Oh, my God. Ben? Why would he do that? How is she? Can I see her?" He wanted to know everything immediately.

"Yes, she has been asking for you, and now that the questioning is over, you can see her. I assume you will want to take your truck."

He nodded and ran over to it. He didn't think to tell Graham, didn't think to change out of his milking clothes; he just thought of Christine. The drive into Redwater was the longest he had ever taken. He wanted to speed, to get there now, but he had to follow the police car at the speed limit. Couldn't he put on his siren? Didn't he know this was important, that Christine needed him?

At the station he dashed through the doors, not waiting for the officer to show him the way. Inside he looked wildly around, expecting to see her sitting on a bench or in a chair. She was nowhere in the room.

"Where is she?" he demanded of Constable Keeley when he came in.

"She's in her cell."

"In her cell? What for?"

"She's been charged with murder."

"Murder? I thought you said she was attacked."

"She was." Constable Keeley put his hand on Wayne's shoulder. "Maybe you had better talk to her about it."

He followed the officer into a room with a small, square table and two chairs.

"I'll be back with your wife."

When Christine entered the room, he was dismayed to see her face pale and drawn, her clothes rumpled, her hair dishevelled. He put his arms around her, and she laid her head on his shoulder.

"Christine," he whispered, hugging her close. "Oh, Christine."

They stood like this for a few minutes, and then he led her over to a chair at the table. He sat across from her, holding her cold hands in his.

"Tell me what happened."

Christine shook her head, tears in her eyes.

"Please, Christine. I want to help you."

"You won't after you hear this. You'll hate me."

"No, I won't. My feelings for you will never change."

He listened quietly to Christine as she told her story. She began with how she had gradually begun to hate the farm because of its oppressiveness and how she had dreamed of seeing the world. She told of the affair that had started two years ago because she needed some excitement in her life. She explained how after a year and a half she had told Ben it was over, but Ben had refused to accept that, saying she was now a part of his life. She decided to end the affair and because she didn't want anyone to find out about it, she knew she would have to leave the area. So with Graham gone and her course just about over, she had decided to carry out her dream of seeing more of life. The only obstacle was Wayne.

She had told him to sell the farm and come with her, knowing he wouldn't. When she had told Ben their affair was really over he, like Wayne, had tried to talk her out of it. But he had been more forceful, using physical violence. And last night, fearing for her life, she'd stabbed him.

While listening, Wayne progressed from feeling shock to anger to hatred, and then finally, he was overcome with a sense of deep loss. Up until tonight he had thought there was still a chance for him and Christine to get back together. He'd held out hope, even against all that she'd said.

Now he sat in silence, having long ago withdrawn his hands from hers. How funny that he had thought his life was over when Christine moved out. Hell, he hadn't even known the true meaning of the word "over." Then, it hadn't meant his feelings would be so totally, completely, thoroughly extinguished. Now, it did. He had no sensation, just a huge void.

"Wayne?" Christine's voice was timid, frightened, beseeching. "I'm so sorry for this. I had hoped to get away from here without anyone finding out. I didn't want to cause anyone any pain."

He couldn't answer. There was no answer to her statement. He looked at his wife. The only thought in his emptiness was that she still looked as beautiful as ever.

Wayne suddenly felt tightness in his chest, as if someone had struck him a blow. The hollow feeling of a minute ago was quickly filled with a crush of thoughts and emotions. Ben, his childhood friend; his best friend for over forty years. Ben, who had been his best man at their wedding, who had farmed beside him for almost thirty years. Ben had been having an affair with Christine for two years. Christine killed him. Ben was dead. It was too much, just too much. He stood.

"I have to go."

Christine nodded.

He left the room. Outside, in the cold air, he inhaled deeply, feeling as if he had been holding his breath for a long time.

"Are you finished?" Constable Keeley asked.

He nodded, still unable to speak.

"Let's get a coffee, and then I have some questions to ask you."

He followed him numbly, wondering when he would wake from this dream.

Chapter 35

"Tell us about the day of Anna's death."

Elizabeth had been holding off asking that question. She thought it was up to Jared to bring that day up, but while he'd agreed earlier that he wanted to know, he hadn't opened the conversation. And since time was running out for her, she decided to do it.

"We were eating lunch when the phone rang," Sarah said. "Nick got up to answer it. It was Paul, wondering if Anna was here. At first we thought she'd left him again but when he said he'd come home from the field and found Jared alone in the house, we figured she'd never do that."

"So what happened?" Elizabeth asked.

"We waited, and when he called again he said he couldn't find her anywhere and he wanted us to come and help look for her."

"I asked him if she'd gone to her parents alone this time," Nick said. "But he said he'd called there, and they told him she hadn't phoned them.

"Wayne and Graham were already there, along with some other men," Nick continued. "There wasn't any news. I asked Paul where he had already looked, and he said he'd done a quick check of the buildings and drove up and down the road."

"While the men began to search, I went into the house." Sarah looked at Jared. "I don't know if you remember, but you were watching *Sesame Street*."

Jared, who had sat through this without any expression, shook his head.

"You asked me if I had come to see your mother, and I said yes. You told me that she wasn't there and that your daddy had gone to find her, and you were being good for him.

"I asked you if you were hungry and you were, so I found a can of soup and heated it up. By then, more women had arrived. Meredith had brought a whole bunch of bread and ham, so while some of the women went to help with the search, others came in the house to make sandwiches."

"Did the police come?" Elizabeth asked.

"Not at first. Someone said Paul had to wait forty-eight hours before he could report her missing."

"How long did the search last?" Elizabeth asked Nick.

"It lasted until almost dark."

"How was she found?" Jared asked. His voice was passive, almost lifeless. This was obviously hard on him.

"You went out to the well and said she was down there," Sarah said.

"I did?" Jared asked, astonished.

"Yes. They pushed the rock off, lifted the lid and saw her floating."

"I don't remember that," Jared said quietly. "You'd think something like that would always be in my memory."

"Maybe it was so traumatic that to protect you, your mind erased it," Elizabeth suggested.

Anna's Story

Anna was dishing the bacon and eggs on to Paul's plate when he came up behind her and slapped the side of her head. The blow caused her to stagger sideways, and she almost dropped the plate. He put both his hands on her shoulders, squeezing hard, while he whispered angrily.

"First you drive Willy away, and then you try to make a fool of me by leaving with Jared." He shoved her against the stove. "And now you're telling people that Jared isn't my son and neither is that kid." He pointed to her belly. "Will you never stop causing me pain?"

Paul turned and slumped on to his chair at the table. He put his head in his hands.

Anna's ear and side of her face stung, and she blinked back the tears as she dropped hash browns beside the eggs. She put the plate on the table and left the room. He'd been gone for a few days after the dance, and it had been heaven. Now he was back, and she knew it was to stay.

When he'd gone to the field, Anna picked up the receiver and dialled a number. Meredith was the only one she could think of to call, the only one who might do as she asked. She listened to the phone ringing at the other end and was just about to hang up when Meredith answered, her voice breathless.

"Hi, Meredith, it's Anna."

"Anna. Where are you? Are you okay?"

"Yes." She hated to burden Meredith right now; she was probably in the middle of packing for her move into town. But Meredith was her only friend. She knew what Anna had been going through, and she would understand.

"I'm sorry that I didn't call you," Meredith said. "I've been so busy with my move."

"That's okay. I was wondering if you were going to be there for the next little while this morning."

"Uh, yes." Meredith sounded confused. "We're loading boxes, but we still have lots to do."

"Do you mind if I come over for a few minutes?"

"Of course not. Come when you can."

"Thank you."

Paul was in the field and, other than coming in for lunch, he would be there all day. Anna dug out the paper and pen and finished the letter. It was important for her and for Jared that she do this. She signed it and put it in an envelope. She tucked the envelope in her shorts pocket and called Jared.

"We're going for a ride," she said to him.

"Are we getting on a bus again?"

"No, not this time."

"I liked riding a bus. Can we do it again?"

"Sure we can, someday."

She pulled into Meredith's yard. A pickup was backed up to the door. She could see Brittany and Tylar helping Meredith load her furniture. Anna walked over to Meredith. When Tylar and Brittany had gone into the house, she pulled the letter out of her pocket.

"What's this?" Meredith turned it over in her hand and read the names of Victor and Olga Dombroski on the front.

"Will you give it to my parents when they come?"

"When are they coming?"

"Sometime soon."

"Can't you give it to them?"

"I think it's better if you hold it for me. I don't want Paul to find it."

Meredith stared at her. "Is there anything I can do?"

"Don't tell anyone about the letter," she pleaded.

Meredith hesitated.

"Promise me you'll tell no one." She had to promise, she had to.

"I promise."

"Good." Anna said with relief.

"But ..."

"I'm sorry I can't visit," Anna said, turning away. "I have to get back."

Meredith reached out and touched Anna's arm. "I wish there was something I could do."

Anna nodded. "You've done a lot for me, and I want to thank you."

On her way back, Anna saw Sarah walking along the road. She waved, but Sarah ignored her. At home she didn't hurry. She knew she'd exhausted all avenues, and there was nothing more she could do. She felt so much calmer now. She put Jared down for a nap, and when he was asleep, she went out to get some water from the well. The heat of the day was getting to her.

At the well, she looked down into the serene water. She could see her reflection looking back. The water was so inviting. It would feel so good to sink into its depth, to have it cool her all over. Suddenly, she was falling towards the water, seeing her startled face coming at her. She knew she was going to die. She was facing head down. With her bulk, there was no way she could turn around and get her head above the water. She'd heard drowning was an easy way to go. She hoped it was true.

Chapter 36

"I don't think Sarah told us all of it," Elizabeth said, after they'd left the Munter-Thompson place. "Do you want to go and find out if Meredith's version of the search is different?"

Elizabeth waited a few moments. "Jared?"

Jared took his eyes off the road to look at her.

"I'm sorry," he said. "I'm having a hard time concentrating this morning. I'm just getting overwhelmed with everything that I'm suddenly learning."

"We can quit any time," Elizabeth assured him. "You can go home and digest everything, then come back and try again. I think everyone will be around for a while yet."

Jared shook his head. "I just have to pull myself together and keep going because I do want to find out the truth."

"What do you suggest we do next?" Elizabeth had run out of ideas. She had the feeling that they were going in circles. Everyone was giving them the same message: Anna killed herself, Christine killed Ben. It was getting to the point where she could think of nothing more to ask.

"There's something that's trying to break through my memory. It almost makes it, and then disappears again. Maybe a chat with Meredith will bring it out into the open."

"Okay," Elizabeth said, nodding in agreement.

"Do you mind asking the questions?" Jared entreated, when they got there. "I'm hoping that by listening, that niggling in my mind will develop into something concrete."

"Sure, but jump in whenever you want."

"So have you had a chance to read much of my new book?" Meredith asked, when they were settled. Apparently, her anger from the last visit was gone.

"I have, and I liked it as much as the first two," Jared said. "I'm really interested in what your last book will be about."

"I'm glad to hear you say that, because I emailed you some poems from that book just five minutes ago," Meredith said. "My publisher is getting anxious, and I need the feedback quickly. If you could read them as soon as possible, I'd appreciate it."

"Okay, I'll look at them when I get back to the B and B."

"Thank you."

"Have you read any of my poems?" Meredith turned to Elizabeth.

"Yes." Elizabeth nodded.

"What do you think of them so far?"

Elizabeth wondered why she was so curious about her reaction. As a writer, she understood how great it was to have a reader appreciate your work. But she didn't think she herself could push so much for a comment. Elizabeth decided to be honest.

"I've never been a fan of poetry, but I really like yours. The script poetry approach is different, and you get very personal about your love for Ben."

Meredith beamed. "How far have you gotten?"

"I've finished them all too," Elizabeth replied. She wasn't sure if she should state that she found them very sad. She didn't want to make that sort of comment on Meredith's life.

"Good." Meredith seemed pleased. "Feel free to read the ones I emailed Jared."

"I will."

"So what do you want to know today?" Meredith asked Jared.

Elizabeth answered for him. "We heard that you went to Paul and Anna's place on the day Anna disappeared."

"Yes, that's right. I was in the middle of moving. Brittany and Tylar were helping me. We stopped loading their truck to go and see if there was anything we could do. I didn't really know what was happening, so I started making sandwiches and coffee. People always have to eat."

"Can you describe what the day was like?"

"Pretty chaotic. People were randomly wandering around the fields and up and down the roads, calling her name."

"Did you mention the envelope to anyone?"

Meredith shook her head. "I carried it with me but it was addressed to her parents, and I had promised Anna."

"Can you tell us how Mom was found?" Jared asked.

She looked at him quizzically. "You don't remember?"

Jared shook his head slowly. "Sarah told me I was there, and something keeps trying to surface in my mind, but so far it hasn't. I'm sure that whatever is on the outer edge of my memory has something to do with that day."

"You were looking out the living room window when I arrived. You looked so small, and my heart went out to you. I wondered if I should say something to you about your mother or just let you continue your vigil. I did go over and put my hand on your shoulder, but I don't think you even noticed.

"Then I got busy making sandwiches with the other women. We set up a table outside and put the sandwiches and coffee and juice on it so that the searchers could help themselves as they wished. When I looked again, you were still at the window."

"I remember," Jared said suddenly. "I had woken up from my nap and couldn't find Mom anywhere in the house. She'd always told me to stay in the house if I woke up and she wasn't there. So I went to look out the window and see if I could find her. Then Dad came home and wondered where she was, and then a lot of people came." His face clouded. "That's all I remember."

"All at once you started for the door," Meredith resumed her story. "I reached out to stop you because I didn't want you getting in the way. But you kept saying that you wanted to see your mommy. I didn't know what to answer to that. How could I explain to a four-year-old that his mother was missing? So I told you that she wasn't there right now."

"And I said, 'Yes, she is,'" Jared jumped in, excited.

Elizabeth leaned forward to catch every word. It looked like Jared's memory was coming back.

"And I wrapped my arms around you and told you again that she wasn't. But you kept insisting that she was, and you asked that if you put on your shoes, would I let you go see her?'"

Elizabeth watched them relive this thirty-year-old conversation. Maybe they were close to getting to the bottom of what had happened.

"And you agreed. I remember you tying my laces, and we went outside."

He began to slow down and put his head in his hands. "There is so much flooding my mind right now. I need time to sort it all out."

Elizabeth was glad Meredith waited for him to continue.

When he didn't, Meredith said, "Outside, the men were discussing how they should organize the search. You ran across the yard to the old well and began to push at the large rock on the lid."

Jared looked up. "Yes, I asked you to get it off for me," he said. "I'm slowly picking out the sequence in my mind."

"'I don't think we'd better,' I told you," Meredith prompted. "'You might fall in.'"

There were tears in his eyes as he said, "I said that my mommy was down there, and I wanted to go to her."

"When I asked you what made you think your mommy was down there, you said ...?" Meredith left the sentence open.

"Because I saw her." He pressed his chest.

Elizabeth immediately stood and went to him. "Are you okay?"

"I've got a terrible pain in my chest," he whispered.

"You should quit now."

Jared took a deep breath. "No, I can't. I just can't."

He looked at Meredith. She stared back at him intently.

"It seemed to take forever to get someone's attention," she continued. "I didn't want to look because you were right there. I finally saw Nick and yelled for him to come. He wanted to know what the matter was, and he didn't understand at first when I said Anna was down there. He finally pushed the rock off the lid and lifted it. Paul had also come over, and the two of them looked down.

"They stared into the well, and then Nick looked away. It seems your mom used to get water from there to cool her feet, and when your dad came home he saw that the lid was off. He replaced it, not thinking to look down."

"I remember running to the edge of the well and someone picked me up," Jared said. "I wanted so badly to get to my mom."

Meredith nodded. "You were screaming, 'I want to see my mommy! I want to see my mommy!' I picked you up and took you back to the house so that you wouldn't see your mother being pulled out of the well." She smiled slightly. "You fought hard. You punched and kicked me all the way."

"I ran to the window. I saw the flashing lights of the police cars and ambulance."

"You asked what they were for, and I said they were going to get your mother out of the well. You wondered if your mother was coming into the house after that and ..."

"You told me that Mommy was all wet, and she wouldn't be able to come see me. Then you said she had to go to the hospital."

"You wanted to know if she was sick, and I said yes. I just couldn't say that she was dead."

Jared nodded.

Elizabeth was worried about him. He looked so pale, so drained. How much more could he take this week before collapsing?

Jared sat back in his chair. "Finally, I've remembered, and now I wish I hadn't." He looked at Elizabeth with tears in his eyes.

There was silence as Jared breathed deeply, trying to pull himself together. Suddenly he stopped, his face contorting in a frown.

"There's something more, something else that I need to remember." He shut his eyes. After a few moments he opened them again. "It just won't come."

"Do you have any idea what it's about?" Elizabeth asked.

"Well, how did I know she was in the well? I must have seen her go there." He shook his head as if trying to clear it. "Why don't I remember that? What happened that my memory has blanked it out so completely?"

"Do you think you're ready to dig for it?"

"From the beginning, I've never been sure where this week was going to take me, and so far it hasn't been pleasant. I guess it can't get any worse."

Elizabeth waited for him to say more. When he didn't, she asked Meredith, "Do you think Paul had something to do with her death? After all, he did admit to putting the lid back on the well."

"I don't think he killed her, if that's what you mean," Meredith said.

"Do you think someone else may have?"

Meredith hesitated.

"What?" Jared asked, coming back into the conversation.

"Well, it's just something I overheard. I forgot about it until now. There was a benefit dance for a family whose house had burned down. I was sitting with Anna, and then we went outside because it was hot. She went to talk with Sarah. Sarah asked her what she'd meant by their first conversation, and Anna told her that Nick had been a bit of a playboy when he was younger, and she insinuated that he might be the father of her unborn baby."

"Why would she say that?" Jared asked.

"I don't know. But other people must have heard it because it wasn't long before the rumours were flying that she was pregnant again with a child of Nick's."

"What do you mean 'again?'" Elizabeth asked. She was looking for confirmation of what they had been told yesterday.

"Just that everyone thought Jared was Nick's son."

"Do you think he is?"

Again Meredith paused. "I did overhear her tell Sarah he was."

Elizabeth watched Jared. He just nodded his head.

"How did Paul and Nick feel about the rumours?" Elizabeth asked.

"I never really saw them after I moved into town. But according to the gossip, Paul was livid and embarrassed, especially since it was just after he had gone to pick Anna and Jared up in Edmonton. And Nick went around telling people he was not the father of either of her children."

"That must have caused a lot of hard feelings."

"It did, but the one I really felt sorry for was Sarah. She'd just gotten married, left her family and the life she knew and moved to a farm where she knew no one, all for the man she loved. And then to find out that he may have fathered one child, and while they were planning their wedding may have had an affair with his old girlfriend and fathered her second child?"

"That must have been so hard on her," Elizabeth agreed. "But she stuck it out with Nick."

"Yes, she has. But she has become a very bitter woman."

As they headed towards the van, Meredith called, "Let me know what you think of the poems when you finish them."

Elizabeth didn't say anything when they were in the van. She imagined Jared had too many thoughts running through his mind. His mother at the well, the possibility that Paul was not his father, his mother being so spiteful to another woman. When he didn't start the van she decided she had to know.

"How are you doing with all this? Do you want to talk about it?"

"It's just so hard to digest it all because it isn't even close to what I'd expected to discover about Mom. The memories of her that have been coming back are of her sweetness, her bathing me in bubble bath, her hugging me, her playing games with me. I guess I expected to find out that she was an angel who was mistreated by everyone around her. That image of her is slowly being crushed."

Elizabeth was determined to try and divert his attention. "Do you want to know my thoughts about what we've learned?"

Jared shook his head. "I appreciate that you are trying to distract me. I'm just not sure if I can discuss my mother right now, with all I've been finding out recently."

Elizabeth waited, willing him to say more.

"Okay. Tell me your thoughts," he finally said.

"We know your mother dated Nick before she married Paul," Elizabeth said, wondering if he was really paying attention. "She was pregnant with you when she got married, so Nick may be your father. Then four years later, Nick moves back to the farm, and she suddenly gets pregnant again."

"And she tells Sarah that Nick had made her pregnant just before they married," Jared added.

"Maybe she was trying to get Nick back," Elizabeth said. "After all, her marriage wasn't very good. I wonder if at some point she told him outright that he was your father."

"And what would his reaction have been?" Jared asked.

"There is the possibility that he may have killed her," Elizabeth pointed out gently.

"Oh, no," Jared sobbed. "Do I want to find out if the man who may be my father killed my mother? Jeez, what will I do if it's true?" He rubbed his eyes with the heels of his hands.

Elizabeth stopped. Was she pushing him too far? Should she wait, let him recover from today's bombshells? She looked at Meredith's house, expecting her to be peeking out the window, wondering what was happening. No one was there. She glanced up and down the street. Cars were driving, people were walking. Everything else was normal. It was just in this van that things were in turmoil.

"We could go back to ..."

"I don't want to see Dad tonight," Jared said quickly, as if knowing what she was going to say. "I'm really not sure if I want to learn the truth about that. If he is not my dad and Nick is, then where does that leave me? Without the man who raised me and having no bond with the man who is my father. Before I pursue it, I really have to be certain that I can deal with it if it is true."

Suddenly, Jared slapped the steering wheel. "I know what it was that I've been trying to remember," he said.

"What?" Elizabeth asked quickly.

"There was someone else with Mom at the well on the day she died."

"There was? Who?"

He shook his head. "I don't know."

Chapter 37

Wayne's Story

Wayne had stopped in at a convenience store for two packages of cigarettes and then went to the liquor store for a bottle of whiskey. He and Meredith were going to need both in order to get through this. He'd been told she had been in earlier to identify the body and then had quickly left after learning about the affair.

His feelings had returned and galvanized into one searing ball of hatred. How he hated Ben, and there was nothing he could do to get rid of the feeling. There was no Ben to hit, kick or throw across the room, like he'd done to the man who had made those calls to Christine. Last he'd seen of him, he'd been out cold on his living room floor. If he reported it to the police, Wayne never heard about it. Wayne wished he had the opportunity to do the same to Ben. Even a substitute would work, someone who deserved a good beating.

Wayne pulled into Meredith's yard. The cows were bawling at the fence. He walked into the house without knocking. Meredith was standing at the sink, her eyes red from crying. He held up the cigarettes, and she grabbed a package and immediately lit one. He showed her the whiskey, and she carried two glasses to the table.

"Have you seen Christine?" Meredith asked.

"Yes. I just left her before coming here." Wayne poured them each a drink. He drank his in one gulp.

Meredith downed hers. "Did she really stab Ben? Did she admit it to you? Is it really true?"

"Yes." Wayne was trying hard to keep his voice neutral. He knew that if he gave in to his anger, he would wreck her place, Ben's place.

"Did she tell you about the affair?"

"Yes."

They had another drink, and then he stood. "Come on. We've got to feed and water the animals."

Meredith looked up at him and shook her head.

"They need looking after," he said.

"I can't." She inhaled deeply.

"Yes, you can. What happened is not their fault."

"You do it."

"We'll do it." Wayne had no desire to go out into the cold, but he wasn't one to neglect animals that supplied a person's living. He pulled Meredith into a standing position and guided her over to where her winter coat hung. She listlessly put it on and slipped her feet into her boots.

While she went and started the pump, Wayne threw some bales over the fence to the cows. Then they carried pails of chop and water to the pigs.

"Will you tell me?"

"Are you sure you want to hear?"

Meredith breathed in a lungful of the cold air and let it out. "Yes."

"It's not very pleasant."

Meredith glanced at Wayne. "Tell me."

"They've been seeing each other for two years." Wayne paused at the agony it caused him to say it and at the pained expression on Meredith's face.

"Two years?" she whispered.

Wayne nodded.

"Two years." Meredith shook her head. "That's a long time for us to not know or even suspect."

"I've thought of that too," Wayne agreed. "They'd get together at lunchtime or on some of the evenings when Christine told me she was working late."

"Probably the same evenings Ben said he was going to see his father at the bar," Meredith said in a quiet voice.

"She said he wanted his wife and girlfriend too."

"Well, I definitely feel better that I was ranked as high as his girlfriend." Meredith dumped the chop in the feeder and watched the three pigs come out of their house. "I always thought his possessiveness was only for me. Apparently, it was for any woman who came within his grasp."

"When she moved out on me, she also tried to cut all ties with Ben." Wayne poured the water on top of the chop.

"And he wasn't happy about it," Meredith said. "He didn't like the idea of her calling the affair off."

They went and gave the chickens some water and grain. Once the animals were taken care of, they returned to the house.

Wayne poured each another glass of whiskey, and Meredith lit two cigarettes. They blew smoke into the air and drank.

Meredith shook her head. "This is so unbelievable, so horrible. Ben is dead, and Christine killed him. And they were having an affair." Her eyes misted over. "It's just too much to take in."

Wayne wasn't sure if she wanted to hear more. He wasn't sure if he could tell her more. He waited in silence.

"What did Ben do to try and keep Christine?" Meredith asked. She got up and began to pace the floor.

"He made phone calls to her, and when she got an unlisted number, he started going to her place at night."

As Wayne spoke, he wondered if Ben had seen him make his own evening visits.

"Apparently, she wouldn't let him in, but the night before last, he snuck up on her when she was entering. He actually hit her and he also threatened her if she didn't see him again. When he came last night, he broke the door down to get in, and she thought he was going to kill her. She got a knife and begged him to leave, but he wouldn't. He just kept coming at her until she stabbed him. Then she says that someone hit her on the head and she blacked out."

"Where did they meet for their little love fests?" Meredith stopped her pacing to pour herself another drink.

"At lunch, Ben would buy hamburgers or something, and they would meet along a dead-end road. In the evenings, they'd go to a hotel in Smoky Lake."

"Sounds like they were acting like a couple of teenagers." Meredith took a gulp of her drink, and then suddenly she threw the glass across the room. It splintered against the wall, and the remains of her whiskey slowly trickled down the paint.

"How could they do that to us?" she cried. "How could they betray us like that?"

Wayne went and put his arms around her. He held her until the tears stopped. She stepped back and wiped her eyes.

"How could they?" she asked again.

"I don't know," Wayne said, keeping his arms lightly around her. "I've asked myself that too."

"Didn't we mean anything to them? Didn't our marriages mean anything?"

"I guess not enough to stop them." He really should go. He felt himself losing the battle with his anger.

"Do you realize how trusting we were, how gullible? We actually sent them to that concert in Calgary together because neither of us wanted to go to it. I'll bet they laughed all the way into the city."

"And what were we doing that weekend?" Wayne asked gruffly.

Meredith reddened and pushed herself away from him. "That wasn't an affair. That wasn't even a one-night stand."

"Yes, but we were thinking of doing the exact same thing they were doing."

"They had an affair for two years," Meredith yelled harshly, pounding the table with her fist. "We got drunk and went to a motel room only to find out we didn't have the guts to cheat on them."

"But we were thinking about it."

"How can you say that?" Meredith paced the floor again. "They were seeing each other long before we even thought about it and long after we decided we loved them too much to do it." She looked at him. "But you know what? Right now I wished we had done it. I wished we had spent the whole night screwing instead of running home like two honourable married people."

"It wouldn't have changed anything."

"Maybe not, but right now I would feel like I'd gotten a little revenge on them." Meredith reached for another cigarette. "Why aren't you mad? Why aren't you throwing things and yelling?"

"I've come close, believe me. It's taking all my willpower to stay calm. Christine told me that during the affair, she realized she didn't love me."

Meredith put her hand on his arm. "I'm sorry."

"Me too."

"Then why did she want you to sell the farm and move away with her?"

"She said she used that as an excuse to end our marriage. She knew I wouldn't."

"Do you think Ben loved me?"

"He acted like he did."

"Yes, acted." Meredith got another glass and filled it. "We had a conversation a while ago, and I thought he was mad about Christine leaving you, but now I see that he was mad about her leaving him."

They had just about finished the bottle, but neither of them was close to feeling drunk. It was as if their bodies wouldn't let their minds block out the devastation that had invaded their lives.

"Did Christine say how they got together? What, after all these years of being friends, had sparked them into having an affair?"

"She said that Ben came into the office one evening when she was working late to drop off his income tax papers. He told her she looked tired and asked if she wanted to have a drink with him. She accepted and somehow, after a couple of drinks, they ended up in a motel room."

"That's the way we almost had our fling," Meredith said. "Only you bought me supper first and then the drinks."

Wayne smiled at the memory. They had decided to go into Gibbons for supper and a stroll along the riverbank while Ben and Christine were off enjoying themselves at the concert. They had the supper but didn't get as far as the stroll. The few drinks they'd consumed had left them giddy and feeling a little reckless. On the spur of the moment, they'd rented a motel room under the names Mr. and Mrs. Wayne Dearden. They'd giggled as they opened the door and went in, but once inside they had quickly sobered as the realization of what they were doing hit them.

The man behind the desk looked puzzled when they handed in the key ten minutes after they had gotten it. Wayne had saved the motel receipt as a souvenir, a reaffirmation of his love for Christine.

"So what made them take it further?"

Wayne shrugged. "I don't know. Christine said it just kind of happened. They felt bad after the first time, but when Ben came in to pick up his completed tax form they went for drinks again."

"Did you tell Christine about our feeble attempt at an affair?"

"No."

"Are you going to?"

Wayne shook his head. "What good will it do? It won't change anything."

"No," Meredith agreed. "It won't."

"Have you told anyone about Ben?" Wayne asked.

"I phoned Brittany and Tylar as soon as I got home. They said they would call the rest of the family."

"Did you tell them the story?"

"Only what I knew at the time, that Christine had stabbed him. I also said I didn't want to see anyone. What about you? Have you told anyone?"

"No. I don't know what I'm going to say to Graham."

"It's going to be very hard on him. What's going to happen to Christine?"

"She'll go before a judge and if he sets bail, I'll put it up, and she'll come back home until her trial."

"You're letting her move back in with you?" Meredith stared in disbelief.

"She has no place else to go. She won't be able to go back to work after this, and she won't have any money to live on."

"But to let her back into your life after what she has done, knowing she doesn't even love you."

"I can't abandon her."

"That's what she was doing to you."

"The circumstances are different now. And she is Graham's mother. I have to do it for him too. Besides, she does own half the farm. She has a right to come home."

Meredith smiled for the first time. "You're an amazing man, you know that."

"No." Wayne shook his head sadly. "If I was an amazing man, Christine wouldn't have fallen out of love with me in the first place."

Meredith put her hand on his arm. "I'm truly sorry. At least on good days I'll be able to delude myself into believing Ben still had some love for me."

Wayne stood. "I'll send Graham over this evening to help with the chores." He paused at the door. "What are you going to do now? With the farm, I mean."

Meredith shrugged. "I'm not even going to think about that until after the funeral." She stood and kissed Wayne on the cheek. "Thank you for coming over. I really needed this."

Wayne patted her on the shoulder. "We'll get through this together."

At his vehicle, Wayne kicked the tires hard. It didn't even begin to alleviate his burning rage.

Chapter 38

When they got back to the B and B after grabbing a bite to eat, Jared said, "I need to quit thinking about Mom for a while. My mind and body both need a rest."

"Yes," Elizabeth agreed. "We've learned a lot today but discussing it over and over is not going to make it any clearer. I'll help you into bed, and then I'll go do some work on my article."

When he was settled in bed, Jared asked, "Could you pass me the laptop? Meredith really pushed her poems on us today, and it's the first time she's let me read her poems-in-progress, so I'm curious. Once I'm finished that I will do some editing on mine."

Elizabeth headed out with Chevy for a walk, disappointed that Jared hadn't asked her to stay.

"Well, you told him you needed to do some work," she chided herself. "And he feels bad about keeping you from your writing."

She hadn't gone very far when suddenly her cellphone rang, startling her. Chevy barked at the noise. She looked at the display. Jared. Was something wrong?

"Hey, Elizabeth," Jared said, excitement in his voice. "You have to come and read this."

Meredith's poems, she thought immediately. What had he discovered? Elizabeth picked Chevy up and hurried to Jared's room. When she arrived, he pointed at the laptop with Meredith's poetry on the screen.

Act One
Fade In
Interior–Kitchen–Evening

Two women are sitting at a kitchen table. There is a teapot and two cups on the table. One pours the tea. The mood between them is strained.

I go that evening to visit Christine.
She is quiet, cool, unfriendly.
I am hurt. I do not understand.
She is my best friend, the one
I had picked berries with, the one
I had raised chickens with, the one
I had confided in for many years.
Why has she changed, I wonder?
What has happened in their marriage?
Why is she leaving?
I have yet to know why she needs
my forgiveness.

Fade Out
End Act One

Act Two
Fade In
Exterior–Street–Night
Snow is piled high in the yards. Vehicles are parked in front of those yards, some of them hidden by the snow. The street lights illuminate everything. One truck is parked and running. It is cold, and the exhaust rises. A man is sitting in it watching a house. A few houses back, another vehicle is running. A woman is watching the man.

I am driving away from Christine's
when I see you pass by.
You do not notice me, so intent are you.
I turn around and follow,
wondering where you are going.
I see you park near her house.
Have you come to talk with her
to try and help, like I have?

But you sit and watch her place.
When Graham leaves, then you go
to her door, pound on it.
She is there, yet she won't let you in.

Fade Out
End Act Two

Act Three
Fade In
Exterior–Night–Porch
A man is yelling and banging on the door of the house. Then he begins kicking it with his foot. Finally, it breaks. He enters the house.

I cannot believe that you broke her door.
Why would she not let you in?
I have to find out. I creep on to the porch.
I listen to you begging her to stay,
begging her to love you again.
Pain grips my heart. You love her, not me.
She has a knife, stabs you.
I grab her toaster, strike her.
I go to you, ask you,
"Do you not love me?"
You laugh and say, "Help me."
I reach over and pull out the knife.

Fade Out
End Act Three

Elizabeth looked at Jared. "It sounds like a confession," she said.

"Yeah, that's what I thought," Jared agreed. "She doesn't actually say that she plunged it back into him four times, but she is admitting to being there."

"We just may have to see her again tomorrow," Elizabeth said, taking his hand.

Chapter 39

Christine's Story

Every night, for weeks after the murder, Christine just lay on her bed and stared up at the ceiling of the basement of their house. She hadn't wanted to move back to the farm, hadn't wanted to be under the same roof with Wayne, hadn't wanted to face Graham, but Wayne had insisted, stating she couldn't live on her own. As soon as she'd been charged, she was let go from her job. She'd hired a lawyer, and when she heard how much it would cost, she'd given a month's notice to her landlord. Since all the money she had saved to move to Vancouver was now going to her lawyer, she'd moved back to the farm.

As far as she could see, there wasn't much difference being on the farm or in jail. She was in a prison here, even if it was a prison of her own making. This room was her cell, and she left it to make the meals, do the dishes and wash the clothes. Once those duties were performed, she returned to the room.

The few times she left the farm were for the visits she made to her lawyer.

Sometimes, Wayne accompanied her. She never went outside to help with the cows or to get the garden ready for planting, she never stayed upstairs longer than she had to and she never watched television or listened to the radio.

The only thing she did was lie on the bed, stare at the ceiling and run the events of the past two years over and over in her head. She always began with the first night she and Ben had spent together and how they had agreed never to do it again. And then on to the second time, when they had vowed that was the last time. From there, she pictured them meeting at the hotel and how romantic it seemed to have a lover. She heard herself justifying her actions by saying she didn't like the farm, didn't love Wayne anymore and she had a right to find love somewhere else.

The first feeling of guilt had come when Wayne and Meredith had insisted she and Ben go together to the concert they wanted so badly to see in Calgary. She had felt so moved by the total trust Wayne and Meredith had in them that she and Ben took separate hotel rooms and stayed in them all night.

Then she reached the point where she understood that it wasn't the affair she wanted, it was the stimulation, the rush it brought to her mundane life that appealed to her. That's when she had decided she really wanted to fulfill her lifelong desire to see more of the world.

It had been hard telling Wayne that their marriage was over. Harder yet convincing him that it was true. She'd thought Ben would agree that their affair had run its course, but he didn't want it to end. He had been just as adamant as Wayne that she stay.

Her move into Redwater followed, and then the phone calls she began receiving and the visits from Wayne and Ben. The last act was that night with Ben, and she saw each and every detail in full colour, heard every word spoken, felt every touch until the final scene of Ben's face as he realized she'd actually stabbed him. It was what had happened after that she still couldn't face. She couldn't even bring herself to tell her lawyer. She couldn't tell anyone.

And then time was set aside for the feelings of the day, and any number of them would clamour for attention. She had her choice: shame, regret, sorrow and so many more. She had screwed up her life and the lives of her husband and child. Oh, how she wished that she had never begun the affair with Ben.

She was in limbo, with no marriage, no work. She'd told Wayne that she wanted to move to Edmonton until the trial and she would sign the farm over to him totally if he would give her some money. He'd agreed to buy out her share. That, at least, was a relief.

Christine was startled out of her reverie by the alarm on her clock. She reached over and shut it off. Time to make supper. She knew that if she didn't set the alarm, she would never know how much time had passed. She climbed off the bed and headed upstairs. The house was silent, but she didn't wonder where Wayne and Graham were. She didn't have that right anymore. She peeled and cooked the potatoes, fried the chicken and set the table. When the food was ready and no one had shown up, she dished up a plate for herself, ate, and went back downstairs. The men would reheat the meal when they got in.

Wayne's Story

Wayne walked up to Meredith's house. At the door was a pile of bags and boxes, and he wondered what was in them. Had Meredith cleaned out all of Ben's things already? He knocked and heard her call. When he pushed the door open, he felt a difference in the house. Although the furniture was still in the same places, it seemed empty somehow. Meredith was polishing the wooden table in the dining room.

"Got a spare cup of coffee?" Wayne asked.

Meredith smiled. "You bet."

She put the spray can and cloth down and went to the kitchen to make a fresh pot of coffee while Wayne sat at the table.

"How are you doing?" he asked.

"Surviving." Meredith put two mugs on the table. "I did a little house-cleaning," she explained.

"Yes, I saw the pile outside," Wayne said.

"I've got some more to add to it, then I'm going to haul them to the dump."

"If they are Ben's clothing and stuff, why don't you give them to the second-hand store."

"I don't think they'd appreciate the condition they're in."

"Why not?"

"Well, I may have wrecked them a bit," Meredith said mischievously.

"Oh, I see." Wayne smiled. He was glad to see her humour had returned. He just wished he could recover as quickly. But then Ben was gone, and she could begin her life again, whereas he had Christine as a constant reminder. And that had been his choice, although at the time he hadn't realized how hard it would be on him.

"Where are your seedlings?" Wayne looked in the corner of the dining room. He was sure he had seen them on the day he'd come after finding out about Ben. He was surprised that he even remembered it. There were lots that he didn't—or wouldn't—recall.

"Well." Meredith looked a little sheepish. "They kind of fell on the floor."

"Your figurines are missing too." Wayne looked at the empty china cabinet. Meredith had been so proud of them.

"They kind of had an accident too."

"Sounds like a hurricane went through here."

"I guess a Meredith betrayed is a little like a hurricane."

They both laughed.

"Do you want to tell me about it?" Wayne asked.

Meredith got up and opened the cupboards, showing the near-empty shelves.

"Follow me," she said and led him upstairs to the master bedroom. "I haven't finished cleaning in here yet."

Wayne saw the shredded clothes, curtains and sheets in a pile on the floor.

"Looks like you were busy."

"It took awhile. What about you? How are you holding up?"

"It's tougher than I thought." Wayne followed her back to the kitchen. "Christine is polite and I'm polite and Graham is polite. We're like three strangers not knowing what to say to each other. Christine wants me to take a mortgage on the farm and give her some money so that she can move to Edmonton."

"Not Vancouver?"

"No, she has to stay close because of the trial."

"Are you going to?"

Wayne nodded. "I've been to the bank. The farm has to be appraised, and then I have to prove I can pay it back with just the milk income. It will be a few weeks before the paperwork is done."

"Maybe once she's gone, you can clean house like I did. It would make you feel better, at least for a while."

"So it doesn't last."

"No. A sudden thought will enter my head, and I'll feel hatred, then later another thought will make me feel love, and they keep coming until I've gone through most of the emotions. It can be very upsetting."

"I know. My feelings are so mixed up that I never know what to feel. Sometimes I want so badly to get away from my thoughts."

They drank their coffee in relaxed silence. Wayne was glad he had come over. This was what he needed. A person he was comfortable with, to whom he could talk and who understood his feelings. This was the first time in days that he had actually felt at ease. He didn't have to be on his guard here, worried about saying or doing the wrong thing. He wondered if she would mind if he came here when his brooding threatened to overpower him.

Chapter 40

"So ... it was you who killed Ben," Elizabeth stated, when they were settled in Meredith's backyard the next morning.

Meredith smiled slightly at them. "Yes," she said easily.

Just like that. Elizabeth had expected her to deny it, to say it was just a poem. "Why?"

"Why? Why?" Meredith's voice rose as she spoke. "He was having an affair with the woman I had considered my best friend. Is that a good enough reason for you?"

"So you went there and hit her over the head then pulled the knife out of him and stabbed him again and again."

"Yes," she said.

"Why are you confessing now?"

She looked down at her hands in her lap. "I could say I'm dying from some terrible disease, but I'm not. I could say that I've found religion and need to confess my sins, but that's not true. The simple truth is that I believe Christine has suffered for enough years."

"Suffered, as in thinking she killed someone that she didn't?"

"I'll answer that by letting you read the last poem for my last book."

She picked up two pieces of paper from the patio table and handed one to each of them. Elizabeth read.

Act One
Fade In
Exterior–Backyard–Day
A woman is on her knees, pulling weeds in the garden. She stops and sits back on her heels. She looks around the yard and her shoulders slump. A tear runs down her cheek.

I work in my garden,
I clean my house, I go shopping,
but always I am alone.
Thirty years of flowers and vegetables.
My life is no life.
Your death was my death.
People ignore me like I am not there.
Even my whirlwind success as a poet
is not what I want from life.
If I had not killed you in anger,
I may have taken you back.
Because you were my life.

Fade Out
End Act One

Act Two
Fade In
Interior–House–Day
The woman is sitting at her desk. Her computer is on, and she is typing on the keyboard. She stops and reads what she had written.

You were stabbed once by your lover.
Then once by me for the pain,
Twice by me for the faithlessness,
Three times by me for the loss of trust,
Four times by me for the loss of love.
I have often wondered, pondered,
as your eyes watched me,

what were your last thoughts?
Did you have any regrets about what
you had done to me, to our marriage?
Or was it Christine who occupied
those final moments of your life?

Fade Out
End Act Two

Act Three
Fade In
Interior–House–Day
The woman at the computer lifts her head and looks into the distance. She shakes it, then continues typing.

Why did I keep quiet, not admit it was me?
I thought the police would discover it,
but they never believed her story
that someone had hit her, and they never came for me.
So I kept my secret all these years,
And she kept hers, for when she fell to the floor
I heard her whisper "Graham."
And knew she thought I was him.
So you have not been protecting your son
these thirty years, Christine.
You have been protecting me.
A fitting sentence for your betrayal.

Fade Out
End Act Three

Elizabeth sat and absorbed what she had just read. She'd known that Meredith had loved Ben from the other poems. This poem showed the hatred she must have felt at the moment she discovered the affair, and she killed Ben in that passion. What malice she had harboured for Christine all these years.

"What are you going to do now?" Elizabeth asked.

"I'll go to the police and tell them. I've just been waiting for someone to come to me and let me know they had reasoned it out. I was sure I had made it clear how much I loved Ben. I thought some reader would put that together with him having an affair, being stabbed by Christine and then Christine claiming that she'd been hit over the head by someone who had finally killed him. Following that thread they would suspected me. After all, isn't it the spouse who is the first suspect?"

Meredith sighed. "When that never happened, I was beginning to think I was too subtle, or worse yet for a writer, that maybe no one was reading my poetry. But when you two came here to try and find answers about Anna and started asking questions about Ben's death, I knew it wouldn't be very long before you clued in."

"Did you send that photograph to Jared?' Elizabeth asked. If Meredith was looking to be found out, maybe she used that as a means of getting Jared here and asking questions.

"You're smarter than I thought. Yes, I sent it."

"So you really know that Anna was murdered."

"I don't know for certain, but I strongly suspect she was."

"Why? What makes you think so?" Could they finally be getting somewhere?

"Because, when she brought me that note, she said she wished he would understand why she had done it. That she was trying to do the best for her son."

"Who did she mean?" Jared asked eagerly.

"I don't know. She didn't say."

"Do you know what it was that she did?

Meredith shook her head. "Sorry, no."

Jared sat back, dejected.

"Why didn't you tell us this before when we asked?" Elizabeth thought it would have saved them a lot of time.

"I didn't have my last poems ready yet for Jared to read." Meredith looked at Jared fondly. "We've become good friends during our poetry sessions together. The few times you spoke of your mother, I realized how much you had missed in your childhood and how terrible it must have been to grow up not only without a mother but also with her suicide hanging over you."

"Why didn't you just tell me what you knew?" Jared asked.

"I needed time to finish the last book. I didn't want to scoop myself too much before publication ..."

Meredith smiled.

"Well, I never thought it would end that way," Elizabeth said, as they left Meredith's place. "So Christine thought all this time that she was protecting Graham. I wonder what made her think it was him."

"Probably only she can answer that."

"I guess the question now is, do you want to go see Paul or do you want to let it rest awhile?"

Elizabeth had asked him this question before, and he had opted to continue. But now they had uncovered things that might be better left alone.

"I thought about it all night," Jared said. "I guess I have to know."

On the way, Elizabeth told him it was going to be her last trip. She was going back to Edmonton tomorrow. "You'll have to decide if you want to stay longer."

"Okay," he agreed. "Thank you for spending this much time with me on this. I don't know what I would have done without your support."

When they got to the farm, Jared got right to the point. "We've heard the rumours that Nick is my father," he said.

He's given up trying to be diplomatic about the whole thing, Elizabeth thought.

Paul put his head in his hands. His shoulders drooped. He looked defeated.

"Is he?" Jared asked, leaning forward.

Elizabeth watched him as he tried to prepare himself for the answer.

Paul looked up at him. "I really don't know. All I do know is that you are not my son."

Elizabeth watched as Jared slumped back in his chair. He closed his eyes, and then put his hands over his face. When he pulled them away, there were tears in his eyes.

"Could I have a drink of water?" he whispered.

Susie hurried to the sink and returned with a glass. She handed it to him. His hands shook as he took it. After a couple of sips, he set it on the table.

"Are you okay?" Elizabeth asked, bending over him.

He lifted his head and looked around at them.

There was silence. Elizabeth realized everyone was waiting for Jared to make the next move.

Jared took a deep breath.

"I'm sorry." His voice faltered. "In spite of all that I've learned, deep down I really wasn't expecting that for an answer."

"And I'm sorry that I couldn't have said it in a gentler way."

Did she hear right? Did Paul just apologize?

"Knowing you were someone else's kid kind of messed with my mind," Paul continued. "I began to drink and carouse, and God forgive me, I hit her. Then when she committed suicide, I began to feel guilty that I had driven her to it. I tried to be a good father to you. I just couldn't love you."

"What about the unborn child?" Elizabeth asked. "Was it yours?"

"I thought so, until she began hinting to people that it was Nick's. Then I think I lost it. I didn't come home for days, spending my time at my mothers. When I did come back, it was all I could do not to punch her."

"What about ..." Oh, how to ask this? Elizabeth tried again. "Did you ...?" She held her breath and was surprised when there was no outburst at her unspoken question.

"No," Paul said slowly. "I may be a lot of things, but I'm not a murderer."

"How do you feel?" Elizabeth asked on their way to the van. "Do you think you can drive?"

Elizabeth watched as Jared did his best to smile at her.

"Yes."

"Do you believe him?" Elizabeth asked.

"About him not being my father? Yes," Jared said quietly.

"What about whether he killed your mother? He certainly admitted he had good reason to."

"I don't know what to believe about that. It's as if my life is not my life anymore. It's all surreal. They feel like strangers to me now. Paul isn't my father; Willy isn't my half-brother; Susie isn't my stepmom. I know them, yet I don't know them. I've effectively lost my past."

Elizabeth put her arm on his shoulder. She wished now that she had never agreed to do this for him. The pain he was going through was hard on her. She hated to see him suffer like that.

"At least I now understand the parental distance while I was growing up."

"Wait," called Susie, coming up behind them as Jared wheeled on to the lift. "I'm so sorry about all of this. I know it's a lot for you to grasp in such a short time." She bit her lip. "I may have come late into your life, but I just want you to know that you and Willy are the only children I have. I really don't want to lose you, and I don't think Paul and Willy do either. Give them time."

Elizabeth felt the prick of tears in her eyes, and she could see that Jared was just as moved.

"Thank you," Jared said, wiping his eyes.

Susie leaned over and gave him a hug. "I love you."

Paul came up behind Susie and put his arm around her. Elizabeth waited expectantly. What was he going to tell Jared?

"We have a lot to talk about once you've had time to absorb this. But right now, I just thought you should know that Nick has terminal lung cancer. If you want to do anything about finding out if he's your father, you should start soon."

Chapter 41

"Do you want to go and talk to Nick?" Elizabeth asked as they headed to the B and B.

"No. I just want to go home and hide for a long time."

He drove into the B and B yard and undid his seat belt. "I want you to put me to bed, draw the curtains, turn out the light and leave me there."

Elizabeth smiled. "I don't think that would be very ethical of me, a caregiver, to do that to you."

"But it might make me feel better."

Jared suddenly went still. "Some of it's coming back to me."

Elizabeth wasn't sure what he was talking about. She waited.

He turned to her, excited. "I saw someone. I saw someone at the well with Mom on the day she died. I knew it. There's no way she committed suicide. After all we've been finding out these past few days, and in my own gut, I know my mother did love me. She wouldn't have left me."

"Can you tell who it was?" Elizabeth asked. This was a definite breakthrough. "A man, a woman?"

Jared shook his head. "But I'm sure I would have known if the person was someone familiar to me like Paul or Willy."

"What are you going to do?" Elizabeth asked.

"I have to tell the police," he said, doing up his belt. "I have to get them to open the case again."

They drove to the RCMP detachment in Redwater. Elizabeth could see the excitement on his face. Could the police just ignore them? After all, he was an eyewitness, even if he was only four at the time, even if he didn't actually see her get pushed. Sure, the fact that someone else had been there with her immediately before her death must count for something. Nobody had admitted to it at the time, so someone obviously had something to hide. As far as she could see, this was practically proof that someone had killed his mother.

However, once they were in front of an officer, try as he might, Jared could not get the words to come out right as he described everything up until this moment. Elizabeth did her best to fill in the blanks, but between them she could tell that the officer was totally confused.

"Just one person, please."

Elizabeth waited while Jared told the officer of his mother's death thirty years ago and then showed him the photograph with the message on the back. The officer listened intently as Jared explained about remembering seeing someone with his mother out by the well just before she died.

"How old were you?"

"Four."

"Can you describe the person? Was it a man or woman?"

Jared shook his head. "I only know he or she didn't seem to be as big as my dad," Jared stopped. "Uh, as Paul Jones."

The officer looked at Jared. "That really doesn't give us much to go on. If you could recall more about this person, hair colour, anything like that, it would greatly assist us."

Jared shook his head. "I can't."

"Well, if you do, come back and see us."

Their excitement quickly died as they comprehended that the officer wasn't going to help. Jared wheeled out of the building, Elizabeth behind him.

"What more did they want?" he asked angrily. "An outright confession from the murderer?"

"So we know the person wasn't Paul or Willy, right?" Elizabeth prodded, when they were in the van.

"Right," he nodded. "From where I was, I could tell the person was too small to be either of them."

"We've met a lot of people who are smaller than them," Elizabeth said. "In fact, I think everyone has been."

Jared nodded again. "I see your point."

"You know, the one who has been willing to talk to us is Sarah," Elizabeth pointed out. "I wonder if there's more we can learn from her. It also might be an opportunity for you to approach Nick."

"We know that Meredith sent the photograph," Elizabeth said to Sarah when they were seated in the gazebo.

Sarah nodded. "I guessed it would be her."

"She also admitted to killing Ben."

"She killed him?" Sarah asked. Her eyes widened. "It wasn't Christine?"

Elizabeth shook her head.

"Are you sure?"

"She confessed to us. She was the one who hit Christine over the head."

"I didn't expect that," Sarah said, thoughtfully. "So that's one of your mysteries solved."

Elizabeth nodded. She wondered if she should mention that they also knew about Nick's condition.

"I don't imagine that's the reason you came to see me."

"We actually came to see Nick," Jared explained.

"He's not here right now."

"We've heard he has cancer," Elizabeth said.

Sarah nodded slowly. Was there a tear in her eye? Elizabeth wondered.

"Yes," Sarah said. "The doctor gives him six months. He's gone to the drugstore to renew his painkillers." She waited for them to say more.

"Anna told you that Jared was Nick's son and that she was pregnant with another of his children," Elizabeth said.

Sarah held up her hand. "Let me explain. Anna told me that Nick dated a lot of girls when they were in high school, even when he was seeing her. Then she told me about Jared and the baby she was expecting. I didn't believe her. When I confronted Nick, he denied the baby was his, but he couldn't deny that Jared might be his son. He did say that Anna had other boyfriends in school, like Graham Dearden, that he'd found out she had slept with, so Jared could have been someone else's for all he knew."

"Oh, my God," Jared exclaimed.

Elizabeth knew there was nothing more she could do to help Jared, other than just be there for him. They had opened Pandora's box, and he had to deal with the dreadful picture that was slowly being drawn of his mother.

She did file away the name Graham Dearden. The man kept cropping up in conversations. He'd been in the graduation photo with Anna too, she remembered.

"Well, knowing that Nick may have had a son in the past by another woman was okay," Sarah continued. "Those things happen. But thinking that he had been fooling around with her again just before we married and that she was pregnant with his child totally ruined my fledgling marriage."

"But you remained here."

"There wasn't much I could do. I was too embarrassed to go back to the city and tell everyone. So I acted like I didn't believe what she had said, that I believed in my husband. But it has eaten at me every day of my life since," she said harshly. "Look at me. I was a slim child. I was a slim bride. I used to walk a lot when I first came here. Knowing has made me into this."

She glared at them. "But I made him pay. I wouldn't have his kids, even though he really wanted some." Then she laughed, mirthlessly. "And he didn't want to give me half the farm, so he had to stick it out with me."

A vehicle drove into the yard.

"There he is now," Sarah said.

Elizabeth didn't know if they should talk to him in front of Sarah.

"Nick," Sarah called.

Elizabeth watched Nick come towards them. He didn't seem sick, but then again her mother hadn't looked sick until the final few months.

"I told them that you think you could be Jared's dad," Sarah said.

Nick didn't show any reaction to that. He just sat down on the gazebo bench.

"I do admit that I could be your father," he said to Jared. "Your mother and I had a relationship of sorts during high school, but I know she did see other guys to spite me because I wouldn't be faithful to her. She had always wanted us to get married as soon as we graduated, and I didn't. I left here not knowing she was pregnant."

Elizabeth expected Jared to ask if Nick would have stayed if he'd known. She agreed with his choice to keep silent.

"I also told them that you were the baby's father too."

This time he did react, waving his arms in the air. "I was not! How many times do I have to tell you, I didn't have an affair with her before we were married. I didn't."

He fell silent and stared at the floor.

"It wasn't mine," he said again, looking up. "Not that she didn't try to get back together again after I moved back to farm. But I was already engaged and didn't want anything to do with her."

"What happened?" Elizabeth asked.

"She came to the farm and tried to seduce me, said that we would make a good couple."

"When did she tell you about Jared?" Elizabeth asked.

"That same day. When I wouldn't go along with her plans, she brought Jared out of her truck and told me he was mine. She said that I would regret not getting back with her."

"So, if it was just after you moved out here, it was before you were married."

Nick looked at Sarah. "Yes."

"You knew, and you didn't warn me," Sarah spat out. "You let me find out at a dance with the whole neighbourhood listening in."

"I didn't think she would tell you," Nick said lamely.

"Well, if you didn't tell me that, then maybe you've never told me the whole truth. Maybe you and Anna did go further for old time's sake. The time frame was right for you to have fathered her second child."

Nick turned to Elizabeth and Jared. "You know, we've had this conversation about once a month for our entire marriage. She has never believed me, and she never will."

"I was about to tell them that you killed Anna when you drove up," Sarah said suddenly.

"Oh, please." Nick dropped his head into his hands. "Not that too."

"Yes, that too."

Nick turned to Jared. "Don't believe her. I didn't kill your mother."

Elizabeth noticed a smirk on Sarah's face. It looked like she enjoyed pulling Nick's strings. Was that what kept her here? Total and all-out revenge. How far would she have gone?

"Did you kill Anna?" Elizabeth asked abruptly.

Sarah laughed, but there was no amusement in her voice. "No. I told you, Nick did."

Nick just shook his head.

"And I turned Anna down because I was in love with my bride-to-be."

Sarah stared at him. Elizabeth wasn't sure if she believed him or not, but then she noticed that Jared had a strange expression on his face.

He looked at her. "I think we should go."

Something was definitely up.

"Okay," Elizabeth said.

When they were driving in the van, she turned to him. "What's the matter?"

"I've remembered something else."

"What?"

"It's what Nick said about Graham and my mom. I knew there was something familiar about Wayne's place, that carport. I'm sure I've been there before. And Wayne, there's something about him that makes me uneasy. I don't know for sure, but I have this feeling that something was going on between him and my mom, and it was bad. I remember them shouting ..."

Elizabeth's mind was going a mile a minute as she wondered what this could mean. What could Wayne possibly have against Anna? Surely they hadn't been involved ... she was much too young for him, she had even been dating his son. There was just no way.

"We have to go and see him first thing in the morning," she said with conviction. This may be the last piece of information they needed.

Jared began to shake. "Now what do I do?"

"I don't know" was all Elizabeth could say. She was failing miserably at being able to comfort him.

They sat on the side of the road for a long time, Jared overwhelmed with this coming on top of everything else he'd found out that day. Elizabeth felt helpless, realizing she couldn't really help him. These were things he'd have to come to terms with on his own. Finally, he roused himself enough to drive back to the B and B. Neither of them said anything on the way.

Jared barely spoke to her while Elizabeth helped him into bed. When he was settled, she sat on the edge. She wished she knew something about psychology so that she would know the best words to say to him that would make him feel better.

"It's been quite a week," she said.

"Yes." Jared's voice was subdued.

"Not really what we expected when we started out."

Jared shook his head.

"I think Susie was right when she said to give Paul and Willy some time. After all, you three have a life together that can't be erased just by a few words."

"I know," Jared said softly. "It's just that ..." He let the sentence hang.

Elizabeth waited. Finally, she asked, "It's just that, what?"

Jared shook his head. "I'm sorry. I just can't talk about it yet." He removed his glasses and tucked them under the edge of his pillow.

Elizabeth bent over and kissed him. He barely returned it. She went and pulled the curtains, said good night, and closed the door.

As she walked Chevy, she began to fear that, emotionally, Jared was pulling away from her. This was the second evening in a row that he hadn't invited her to stay with him, not even to discuss what they'd learned during the day. And wasn't it just two nights ago that he'd said talking with her always made him feel better? But she knew that sometimes the bearer of bad news is subconsciously held responsible for it. And while she wasn't bearing the bad news, she certainly was providing the means of uncovering it.

This new information definitely threw a kink into the mystery, she thought. She wouldn't be surprised if tomorrow Jared decided to pack up and head home. The strain must be huge. Maybe it would be better for him to just leave it alone for a while, at least until he could wrap his mind around everything he'd learned.

On her way back to the B and B she realized that neither she nor Chevy had eaten for a long time. They both deserved a hamburger and a shake. Well, Chevy could have water. Then she'd pack her clothes and get ready in case they decided to check out the next morning.

Chapter 42

Elizabeth wasn't sure what to expect with Jared today. To forestall what she anticipated to be a sombre encounter, she filled out the questionnaire that Brandon had given them the first day. Then she grabbed her camera and took Chevy for a quick walk around the yard. She snapped some pictures of the trees, since she hadn't gotten to it before.

After she put Chevy in her Tracker, she went to get Jared up. Brandon needed to know if they were checking out. She knocked quietly on his door.

"Come in," he called.

She peeked around the door, and then entered the still-dark room. She went over and opened the drapes, letting the morning sunshine in. When she turned to the bed, she saw that he was facing the wall. She felt so sorry for him. This excursion had not turned out well.

He turned his head and smiled slightly at her. His face was drawn and pale.

"I've been thinking most of the night," he said, putting on his glasses. "I tried remembering more about the person at the well with Mom, but I couldn't. Then I realized that I can't even be sure that the person was there on the same day she died. It could be another memory that I'm mixing up with it."

Elizabeth nodded. "I never thought of that."

"I've decided that I'll probably never find out the truth, or maybe the truth is that she did kill herself."

"Yes," Elizabeth agreed. "We have to consider that possibility."

"So I just want to see Wayne Dearden today, and then I'll call it quits." He fingered the necklace around his neck. "Because I do have a life that I want to get back to and a girlfriend who I want to spend time with doing things that don't include going around quizzing people."

Elizabeth grinned, and her heart soared. Yes! He hadn't been rejecting her. He'd just been preoccupied.

"Then let's get going," she said, bringing the commode chair over for his shower.

"I'll only shower if you get in with me."

Elizabeth chuckled. "I certainly won't object to two showers in one morning under the circumstances."

After their shower, Elizabeth packed Jared's clothes and left the suitcase and his laptop by the door. They went and had a leisurely breakfast of bacon, eggs, pancakes and hash browns. While they ate, they talked about what they would do when they got back to Edmonton. Now that things had been settled, it seemed they could relax and get back to their relationship.

"When do you expect to head to the mountains?" Jared asked.

"Well, I've been able to do some work on my article, so it shouldn't take me more than two days to get it magazine-ready. Then I have to decide on the pictures to send with it, which will take about a day. So I'm thinking I'll leave Tuesday or Wednesday."

"Not the week you had hoped for," Jared said.

Elizabeth shrugged. "That's okay. There's always next year. Maybe we can arrange to go together."

"That would be fine with me."

"While you are working on your article, do you take time off to eat?" Jared asked. "Or do you work all day like you travel and don't stop for a decent meal?"

"Sometimes I stop to eat if the food is tempting."

"What about the food at Swiss Chalet?"

"That's pretty tempting. What else goes with it?"

"Why, a date with me, of course."

Elizabeth laughed. It felt so good to have their easygoing rapport again. She hadn't realized how much of it had disappeared. Yes, they'd talked this past week but only about Jared's quest and what he was finding out, barely about themselves.

After breakfast, they checked out, and Brandon helped with Jared's bags. Jared was in his van. Elizabeth went up to the window.

"Do you remember anything more, other than being at Wayne's?"

Jared shook his head. "Maybe I will once I get there and we start talking."

"Do you know how your memory of visiting Wayne's place fits with what else was happening?"

Jared thought a moment. "Not really. I don't remember Christine being there, but she could have been at work, or maybe it was after she left him. I remember going through the kitchen, and it was messy."

Wayne came out to meet them when they drove in the yard. Elizabeth climbed out of her vehicle and joined him at the van. Jared rested his arms on his window frame.

"What do you want?" Wayne asked in a belligerent tone.

"We'd like to talk some more," Elizabeth said. "We've learned some things that you might be interested in hearing."

"Such as?" Wayne crossed his arms and glared at her.

"Such as Meredith killed Ben, not Christine."

"I already know that," Wayne said. "Meredith phoned me."

"And we also know that Anna came here with Jared to talk to you."

Wayne looked at Jared and shook his head. "You were never here."

"Yes, I was, and I remember you and Mom arguing."

"Are you Jared's father?" Elizabeth asked, getting right to the point.

"What?" Wayne was flabbergasted. "How could you say such a thing?"

Jared spoke up. "I remember you grabbed my mom and pushed her away."

"All right," Wayne snarled. He put his hands on Jared's van. "You guys were here. Anna tried to blackmail Graham into paying her support money. She claimed that you and her baby were his."

Now this is starting to make sense, thought Elizabeth.

"What did he say?" she asked.

"He denied it, of course, because it wasn't true. Then she said that if he didn't pay her money, she would tell everyone that he was Jared's father."

"Jared saw someone at the well with his mother the day she drowned." Elizabeth chanced a guess. "Was that you? Did you push her?"

Wayne stared from one to the other for a long time.

"That little slut was trying to wreck my son's life," he bellowed. "She'd already gotten Paul to marry her by saying he was your father. When that didn't work out well, she tried to wreck Nick's marriage by saying you were his kid and so was the baby she was carrying. Then she came over here and accused Graham of being the father of both kids. She tried to blackmail us into giving her money."

He got a smug look on his face. "I couldn't have her ruin Graham's life. He'd just come back to farm with me. My life may have been hell back then but at least I did one thing right by getting rid of her."

Once she'd answered all the police questions and given her phone number and address Elizabeth sat for a few minutes in her vehicle. She was amazed at how resilient Jared had been over the past few days. Many times she'd expected him to crumble under the weight of some new piece of information, but he'd kept going. She was just so glad that he'd found his mother's killer, even though it meant that he'd learned there were now two men who could be his father. She wondered if he would try to find out which one he was. However, that was a subject she would leave alone until he broached it.

Elizabeth turned her mind to Christine and Wayne. It was funny how both parents had thought they were protecting their son. One through not saying she thought he had really killed her boyfriend and the other by murdering a young woman he felt would ruin his son's life.

She let Chevy out for a quick run, and then went to find Jared waiting in his van. She climbed in beside him.

"I'm so glad that it's over," Jared said, his hands on the steering wheel. "All the fantasies I've ever had about how lovely my mother was are gone, though. She was not the parent I had so desperately wanted."

"I don't think anyone's parent is perfect. But whatever she was, we do know that she loved you."

Jared nodded. "I can go home knowing that I've done something for her, something that no one else did."

"I'm sure she would be very proud of you."

Jared turned to her. "I can't thank you enough for what you've done for me."

Elizabeth waved her hand. "I didn't do much."

"Yes, you did. Sometimes, it was only because of you that I was able to keep going. I always knew that when I faltered, you would step in to ask the right question. You made this happen for me."

"I'm sorry that it wasn't all good news." Elizabeth changed the subject. "So what are you going to do now?"

"Well, I think I should go and see Paul. He probably needs some support right now too. Plus I want to get the headstone on her grave changed immediately."

"What are you going to have put in its place?"

"I don't know. I've been trying to come up with something, but none of the normal things seem right. She certainly wasn't a loving wife. Or a good friend, for that matter," he said bitterly.

"How about 'loving mother?'"

Jared's face brightened. "I like that." Then he sobered. "I have one last request of you."

"What is that?" Elizabeth asked. This sounded serious. She wasn't sure if she wanted to hear it.

"Would you come with me to Paul's? I don't want to face him alone yet, especially after this news. He and Wayne have been friends for a long time."

"Sure," she agreed. "I'll follow you."

Elizabeth pulled in behind Jared. At the door, he knocked, and then waited while someone came to open it. This wasn't his home anymore, and he was waiting to be welcomed like any visitor. Susie opened the door, and a smile lit up her face.

"Oh, Jared. I'm so glad you came back." She bent down and hugged him. "I was afraid I wouldn't see you again."

It was noon, and Paul and Willy were seated around the table having lunch.

"Please join us," Susie said, getting some plates from the cupboard.

Paul and Willy moved their chairs to fit one in for Elizabeth. Jared wheeled into his usual spot.

There was a long silence, until Jared finally spoke. "I guess you heard about Wayne."

Elizabeth watched Paul. This must have been almost as hard on him as on Jared.

Paul leaned back and ran his hands through his hair. He nodded his head.

"Maybe now it will be all over," he said.

"As bad as everything else is that I learned, I'm glad that I did discover the truth about what happened to Mom," Jared said. "I'm glad she didn't commit suicide."

Paul looked at him. "I was awake all night. Now that the fact that I'm not your father is out in the open, I would like us to ... I really think that ... Oh, damn. I don't know how to say it."

Susie stepped in. "What he is trying to say is that he, we, want you to remain part of our family."

Paul nodded.

"Yes," Willy said. "I'd be lost without a little brother."

Jared beamed. "I would like that too."

Elizabeth knew it was time for her to leave. The past was being mended, and they didn't need an outsider here right now. She said her goodbyes to the others, then leaned over and gave Jared a kiss.

"Call me when you get back," she whispered.

"Oh, you can bet I will. We have a date at Swiss Chalet."

Elizabeth drove to the city. It had been a long day, a long week. But she'd gotten her research done, helped Jared find out what really happened to his mother and strengthened the relationship between them. Not bad for one week.

Joan's Note

I am happy to say that I received many compliments on my first novel, *Illegally Dead*, which is set along the Crowsnest Highway in southern Alberta . Besides liking the mystery, some told me that they enjoyed the book because they had been raised in one of the towns along the highway or had traveled through the area on a holiday and could relate to the places mentioned. A few also told me that they wanted to visit the area after reading the novel. With that in mind, in this book I have included Elizabeth's magazine article for those who would like to know more about the places she visited while doing her research.

If you wish to contact me about either of my novels you may send me an email at mjyarmey@yahoo.com and write "commentary on your novel" in the comment space.

Day Tripping From Edmonton

By Elizabeth Oliver

Author's Note

The following are three loop trips from Edmonton. Each of these drives makes a nice one-day outing. However, this article in no way claims to cover all that there is to see and do on these routes and, due to space constraints, not all places along the highways are mentioned. That doesn't mean, however, that they aren't worth a visit. The intent of this article is to get you, the reader, out and exploring this part of the province. You may discover the perfect antique or a hidden little park.

A map is provided to make the journey easier. A road map for distances between towns is advisable. You may bring your own picnic lunch or stop and sample the foods along the way.

Trip 1: Gibbons–St. Paul–Andrew Loop

Take Highway 28A out of northeast Edmonton and follow it to Gibbons. On the corner of 28A and 50th Avenue is the Emmanuel Anglican Church. The interior, with its U-joint style and large beams, is modelled after the inside of a ship and is unique in Alberta. It was constructed in 1902 and is still in use today.

The Sturgeon River Historical Museum is in Oliver Park on 48th Avenue. Visit the McLean Brothers Store, which has a counter with an antique cash register, shelving full of boxes and cans, books, photographs, desks and an old sewing machine sitting on a hardwood floor. A log building with artifacts from the area and a small home with 1920s furnishings are two of the other buildings on the grounds.

At the opposite end of town is Echo Glen Park. The park is beside the Sturgeon River, and there is a hiking/biking trail that will take you along the high banks of the river.

Continue past the park to reach a stop sign on Highway 28. Turn right and head to Redwater.

One of Alberta's major oilfields was discovered near Redwater in 1948. To honour the oil industry, the town has preserved the Discovery Derrick, which was used to drill the first well. The derrick, which at 51.2 metres high is the largest free-standing oil derrick in North America, is in a park on 53rd Street.

Follow 48th Avenue out of town to the junction with Highway 38, where you turn right. Turn left at the Victoria Trail sign to head towards Fort Victoria itself. The road is fifty-eight kilometres long and mainly gravel, and although it doesn't exactly follow the route, since some of it has been plowed under, it uses as much of the original trail as possible. The Victoria Trail was part of an overland route from Fort Garry (Winnipeg) to Edmonton, dating from the 1820s and called various names such as the Carlton Trail, Winnipeg Trail, Fort Pitt and Saskatchewan Trail, depending on the section. Victoria Trail is the part between Edmonton and Fort Victoria.

There are signs along the road, so don't let the number of twists and turns stop you from taking this enjoyable drive along a trail that natives once walked and, beginning in the 1820s, early settlers travelled in Red River carts. They would probably be surprised at the changes along it: the large, modern homes; the big barns; the rows of metal granaries; the machine sheds with their full line of farming machinery; the open fields of grain and the animals. The biting smell from the barnyards would certainly be unlike the sweet smell of flowers, trees and open air to which they were accustomed.

The road winds through farmland and beside farmhouses and old buildings. You will come to the original site of the Jack Pine Grove School, which operated from 1910 to 1951. Just past that is a cairn for Jack Pine Grove School District, Eldorena, founded in 1909. The church behind the cairn is the Eldorena Ukrainian Catholic Church, built in 1912.

As you continue driving, watch for the valley to your right and the banks of the North Saskatchewan River. At one point, the road is like a country lane with trees lining it. But it is also narrow and winding with blind corners, so keep to your side of the road. At about the halfway point, you reach Highway 31. It goes to Waskatenau, if you wish to get off the gravel road. Proceeding ahead, watch for the road to the left that goes to the church and cemetery of the former Lobstick Settlement.

Return to the Victoria Trail and soon you will come to the RCMP Memorial Sculpture. The thick, plated steel statue of an RCMP officer astride a horse sits on a base made of rock. Some of the names and regimental numbers of the newly founded North-West Mounted Police, like S. B. (Sam) Steele #1, P. Coutts #95, Sub-Inspector S. Gagnon, R. E. Steele #7, are painted on some of the rocks. These commemorate the twenty members of the NWMP who left the main group on July 29, 1874, and headed to Fort Edmonton, passing along this trail in October of that year. The cairn was erected on August 4, 1998.

There are two sharp curves after the cairn and then a dangerous curve, with an old house to the left, so proceed with caution. When you reach SH 855, the road to Smoky Lake, continue across and you will be on pavement heading to the Victoria Settlement. Here there are two cemeteries, the Pakan Church constructed in 1906, and the clerk's quarters built by the Hudson's Bay Company in 1864. The quarters are Alberta's oldest structure still on its original foundation. It has been restored, and on the inside walls you can see where the Hudson's Bay employees carved their initials.

Stroll along the asphalt paths under the spreading branches of the tall maples planted during the early years of the post. If you bring a lunch, have a picnic at a table on the large lawn. Or grab your fishing gear and hike down the wide path to the North Saskatchewan River. You can fish from the banks where the fur traders landed their canoes over one hundred years ago.

In Smoky Lake, the old CN station, on West Railway Drive, is now a museum. Inside are photographs and posters on the wall, an old telephone and telegraph, the original desk and the old wood stove.

The town of Smoky Lake was named for the nearby lake, which was initially called Smoking Lake by the Cree. In one version of how the lake received it name, the Aboriginal people, who stopped by its shores to smoke their pipes during their hunts, called it Smoking Place. In anther story, it was selected because the mist lifting off the lake resembled rising smoke.

Smoky Lake bills itself as the pumpkin capital of Alberta. This is because the town holds the Great Pumpkin Fair and Weigh-Off on the first Saturday in October. Prizes are given for the largest, the ugliest and the best-looking pumpkins.

Drive into Vilna to see the world's largest mushrooms in Mushroom Park. They are six metres high and are from the Tricholoma family. They are called uspale mushroom, which is a traditional mushroom used in Ukrainian cooking in the area. The mushrooms were erected in August 1993.

Glendon bills itself as the Perogy Capital of Alberta. You drive into town on Perogy Drive and in Perogy Park is a giant perogy, the largest in the world. The perogy, which is held up by a fork, is over seven metres in height.

The perogy was unveiled on August 31, 1991, to coincide with the beginning of the 1992 nationwide celebrations commemorating the 100th anniversary of Ukrainian settlement in Canada. If you want a sample of the Ukrainian fare, visit the Perogy House across from the park.

As you drive into St. Paul, watch for unidentified flying objects hovering overhead, waiting for an opportunity to land on the world's first man-made UFO landing pad.

The circular platform, with provincial and territorial flags flying overhead, waits patiently for its first UFO landing on the corner of Galaxy Way. It was erected as a centennial project in 1967, and a time capsule inside the pad is to be opened in 2067.

The land beneath the landing pad has been designated international territory by the town of St. Paul. Climb the steps onto the UFO pad and walk across the pedway to the visitor information building, which has been designed to resemble a UFO. Inside you will see an interpretive display complete with photographs of UFOs and crop circles and write-ups on the different hoaxes that have been pulled. The town operates a UFO hotline. The number is 1-888-SEE-UFOS.

As you enter Elk Point, on your right is a statue of Peter Fidler in the Peter Fidler Peace Park. This park was officially dedicated in 1992, Canada's 125th anniversary of confederation, as part of the Peace Parks Across Canada project.

Fidler joined the Hudson's Bay Company when he was nineteen and studied surveying. In 1792, he helped build Buckingham House and became its factor—a high-ranking fur trader—five years later. He then travelled throughout the West, constructing other fur-trading posts.

As you leave Elk Point, follow the signs to Fort George and Buckingham House. At the parking lot, you will find an interpretive centre with replicas of voyageurs, buffalo, teepees and a gift shop. There is also a map showing the layout of the forts. A short interpretive trail takes you to the sites of Fort George, constructed by the North West Company in 1792, and Buckingham House, built later that same year. Both were fur-trading and provision posts.

They were situated on a plateau overlooking the North Saskatchewan River, and the fur traders had the difficult task of hauling their supplies up the hill from their canoes. The posts did, however, have a beautiful view of the river valley.

Follow the scenic highway to Two Hills, and check out their museum on the corner of 51st Street and 52nd Avenue. In Willingdon is the Willingdon Tourist Park with a campground, picnic tables and a mural on a huge rock. At the end of town is Secondary Highway 857, which will take you north to the Historical Village and Pioneer Museum at Shandro. The more than twenty buildings to tour include a blacksmith shop, post office, funeral home and a reproduction of a sod house, all of which are furnished appropriately. You will also see the ferry used on the North Saskatchewan River, north of the museum before the Shandro Bridge was constructed.

There is a small park in the village of Andrew. Besides a caboose, playground, minigolf course and tennis courts, there is a statue of the world's largest Mallard duck. The colourful duck was chosen as a symbol for Andrew, and this likeness was erected on April 29, 1992.

On the corner of Highway 45 and SH831 is the Skaro Shrine. The shrine was designed as a replica of the Grotto of Lourdes in France and constructed in 1919 by local residents. The first pilgrimage was held on August 14, 1919.

And this ends your journey for today.

Trip 2: Radway–Lac La Biche–Athabasca Loop

You can follow the beginning of Trip 1 to Redwater and then carry on Highway 28 to Radway. In this village is an old, red-brick school that now houses the John Paul II Catholic Bible School. People come from across North America to live here for a year, learning to pray, study, heal and incorporate the Bible into their lives. Some have been computer experts, some have been retired. The bible school opened in 1984 and accepts twenty-one students each year. While most students apply for entry themselves, some have been recommended by the Vatican, while others have come from Germany, Zambia, Ireland and Kuwait.

Also in the village is the Krause Milling Company in the tall, white grain elevator. This elevator has been restored to show the process that is used to mill the grain into flour. In the building next to it is a museum and gift shop.

Stop in at the Waskatenau Creek (also known as Pine Creek) Nature Trail in Waskatenau (pronounced wa-SET-na) for a pleasant stroll on an asphalt trail. The first section is through trees, and then you slowly work your way down until you are beside the creek. There are interpretive signs that tell you more about the wildlife and plants.

Continue along Highway 28 to Highway 36 and turn north to Lac La Biche. Soon after Highway 36 becomes Highway 55, you cross the Beaver River and come to the Continental Divide with an elevation of 575 metres. This narrow height of land between Lac La Biche and Beaver Lake separates the Hudson Bay and the Arctic Ocean drainage systems. The Beaver River drains Beaver Lake and flows east to Hudson Bay. La Biche River issues from Lac La Biche and eventually spills into the Arctic Ocean.

You enter Lac La Biche on 100th Street. Turn right on 91st Avenue, and Portage College is to your left, halfway down the block. Here you will find the Native Cultural Arts Museum Collection, with Native handicrafts showing much of the Aboriginal culture.

On Churchill Drive is a statue of David Thompson and two companions as they arrive at Lac La Biche, then known as Red Deers Lake. Thompson explored, surveyed and mapped most of Western Canada. He is the first recorded non-Native in the Lac La Biche area, and his exploration here led to the building of Red Deers Lake House by the North West Company in 1798.

East of the town is the Sir Winston Churchill Provincial Park, reached by a man-made causeway. Watch for pelicans as you drive to the park and enjoy a picnic at one of the sandy beaches.

Go west of town on Highway 55 to the Old Mission Road to reach the Lac La Biche Mission on a slight hill overlooking the lake. The original Mission Church and some other buildings were destroyed in a tornado in 1921. The present church was built the next year and contains the altar, which was undamaged, from the first church.

It is about a one-hundred-kilometre, picturesque drive to Athabasca. Just before reaching the town, you will pass through Amber Valley, the home of Alberta's first black settlers. In 1910, almost two hundred African-Americans were led into the province by Jefferson Davis Edwards, and they settled on land in what was then known as the Pine Creek area. They had left Oklahoma and the discrimination against their race for what they hoped was a better life.

Athabasca has many historic buildings dating back to the beginning of the early 1900s, including the Union Hotel and the Canadian National Railway Station, both on 50th Street, and the United Church on the corner of 48th Street and 49th Avenue. At Riverfront Park, you can stroll beside the Athabasca River.

Head south out of Athabasca on Highway 2. Turn off the highway at the sign for Perryvale. From Perryvale to Tawatinaw, you will be driving on part of the historic Athabasca Landing Trail. The Hudson's Bay Company developed the trail at a cost of $4,059 in 1877. The trail followed a Native path and was really a 161-kilometre portage between Fort Edmonton on the North Saskatchewan River and Athabasca Landing on the Athabasca River.

Legal has a large collection of murals on their downtown buildings that show the contribution of the Francophones to the West. The murals were sponsored by the descendants of the early pioneers, who are shown in the murals.

As you travel south towards Morinville, look ahead to your left and you will see a tall spire rising above the trees. This is from the St. Jean Baptiste Roman Catholic Church of Morinville. Completed in 1907, it has been modified over the years with the brick exterior added in 1929.

In St. Albert is the massive, three-storey Grandin House on St. Vidal Avenue. Initially, the building, completed in 1887, was to be operated as a Grey Nuns hospital, run by a Canadian order of Catholic religious sisters, but the design was unsuitable, so it became the official residence of Bishop

Vital J. Grandin.

Just past it is Father Lacombe's log chapel, constructed in 1861. It was moved in 1871 and some restoration work was done in 1927, with about forty percent of the original material being replaced. In 1977, the chapel was returned to its original site on this hill above the Sturgeon River.

On the other side of the chapel is St. Albert Parish Church, erected in 1922. Walk behind the church and view the crypt, where the body of Father Lacombe lies in honour. Then take the long, flower-lined path to the grotto, a replica of La Grotto des Apparitions de Lourdes (the Lourdes Grotto) in France.

During the summer, what is called Western Canada's largest outdoor farmer's market takes place on St. Anne Street. Here you can buy meats, vegetables, fruits and dessert for your evening meal at home.

Trip 3: Elk Island National Park–Wainwright–Tofield Loop

Watch for wildlife, especially bison, roaming freely as you drive through Elk Island National Park. If you see one, take your picture from your vehicle, or just sit and admire it. Do not get out and approach the animal, and do not feed it.

Besides the animals to see, there are a number of walking or hiking trails, a Ukrainian pioneer home and a monument to the Plains buffalo, which provided food, clothing and weapons for the Natives, and meat (in the form of pemmican) for the fur traders and explorers.

The Ukrainian Cultural Heritage Village can be a quick stop on this tour or a full-day visit. Each building has its own history, and interpreters, who are dressed in period clothing, will converse with you only about events that took place in that era.

In Mundare is the Basilian Father's Museum, where you will see Ukrainian clothing, photographs, stamps, typewriters, books and a display of Ukrainian liturgical books from the sixteenth and seventeenth centuries.

Sts. Peter and Paul Monastery is across the road from the museum. It was built in 1922 and is one of the oldest Basilian monasteries in Canada. Beside it is the Grotto, built in 1934. Steps lead up to alcoves housing statues. Follow the side paths up the back of the hill, which represents Mount

Calvary, to different levels and the fourteen Stations of the Cross. Ivy hides much of the walls, and colourful flowers adorn flower beds.

Vegreville's most famous feature, the Pysanka, is at the east end of town in the Vegreville Elks/Kinsmen Community Park. The Pysanka, or giant Easter egg, was erected in 1974 to celebrate the centennial of the RCMP in Alberta and to honour the early Ukrainian pioneers of the area. The egg is suspended over a lovely park, with red rock paths through green grass and a footbridge over the river. The park also has a pond with ducks and swans swimming in it, two gazebos and a picnic area.

The Vermilion Provincial Park in Vermilion has camping, a wading pool, walking and equestrian trails and a man-made lake. When a bridge was built over the Vermilion River, part of the river was dammed to form this lake.

On Main Street in Wainwright, you will pass the large statue of a buffalo and drive to the Memorial Clock Tower, a cenotaph. It was built as a memory to the men who died in the two world wars and stands in the centre of the intersection. The Wainwright Museum, with over fifteen rooms of exhibits, is on 1st Avenue in the old railway station. The Wainwright Railway Preservation Society grounds, across the tracks from the museum, has numerous displays about the railway history in the area and the province.

Camp Wainwright is one of Canada's largest training facilities for the Armed Forces. During the Second World War, over one thousand German officers were interred at the camp. A reconstructed POW tower, with artifacts, commemorates that time.

On the highway again, drive to Fabyan and turn left into town. Follow the signs to the viewpoint for the Fabyan Trestle (also know as Battle River Trestle). The trestle, which is 845 metres long and stands 59 metres above the water, was constructed from 1907 to 1908 for the Grand Trunk Pacific Railway. The first train crossed it on December 15, 1908.

Back on the highway, you begin your descent into the Battle River Valley. The river was called Chacutenah by the Cree Natives, which means "the river that flows through the tremendous valley."

To see the Viking Ribstones, watch for a historical sign on the left side of the road. After reading the sign, retrace your drive along the highway to the first right turn and follow the signs to an area surrounded by white posts with red tops. Park here and climb a slight hill to the ribstones and a cairn.

The large, quartzite stones have markings similar to the ribs of a buffalo, and they were carved as a monument to Old Man Buffalo, whom the First Nations people believed was the spirit protector of all the buffalo. While on top of the hill, turn in a circle and enjoy the panoramic view of the surrounding farmland.

The Viking Museum, founded in 1966, is inside the former hospital on 60th Avenue. The hospital was built in 1921, and each room depicts a different time period in the hospital's, and the town's, history.

Holden has the Beaver Regional Arts Centre with a 285-seat capacity on 50th Street. Here a "Chautauqua" (similar to the theatrical groups that toured in the early part of the 1900s), a Christmas concert and a comedy or mystery thriller are each held annually. Besides the professional performers who come to the theatre, the Beaverhill Players, a community theatre group, also puts on many performances.

George's Harness and Saddlery in Ryley is a working museum on 50th Street. As you enter, the smell of leather overwhelms you. Look up and see the tin ceiling brought from an old schoolhouse in Saskatchewan. Walk along the aisles to view the harnesses, bridles, hats and saddles, many of which are antiques.

At the Beaverhill Lake Nature Centre, located along the highway at Tofield, you can see stuffed birds, look at pictures of birds, read books on birds and gather information on Beaverhill Lake, one of the best places to see snow geese on their spring migrations. If you are a birdwatcher, you can pick up a pamphlet at the centre listing the more than 250 recorded bird species that have been sighted on or near the lake.

The Cooking Lake–Blackfoot Grazing, Wildlife and Recreation Area has 150 kilometres of trails for equestrian, hiking, bicycling, snowmobiling and cross-country skiing adventurers. There are a number of staging areas, and the trails from each are designated for the different activities. Coyote, elk, moose, deer and more than 200 varieties of birds occupy the reserve along with cattle.

After a hike along the trails, you can head home.

Acknowledgements

I wish to thank Jennifer Day for her insightful editing and all the staff at Sumach Press for their great work in taking my words on manuscript pages and turning them into a book.

Many thanks to Mike and Noreen for their proofreading skills.

More Fine Fiction from Sumach Press...

ILLEGALLY DEAD
Mystery Fiction by Joan Donaldson-Yarmey

RAGGED CHAIN
Mystery Fiction by Vivian Meyer

IN A PALE BLUE LIGHT
A Novel by Lily Poritz-Miller

THE EXCLUSION PRINCIPLE
A Novel by Leona Gom

THE SHERPA AND OTHER FICTIONS
A Collection of Stories by Nila Gupta

ON PAIN OF DEATH
Mystery Fiction by Jan Rehner

SLANDEROUS TONGUE
Mystery Fiction by Jill Culiner

BOTTOM BRACKET
Mystery Fiction by Vivian Meyer

THE BOOK OF MARY
A Novel by Gail Sidonie Sobat

RIVER REEL
A Novel by Bonnie Laing

ROADS UNRAVELLING
Short Stories by Kathy-Diane Leveille

OUTSKIRTS: WOMEN WRITING FROM SMALL PLACES
Edited by Emily Schultz

GRIZZLY LIES
Mystery Fiction by Eileen Coughlan

JUST MURDER
Mystery Fiction by Jan Rehner
Winner of the 2004 Arthur Ellis Award for Best First Crime Novel

Find out more at www.sumachpress.com